CONSTELLATION

THE FINAL LEAP

WILLIE HIRSH

Author of
Regicide: the Shadow King
Amongst and Above All

HILDEBRAND BOOKS

an imprint of W. Brand Publishing

NASHVILLE, TENNESSEE

Much of the background information for this story was readily available online. Many thanks to Wikipedia, Space.com, the NASA homepage, and the Smithsonian Institution, to name a few.

Hildebrand Books an imprint of W. Brand Publishing
j.brand@wbrandpub.com
www.wbrandpub.com
Printed and bound in the United States of America.

Cover design by designchik.net

Constellation /Willie Hirsh —2nd ed. Revised
Available in Paperback, Kindle, and eBook formats.
Paperback ISBN 978-1-950385-33-1
eBook ISBN: 978-1-950385-34-8
Library of Congress Control Number: 2020905986

To my parents.

TABLE OF CONTENTS

PROLOGUE

President John F. Kennedy's powerful inaugural speech over half a century ago still stands the test of time. It applied to the entire 20th century during two world wars and a major ongoing conflict in the Middle East, and, unfortunately, it remains true in the 21st century, considering the tensions with Iran and North Korea over their nuclear ambitions.

In terms of nuclear power, the world today is far more dangerous than it was during the Cuban Missile Crisis at the height of the Cold War. Nations during that time used their nuclear arsenals as deterrents; today, countries use them as threats, hiding behind the ideology of religious superiority.

JFK's vision to eradicate religious zealots and ensure freedom for all was shredded in the face of reality, time after time.

In war, there are no winners.

TERMINOLOGY

CSIS: Chinese Secret Intelligence Services

ECHELON: A secret government code name for a surveillance program

Extravehicular Activity (EVA): A spacewalk

Geostationary: A satellite's stationary orbit along its equator

Geosynchronous: A satellite's stationary orbit inclined with the Earth

ISS: International Space Station

LLM: (Apollo) Lunar Landing Module

Mossad: Israeli national intelligence agency

NSA: United States' National Security Agency

Prograde: Satellite moving with the Earth's rotation

Retrograde: Satellite moving against the Earth's rotation

SBR: Space-based radar

Shabak: Israel's internal security agency, also known as the Shin Bet

CHAPTER 1

November 17th, Last Year

T echnology...*one powerful word that changed the world,* Dan Eyal thought to himself after seeing the final preparation of the Russian Proton rocket on the LC-81 launch pad.

"Insane, isn't it!?" exclaimed the scientist seated beside him, busy monitoring the flickering computer screens like he was reading Eyal's thoughts.

The Proton M, a four-stage rocket, was connected to its support tower, shooting its slim, fifty-three-meter-long body up in the air. Its six Stage One, RD-275 rocket engines made it look like a prehistoric dinosaur, stalking for prey on the calm landscape background.

"It's fucking impressive!" replied Eyal from his post in the control room, shaking his head slightly.

The scientist, satisfied with the progress on his screen, caught a quick glimpse of Dan's hypnotized eyes watching the view across the large panoramic window. They witnessed as the rocket rotated to its vertical position after completing fueling procedures.

"Unbelievable," whispered Dan, "never seen this before." He let out a whistle.

"All systems switched to 'Go' mode," said the scientist as the pad technicians checked all systems one last time before leaving the area. From that moment on, all systems were remote. A little over a mile away from the safety of the main control room, everyone watched the metal giant against the spectacular red and orange winter sky.

It was precisely 4:02:47 p.m., T-minus twenty-four minutes and thirteen seconds. The tension in the room was so thick a knife could cut it.

Engineers and scientists carefully watched every gauge in the control room. They focused on any tiny change in weather, temperature, humidity, barometric pressure, and wind direction and speed, as well as all the rocket and capsule's data.

In a secluded section of the control room, two Chinese scientists monitored confidential data without sharing with anyone else. They observed, in secrecy, experimental research equipment on the Proton rocket, which was on the top of the Capsule X satellite. They insisted on keeping it classified as part of the deal allowing the launch from the Baikonur.

Dan took notice, and his Mossad-agent instinct nudged him to watch carefully—but he kept to himself, as not to evoke a diplomatic scandal.

After all, new and dominant world ideological leaders were emerging and creating international tensions regularly.

"It seems like they have a secret or two," whispered the scientist in Hebrew.

Eyal nodded and replied the same way, "China's launch rates put Russia and the United States in the minor leagues."

"Yeah, they said the space missions were for science and exploration; most reported as research satellites, planetary probes, and expeditions into the solar system."

The control room speaker announced loudly, "T-minus four minutes and counting; all systems go!"

The scientist and Dan both glanced at the clock. "China offered the same services to other countries at a cost that NASA and the European Union couldn't afford, creating competition and tension among the rivals," Dan muttered with disdain.

"Honestly, only a handful of countries could offer such technologically advanced services," the scientist replied quietly. "A few other countries offered to manufacture satellites to corporations, mainly in the internet, media, and communications industries. And they'd launch them into space for a lower combined fee."

"True," concurred Dan, "the list of those capable of doing both was even shorter, and it was the elite of the prestigious global space club." Dan waved his fist to show visually how many.

Colonel Dan Eyal, the legendary Mossad agent, and General Gershon "Greco" Bar, who was the head of the military's Inteligence Division 8200, Satellite Division 5200, an arm of the IDF military, wore civilian clothes rather than their formal IDF uniforms. They were part of an Israeli delegation of three engineers sent to monitor the Israeli Amos 5 satellite.

Ezra Maman, the head of the science and development division, chatted with Dan. Ezra Maman had developed a device financed by the Israeli government called Orbixeye. The defense department and Mossad agency showed an intense interest in it due to its intelligent capabilities in space. Secured on top of the Proton rocket, it was prepared to be deployed and tested in space that night.

During that time, China started building the largest Cosmodrome on the planet and planned accelerated, aggressive space missions beyond the satellite belt. They used the old Cosmodrome in Baikonur, Kazakhstan. Their construction work finished and allowed them to take over the title of having the largest Cosmodrome in the world.

The Baikonur Cosmodrome was controlled by the USSR, who leased it from Kazakhstan until 2050; it conducted the entire space race with the United States.

Israel also used the space services of the Baikonur to launch its military and communications satellites due to its availability and low operational cost.

"This is the Grand Central Station of rocketry in the Far East," said Greco with a tense face.

Dan started, "We have something to hide, as well—"

Dan was cut off by Ezra. "The collaboration between China and our technology industry is always a red flag for Washington," Ezra interjected. "We should mind our own business, and they should mind theirs."

"For Washington, it's a national security issue," said Greco emotionally.

"It's natural for both countries to collaborate, especially when using the same Cosmodrome in Kazakhstan," Dan remarked.

"Well, China progressed with one giant step into space; now they're equal with America and Russia," replied Ezra, still focused on his monitors.

"Getting close!" Dan added excitedly.

General "Greco" Bar continued, "When Israel developed the 'Lavi' fighter jet, Washington pulled the plug on the financing. We sold some of its newly developed avionics components systems to China—"

"Oh, yeah," Dan interjected, "I saw the two prototypes test flying." Dan sounded enthusiastic and squared his shoulders, now standing behind Ezra, who remained in his chair.

A few long, thin clouds passed over the red sun briefly and cast shadows that enhanced the natural beauty of the remarkable sunset. *Could not be a more perfect setting for a rocket launch than this,* thought Ezra.

The Israeli science delegation was satisfied with the data displayed on the screens. They were eager to start communicating with their equipment in space once it reached orbit. The excitement was high. Just one minute to go.

Ezra, a brilliant mind, did not look like a prominent scientist. Heavy and short, he always knew better and was very obstinate in team settings. When everyone went home, he always stayed at the office and fixed codes, repaired bugs, tested systems, again and again, all night. By sunrise, he'd fall asleep on the office floor, out cold.

"Brilliant minds that you need to tolerate," the head of the agency that employed him once said. He was focused on his mission and ignored the background noise, whatever it was.

"Ophir 1 and Ophir 2, our advanced communications and military satellites, were supposed to be launched from Cape Canaveral in Florida in a few weeks," General Bar said, changing the subject and gazing at Dan for a reaction.

"Yes, I know, but—"

"After launch, those satellites were supposed to connect with Orbixeye and provide a total of three satellites as a network in low orbit and communicate with each other," the general interrupted, his eyes on the launch clock approaching T-time.

"Two hundred miles from Earth!" exclaimed the scientist, still focused on his monitor. "This network may take up to five years to complete all the phases. Although the first Orbixeye could start sending data right off the bat." Ezra's lips curled arrogantly.

That was not Dan's expertise. His mission was not a scientific one. The kick-off plan was to ensure that there were no issues during the launch. Afterward, the system monitoring would be taken over by the Israeli Defense Force's intelligence division, which was based in Glilot and under the command of the current supervisor, General "Greco" Bar.

Ezra glanced at Greco with a grin and a thumbs-up, signaling that all systems were good to go. Greco and Dan looked again at the big clock displaying the countdown time. They focused on the pad with binoculars, even though a closed-circuit camera system covered the rocket from all directions.

"Good luck to Israel," murmured Greco proudly. Dan smiled and coughed nervously.

Greco made a "V" with the fingers of his left hand and pursed his lips. His gray eyes sparkled with enthusiasm.

Dan had been introduced as a civilian member of the Israeli team. A stubbly beard and eyeglasses covered his face. His black, "Manchester United" soccer hat with its red logo made him look like a British sports hooligan. He wore a casual army coat labeled "Dubon," the nickname of a teddy bear.

"What are they are hiding from us?" asked Dan curiously as he looked again at the Chinese scientists in the far corner.

"There are a few satellites other than ours. Israel did not question the rest of the payload. If it could carry 20,700 kilograms for a low Earth orbit, Amos 5 is only 1,972 kilograms. The assumption was that the Chinese satellites were of similar weight," Ezra explained, turning his torso to see Dan standing behind him.

General Bar continued Ezra's assessment and added, "Officially, its reports read that the remaining payload capacity was for two research spaceships. They would be released in a higher-altitude, geosynchronous orbit in space where only the Chinese equipment was. The Zhengzhou space station would be in a low orbit, and the Tianlong space laboratory consisted of a pressurized-propulsion module with experimental docking."

"Very informative," Dan shot back. "Why did they disclose this info?"

The Chinese scientists shared the live launch from their control room north of Beijing, referred to as Space City, just as their Israeli counterparts monitored the mission.

Naturally, what it held was a subject of riddling curiosity for the Israeli intelligence agency. Dan had been designated to sniff around the Chinese program. *Not an easy task, but one well worth the effort*, Dan thought to himself, his eyes glued to the countdown.

"All systems go," declared the Mission Control manager one more time. His voice was composed.

All the engineers pressed on the "Go" icon on their screens and gave the thumbs-up for launch approval. A green light came on the main control panel. On the wall, a large display illuminated the word "IDTI," the Russian term for "go."

The clock's ticking down felt like an eternity.

"T-minus twenty-one seconds and counting!"

Silence. Only the soft humming of the computer fans was heard.

The space vehicle shone brightly in the impressive high-intensity projectors' beams.

Steam from water sprinkled over the launch pad reduced the noise of the rocket engines that might have otherwise caused damage to sensitive electrical systems, payload, and other supporting equipment. The steam rose and blocked the view of the rocket's base. However, at that point—a few seconds before launch—it was not a concerning factor.

"Eight. Seven. Six. Start engine ignition sequence!" declared the loudspeaker.

The monstrous rocket engines ignited with an enormous roar, rattling the entire pad as if in an earthquake. The large safety-glass window of the control room shook and barely held itself together.

"This is it," whispered Greco eagerly.

"Three. Two. One...and we have liftoff of the Proton," the announcer called aloud. "Liftoff!"

"Here we go!" said Ezra. "We are on our way to history."

"Go, go, *go!*" yelled the engineers and scientists in rhythm.

Then, the unexpected—a deafening, panicked scream covered their energetic cheering.

"We have a malfunction," cried an engineer in front of Ezra's desk. "Abort mission," he screamed again, even louder. "Abort mission at once!"

But it was too late. The six mighty engines thrust flames through the two side-tunnels of the concrete pad, shooting fire and smoke for hundreds of yards. The rocket climbed from the launch pad about twenty feet and froze in midair, confused. It hung there for an endless moment before a massive fireball engulfed the launch pad, exploding and shattering the rocket and its facility amongst the swelling gases.

The explosion resembled a small-scale atomic bomb. The mushroom cloud caused by the mixing fuels created a secondary explosion, and the heat traveled a mile away, setting off sensors. The blast was blamed immediately on a fuel leak, which caused a secondary explosion of the oxygen tanks and other flammable materials assembled in the rocket. No evidence of an apparent malfunction flashed on the control room screens, which left everyone in a state of shock.

The grim faces and glazed looks in the control room said it all. They stared in disbelief at the fireball. They then checked their screens for clues and made sure they would be innocent of the blame for the incident.

The area lit up like daylight as the rocket exploded. The fireball rose quickly into the low atmosphere, shot twisting metal into the air hundreds of yards away in every direction, then fell back to Earth and created small fires around the Cosmodrome facilities.

The looming "Go" sign then flickered red letters: "Malfunction." Computer screens displayed the same. Red alert lights blinked on and off throughout the room. Speechless, everyone sat frozen in their chairs, hoping that it was a bad dream that soon would be over. The large screen displaying the launch pad showed only images of destruction. Black soot covered the pad. Everything was lost.

Eyal and Greco stared in disbelief.

"Four years of effort, development, and one hundred and fifty million dollars...disintegrated into dust in a fraction of a second," mumbled Greco sadly.

"Something went horribly wrong," said Ezra as he nervously watched the red letters glimmer across his screen.

"The headquarters in Tel Aviv probably saw it live!" Greco realized aloud, concerned.

"We should wait for instructions," Dan said through curled lips.

The chatter in the control room grew louder. Everyone exchanged information with the engineer or scientist next to them, demanding answers from the control room chief.

"We lost the fucking deal with China!" remorsefully slurred Ezra, who was supposed to be part of that deal. "China offered to buy the Israeli satellite company contingent upon this successful launch. At this point, the deal is automatically off." He stood up and faced the others for the first time since the launch began.

"I wonder what the Mossad thinks?" asked Greco as he leveled his gaze with Dan's.

"I'm sure the spy games have just started," Dan replied calmly. "Many global intelligence agencies will be pleased to know what's going on in this swamp. I'm sure they are working tirelessly to satisfy the curiosity and paranoia of their governments."

"Including ours!" snapped Ezra.

Greco studied the control room and directed a long glance at the Chinese corner. He said quietly in Dan's direction, "The

United States vetoed the sale due to tensions with China, their main adversary. The CIA informed the State and Defense departments about our new Israeli technology that could map and identify satellites and debris orbiting the Earth, like a space GPS for civilian use. America considered this a threat if controlled by other countries that could convert it to military use—like search and destroy satellites in the future."

Dan inhaled sharply and examined his colleague's faces.

"Orbixeye is a collaboration of Israel, the intelligence community, and the Mossad," explained Greco.

"I can't wait to see it working in space," said Ezra with disappointment as he watched his design burning with the Chinese satellites and its cosmonauts.

CHAPTER TWO

The President of the United States was briefed on the missile explosion in Kazakhstan. It went over his head without additional thought, even though his advisors marked it as important.

"What is this, exactly?" POTUS asked his Chief of Staff, who stood in the oval office beside the President's desk, flipping through the briefing notes.

"It's from the Defense Secretary about the explosion."

"This is the third briefing on the subject since it happened; why should we be concerned?"

"The issue is that the NSA and CIA were monitoring an Israeli device, which was supposed to be deployed into space," the Chief of Staff explained. "This caused a headache for the intelligence world."

The White House chef entered to serve breakfast, and was signaled to put it on the coffee table in the middle of the room. Then both men sat facing each other around the coffee table.

They poured the hot coffee into mugs and took bites of their eggs and bacon.

"Another briefing here mentioned that the explosion might ignite a new conflict due to new developments," the Chief of Staff continued, reading the notes.

"Correct—if the situation is not properly handled. Personally, I am not interested in starting a conflict I wouldn't be around to complete," the President replied, bending slander toward the Speaker of the House, his opponent.

"Wow, here is a good one," chirped the Chief of Staff, his mug pressed to his lips. "This is from the NSA military spy base in Cyprus; they intercepted codes regarding a device codenamed Orbixeye."

The President's eyes opened wide. "What's that?" he asked in curiosity.

"NSA and CIA claim it's a spying device deployed with the Russian rocket," the Chief of Staff said through a deep breath.

"Now destroyed?" POTUS asked, looking up at his assistant.

"Exactly," he replied with a nod. "NSA asked if you could plead with the Israelis for information about their new technology without disclosing how we know about it."

The President scoffed, "You think they're dummies?"

"Looks like no matter how the NSA dressed up their requests for information about it from their counterpart in Israel, they hit a brick wall," added the Chief of Staff. He wiped his mouth with the white cloth napkin.

"I'll call, but not now; they're probably grieving their loss," the President chuckled.

"From what I gathered, the only info regarding the new device was released via the security agencies between our countries. We would benefit from the new technology at no charge," the Chief of Staff read from his report and then handed it to the President.

"No charge?" POTUS asked in dismay. "What is this, a club membership?"

"Yup," sneered the Chief of Staff.

"And what do the boys at Langley think?"

"The CIA Director is probably spitting blood from this. As you know, he is naturally suspicious about any device that can spy on us from an adversary, especially from one he calls a friend."

"I certainly understand him. That's his job," POTUS said with a smile and scraped his plate with his last piece of bacon.

"In other words, Israel intended to charge an annual fee for countries who'd join the club and use the service of the Orbix-eye for civilian purposes. They offer mutual control between us, but we don't know what this Orbixeye does."

The President sat back in deep thought and then asked, "Do you think the explosion was sabotage, given the device's secrecy?"

"Perhaps."

"Inform the CIA Director to search for more information; I authorize using the old method of gathering information, if necessary."

"Mr. President, if I may..." the Chief of Staff began, pursing his lips, "President-Elect Cole will take office soon. This will be his headache. We should get him involved. Soon."

CHAPTER THREE

November 17th, Last Year

"F uck," growled Greco as the Cosmodrome security officers stormed the control room to evacuate the staff and start their initial investigation. Dan and Greco were amazed by the security's speedy response. *They clearly trained for this kind of a scenario,* thought Dan with wide eyes.

"What is this?" asked Dan, watching security aim their AK-47s only slightly to the floor.

"No idea," Greco whispered. "This is probably their routine emergency response."

"I think they are protecting us," Ezra speculated.

The general's encrypted cell phone rang. He listened while holding up his pointer finger. The head of the Mossad agency was on the line, obviously furious.

A minibus was waiting to drive the staff back to their rooms, a one-mile ride from the destroyed rocket. They intended on keeping everyone from sniffing around the facilities.

In Tel Aviv, they had instantly received the news via live transmission. The world intelligence services turned speculation to high gear—they wanted to know who was responsible and why.

"This was not the first time a Proton burned," said Greco into the phone. "The rocket experienced mechanical failures, which had all been corrected since."

"Don't be naïve!" yelled the man on the other end of the line. He was the head of the Mossad, referred to as Meir—or M.

Greco had to agree with his counterpart in Tel Aviv. Suspicion of sabotage—even remotely—was ample reason to quickly gather clues, either by elimination, reasoning, or physical evidence on the ground. No one trusted anyone at that point.

"If it were an accident, the recorded information from the control room would clarify that, but assessing it would take time," said Greco as Dan listened. "Until then, any information will remain classified by the Russians and Chinese."

"I'll send an official Israeli request to assist in the investigation."

"No use. As always, they will deny politely," Greco stated curtly.

"When the malfunction was announced, T-plus one second...the point of no return...it looked like an accident. No one will be sure until the data and videos are analyzed by experts repeatedly," Meir continued over the line. "The Mossad needs answers now. The Orbixeye should be the focus!"

"What do you suggest?" asked Greco and raised his eyebrows at Dan in frustration.

Meir had already shared his theory with his top men. He immediately suspected China or Russia, but he was not quite sure yet—after all, they were under contract to buy the Israeli satellite company.

"The Chinese themselves were part of this launch with three secret satellites of their own. Now they are gone, as well, so there was no motive for China to sabotage and cause the explosion," said Eyal aloud.

"Russia, who doesn't like to be behind on the global stage, was watching China take the lead, filling the void left by America after the cancellation of their space programs," Meir barked.

"It was an opportunity to seize control of space before another American President could take over with an aggressive space agenda," Dan replied toward the cell's receiver.

"After looking at the global threats piling up—" Greco started.

Meir cut him off, "Russia and China knew to use this vacuum to their advantage, just as the United States did when they introduced the first nuclear bomb to the world. It was a way of saying, 'I have it, and no one else will.'"

"We all know that whoever controls space, controls the orbit, and whoever controls the orbit, controls the planet," Greco muttered.

"Precisely," snapped M., who personally believed that global superpowers had started the war in space, decades after President Reagan's announcement of the Star Wars program. "The CIA knew something about this matter and tried to sugarcoat it for the President. Images of the explosion were recorded by a spy satellite monitoring all foreign space activities. Other than that, President Clayton and Henry Thomas lost the election to Cole because they did not show any interest in intelligence information during his campaign. His foreign policy was weak. No plans or new ideas were presented in his campaign. Regardless, he'll most likely let his successor President-Elect Cole deal with it."

And yet, with only a little more than two months left in the Oval Office, President Clayton had decided not to wait. It looked better to transfer the information to the President-Elect immediately and wash his hands of any future steps.

The title of President-Elect was only two days old at that point. Cole hadn't even finished celebrating his fantastic victory over his opponent, the current Vice President, who'd been leading the polls decisively until the very end of the election.

President Clayton had completed two terms, and he thought he'd seen enough briefings and global emergencies. He didn't want to see the United States as the world's police. The presidency gave him prematurely gray hair and a wrinkled face and swiftly aged his body by what felt like twenty years. It was proof of both the privilege and cost of being the leader of the free world.

What the President didn't want to hear from his advisors was that many global territorial disputes had received an anemic response from the administration. That fueled new conflicts alongside the critical war in Syria and Afghanistan involving the major global superpowers.

The Clayton administration was up to its neck in these conflicts whether they wanted them or not. There was endless criticism for lack of action from the opposing party, his political adversaries, and other aggravating entities.

Clayton thought it was time to deliver the headaches to others; eight years was enough. His retirement could not be any sweeter than this. He was still capable of enjoying the simple things in life: writing his memoir for a hefty sum and playing golf all day with his best friends.

Clayton's ghostwriter had joked in private that he hoped someone would read a memoir with zero accomplishments in it. However, Clayton didn't care. He shook hands with the publisher. All Clayton needed was a responsible, amicable, and swift transition out of office. That was what he felt he owed his country.

One of the main reasons his party had lost the election a couple weeks earlier was their weak response to the radical religious groups terrorizing the world. His belief was that if he didn't deal with them, they would not deal with him. That was another unresolved issue he would kick down the road to his successor. "The soft policies toward the rise of religious radicalism caught me by surprise," he said one day in an interview.

Politicians from both sides of the aisle and the world raised concerns that the newly elected Cole would deepen the conflicts and even endanger the world through abrasive policies that mirrored his personality. They feared he would lead a major new war and drain the country's piggy bank.

President-Elect Cole looked at the recession of the country on the eve of World War II and the economic boom after the war as an example of what the country could achieve with good leadership, and he was not concerned about it. *I know where the money is being spent, and I'll change that*, Cole had already thought to himself.

"After me, the deluge," chuckled President Clayton to himself as he read the briefings piling up on his desk.

The intercom buzzed and shook him from his passing thoughts. He gently pressed the button. "Yes?" His voice was calm. He listened, groaned at the mouthpiece, "Got it—get me the President-Elect," and slammed the phone down.

Clayton's National Security Advisor and Secretary of Defense, backed by the CIA, had been warning the President of the massive Chinese military buildup for a while. It seemed that for eight years, the President had ignored the calls under the premise that the country needed to pay for other social programs that, if not treated, would fuel anarchy. President Clayton preferred to reduce military buildup and slow down the replacement of parts. He even cut funding for the research departments of major universities, slowing down the development of technological advancements. The social programs were received well and gained him one of the highest approval ratings for an outgoing president.

Submarines, carriers, ships, and fighter planes were grounded or docked, rusting in ports and junkyards. At the same time, the largest Communist dictatorship in the world was building their nuclear-powered submarines identical to the Akula class 190MW. They utilized salvaged Russian ships with reverse engineering to create new ones and refurbish the others with newly developed systems they bought from all over the world. New fighters and stealth jets were developed to replace the aging Russian equipment in the Chinese military.

Chinese businesspeople were always economically monitoring the United States, which bought the majority of their products. Any change in America would inflict a slowdown as the two major economies in the world were tied together. So, China always made sure to be ahead of the United States by devaluing its currency or raising taxes on their products.

In the G20 meetings and on talk shows, political thinkers were complaining, inquiring when the United States would stop the world's milking of the American people.

No doubt, Clayton listened to senators of his party, who repeatedly demanded investment in cybersecurity to curtail their adversaries' threats. He understood that cybersecurity was only an additional paragraph in the insurance policy—not the policy itself.

"What will you do if Russia attacks the United States with a hundred bombers? Would you hack them?" then-candidate Cole asked his opponent in one of the Presidential debates. "We should have both strong military and cybersecurity so that no one will mess with us," he added.

During the Clayton presidency, the world had chopped itself upon the battlefield, hoping that shrapnel would not reach America, which proved to be the contrary.

Media figures and senators from both sides of the aisle claimed that China was using its proxy, North Korea, to keep the United States on a short leash while they developed new ideas to control the world. Others laughed at the Armageddon prophesies on national television.

Chinese ambitions were subdued, secretive, manipulative, and went unnoticed. Burying his head in the sand played well for Clayton's foreign agenda. The President projected no immediate threat, and his smiling diplomacy would eventually prevail.

China's declarations of ownership over the Senkaku Shallow Islands in the East China Sea were a signal that they were not stepping down, even at the cost of confrontation. Those islands had been under the control of Japan since 1895.

Taiwan claimed sovereignty, as well; the dispute was due to a potential oil discovery in the region. Despite stressing their opinion publicly and the red light of possible war, the Pentagon subdued the flames, as commanded by the Oval Office.

The islands were used to build a strong military base to intimidate and control the China and Yellow Seas.

America's red lines were crossed again and again. There was no response when China announced they had destroyed one of their Fengyun-series weather satellites with an ASM-135 ASAT missile orbiting 865 kilometers above the earth. They'd stolen plans via hacking, thus initiating themselves into the exclusive "Earth-to-Space Missile Club."

Presidential candidates said many things they didn't mean, or didn't say what they did mean; in the end, the bottom line was everyone hoped that everyone knew what they were doing, signaling to the world and admitting that there was soon to be a new crazy sheriff in town.

On the agenda of the last campaign was a subject that was never discussed openly: China's technological advancement had shattered America's superiority in space in just one decade.

The signs of China's doing so were everywhere, starting with their capability to destroy a satellite by kinetic kill, traveling eight kilometers per second at high altitudes.

The Pentagon could not live with that threat. China did not admit immediately to the test, and thus raised the concerns that they were seeking to increase their presence, no doubt for future military applications.

Some high-ranking military officers and Pentagon officials analyzed the situation and shook their heads over the "sitting duck" policy required of them. A few times, they'd taken action without consulting the administration, avoiding a long wait or flat-out refusal.

The phone rang again. The voice of the President's assistant was grumpy. The White House staff didn't like the result of the election, and they made sure the President knew it.

"The President-Elect is on the line," murmured the intercom.

Clayton picked up the phone with a lazy hand.

He was not in the mood for a heavy-duty conversation. Somehow, he managed to start by saying, "Congratulations on your victory, Mr. Cole." It was his first greeting to the victor after the election.

"Thank you, Mr. President. It's a great honor coming from you," the voice on the other end replied respectfully. The President-Elect thought to himself that the POTUS could've congratulated him two weeks earlier, but he let it go.

Soon to be inaugurated, Cole respected the man still in the Oval Office for what he was at heart. However, Cole could be a merciless wolf in political debates, using his quick tongue without control.

This evening, Cole was calm, assured, and tried to transmit a humble and friendly attitude.

Cole had been busy on his ranch since the victory, making phone calls to a shortlist of his proposed candidates for his new administration. It had started taking shape as a hardline government, precisely as he had promised in his campaign.

Cole had left traditional Republican territory with a new, right-wing agenda to keep America in power. "People can change their minds," he'd stated.

"There are urgent matters that can't wait," Clayton remarked. "We need to meet. The sooner, the better."

"Is this evening soon enough?"

Clayton chuckled by how eager his successor was to jump right into the hot tub without checking the temperature first. "Yeah, why not? Dinner's on me. Seven o'clock sharp," he replied.

"You got it. I'll bring wine from one of my cellars," Cole offered proudly.

"Not necessary," Clayton said politely. "We have the best bottles in the White House cellars." Cole wasn't President yet—Clayton wouldn't offer him any power, even regarding beverages.

Clayton covered the phone with his hand and asked to meet with his Chief of Staff right away.

Minutes later, Spanapolous walked into the Oval Office. A short, thin man, he was nicknamed "Spinach" due to his Greek last name. He stood in front of Clayton's desk, waiting for instructions.

"Seven o'clock in the Roosevelt Room. Just you and the security team. We are hosting the President-Elect for dinner. Check who is coming with him and brief me. Thanks."

"Yes, Mr. President."

Then, just before Spinach left the office, Clayton added, "Oh, yeah, and invite CIA Director Gene Bennett, as well."

Spinach left to make the meeting a reality.

CHAPTER FOUR

11:11 a.m., March 3rd, Current Year

John Fisher, a former spaceship-astronaut, was in good shape and made sure he maintained a healthy lifestyle to keep himself strong at seventy-one years old. He was always complimented for his youthful looks. "It's genetics," he'd reply with a shy tone to hide his pride.

On one occasion, when working in a restaurant as a waiter during his student life, a customer asked him how old he was. He said, "Twenty-three."

The customer was amazed and replied, "You look seventeen. But, you see that waiter behind you? He looks twenty-three!"

The waiter behind them turned around and stated, "No, I'm seventeen." The customer laughed out loud, but John never forgot this amusing incident.

For many years, John flew for the Navy, piloting over twenty types of planes in his career. During his last service years, he was a test pilot before joining NASA training for the space shuttle program. He was one of the only 241 astronauts hired at that time for the space program and piloted the shuttles on three missions.

Despite his love of flying, his heart always drew him back to his thousand-acre ranch; he loved handling his cattle and collecting orphaned animals from the grasslands of Kiowa, New Mexico. He liked the quiet, simple life, free from the pressures of modernity and world conflicts broadcast daily in the media. In his golden years, he looked for solace. The hard farm work was one thing that kept him in good shape, even though it'd been a decade since he was last checked by a NASA physician or at a gym. John didn't pursue colonoscopies, stress tests, or routine annual visits. He used to say, "If you see me on the floor, do not resuscitate—just shoot me in the head if I'm still breathing!"

Sophie, his wife, was just the opposite: a gentle, soft-spoken, delicately framed woman who admired her husband blindly and stuck with him for good or ill. She never watched the shuttle launches and declined media interviews and invitations to join the rest of the families on the grandstand of Cape Canaveral. She was never eager to visit the launch pad, which was some miles away from the grandstand. She saved her curiosity for reading books, especially old romance novels by Jane Austen or Nora Roberts. Sophie also never watched the shuttle launches or news on the television. If a problem occurred during her husband's launches, all she did was pray for his safe return home.

John's sculpted jawline and deep blue eyes were as impressive as those of a Hollywood actor; his penetrating gaze could melt a rock. In the Navy, they'd called him "John Wayne." His presence drew attention whenever he entered a room, and his colleagues always fought to join his team—in both the military or at NASA. His bold yet relaxed approach to solving the hardest problems made him the legend that he was in the space program, putting him right up there with the iconic Mercury Seven astronauts.

John was the neighborhood pillar; everyone knew "John the Astronaut." He provided jobs to local cowboys and encouraged the young to go to college. John helped local elders with their financial burdens, and from time to time, he anonymously bought meals for a local shelter, but everyone knew he was the donor. He always repeated something he'd heard from a celebrity ages earlier: "Do the right thing when no one sees you—not just in front of a camera."

John's farm was secluded, located northeast of Springer, New Mexico. From Route 412, there was a one-mile, choppy dirt road leading to the main farm residence and the cowboys' barracks. His cowboys handled his massive herd and the daily routine of a dairy farm.

Behind the residence was a windsock hanging high on a pole beside a dirt runway where he kept his Piper J-3 Cub tied to concrete anchors. The Piper was used almost every day to check on his cattle and keep him flying. He never really knew the exact size of his herd. He'd lost the number long ago, as the cows had multiplied at a fast rate. Mountain lions, wolves, coyotes, and bears living in the area took a bite occasionally, but it didn't seem to bother John at all.

When John was curious to know how many heads of cattle he had, he flew his plane and counted a bunch of them, and then, by extrapolation, came up with a number. He didn't need complete accuracy, as long as his alpha male, a huge bull he called "Hulk," kept the population growing.

"The coyotes have to live, too," he'd say with a chuckle when people asked him about predators.

He'd made emergency landings a few times when the Piper's old engine, although well maintained, didn't quite make it. He'd repaired it in the wilderness when new parts were flown to him by friends.

That day, he was busy repairing his tractor with his niece's husband, Gary. The two were bonded when it came to fixing the farm's equipment and flying the Piper. For Gary, it was the paycheck for his help, and no one was happier than he when taking over the controls.

"Hey, John. You got a visitor," said Gary calmly, looking at the dust cloud raised by a heavy car on the dirt road.

"It's the mailman," answered John when he examined the approaching vehicle. "They come here once a week with all my mail, mostly junk mail, which I use to start my fireplace in the winter." He chuckled aloud.

The mailman's car stopped just feet in front of them, tossing a huge plume of dust into the air. The mailman apologized with a smile and walked the short distance to the mailbox with a stack of letters and fliers.

"The usual crap, Eric?" asked John.

The mailman nodded his head. Then he raised one letter in the air and said, "No, wait a second, John. There's a letter here from NASA!"

"NASA?" John wrinkled his forehead. He hadn't heard from the agency for a long time. *Perhaps another invitation to a ceremony or something,* he thought. After so many requests to participate in public events, he simply declined politely, feeling his service to his country had come to its end. The agency had stopped sending invites but continued mailing holiday greeting cards.

Sometimes he was invited to a local news station to discuss an event; yet, after a while, he stopped doing that, as well.

"Let me see it," said John, and the mailman respectfully handed it over.

Everyone knew that John was the most celebrated shuttle astronaut currently alive, having witnessed a space event that triggered the cult of alien conspiracy theories. He never talked about it in public. "It's all imagination," he would say, but he saw them.

He opened the stuffed letter that was stamped two weeks earlier. As he read it, his tanned face grew serious.

"What's up, John?" asked Gary.

"Not much," he replied, "And thank you, Eric." John directed his blue eyes at the mailman, who understood that he was no longer needed.

"See you next week," Eric answered and was engulfed by the same dusty haze as he left the farm.

John kept the letter's contents to himself.

Suddenly, a chopper rattled the air in the distance. The Black Hawk military helicopter flew very low and headed straight toward John's ranch. It hovered above the house and landed behind it, beside the windsock, throwing far more dust than a mail truck.

"This bastard will have to wash my farm," murmured John as he walked to the landing site. Gary was curious, trailing just behind him.

Sophie came out of the house and stood on the porch with a few curious employees. Then she walked quickly to the back of the house and glanced at the scene with anticipation.

The dust settled, and John saw the pilot's white helmet peeping from his window.

"What's this, John?" asked Sophie, concerned. Her soft voice could barely overcome the noise.

"Don't worry, Sophie," he said, calming her down. "Someone probably just missed me." He chuckled at his own joke.

The chopper's door opened, and a short man with an impeccably ironed Marine Corps uniform stood on the threshold, examining the area. He spotted John and his leather cowboy hat and sooty aviation sunglasses.

"General!" John called out once he recognized the rank on the man's shoulders and his chest full of medals.

The general's short, stocky frame stepped down the aircraft steps and crossed the short distance. He stretched his hand out, his face serious.

"Colonel Fisher. I am General Bradley Bloomfield, NASA's new military Attaché."

"Nice to meet you, General. Apparently, they forgot to tell you that I left the military long ago, and I'm not a colonel anymore." John's forehead wrinkled.

Bradley scoffed and smiled wide as John searched his face for answers.

"What's all this about?" John asked, internally a bit surprised by the grand military entrance.

"You didn't respond to letters from the agency. We sent you a few with no reply, and you don't answer the phone, either," the general reprimanded John like one of his soldiers.

"Well, thank you and NASA for checking on my wellbeing. I just got this letter in my hand ten minutes ago, and it's the first one in ages. The mail is very slow around here, you know." John raised his hand and waved the envelope.

Bradley dusted off his jacket and asked impatiently, "May we talk privately?"

"Sure. Come with me," John replied and signaled his wife to prepare some refreshments in the house.

The two men entered a large foyer leading to a library full of military, space, and shuttle memorabilia. John closed the door behind them and sat himself on the leather couch.

"Some collection you have here, Colonel," the general said with amazement. "Your entire life is here. So many photos, models." He looked around the room with great interest, identifying in his imagination each of the events that carved the space program's history.

"That's my past life, General."

"Of course, and nothing to be ashamed of. You are a legend, Colonel!"

John ignored the general's gesture and asked only, "Drink?"

"Sure. What do you have?"

"Bourbon?"

"I was hoping you would offer," the general chuckled. "That will do. On the rocks, please."

John approached him with two glasses. "What happened to General Hudson?" he asked Bloomfield firmly.

"Retired a year ago. I took his post at NASA."

"So, General, what brings you here? It's not a social visit, I presume?"

The general set his glass on the coffee table and snipped, "No, it's not, Colonel." It seemed that Bloomfield was eager to start the conversation. "Did you read the letter?"

"Just tell me," John insisted and took a sip from his drink, locking his eyes directly on the general's confident expression.

"Frankly, we need you," the general shot back.

"Who is 'we'?"

"NASA and the military...your country," declared the general, raising his tone.

"What's going on? And why me? Are we desperate?"

General Bloomfield leaned back in his chair and relaxed. John remained tense. The general grew excited as he spoke, moving his hand sporadically in all directions.

"Some things I can't disclose here and now—you need to hear it directly from the horse's mouth. I hope you understand, Colonel."

John nodded and swallowed half his glass of bourbon. "I guess I needed this shot," he mused. "Now, this must be very important if they sent you in a private chopper. What do they need me for, and when exactly do they need me?" John assumed that NASA sought his expertise and wanted a consultation.

"If you agree to hear what NASA has to say, you are coming back with me," the general's face was stone still.

John snorted and asked, "You're not serious, are you?"

"Dead serious. I was told to bring you in by hook or by crook." Bloomfield's expression didn't change. He raised his glass and swallowed the rest of his drink. John was impressed.

"Yes, the bourbon was a nice addition," the General said with a satisfied smile. "Colonel, do you remember the famous World War II poster? 'Uncle Sam Wants You!' Well, my message is the same. It's not a question. It's an order. I'm bringing you to Houston, no matter what."

John stared, his words dissipating on his tongue.

"Do I need to use my handgun?" the general asked, grinning below a raised eyebrow.

CHAPTER FIVE

10:00 a.m., March 6th, Current Year

The NASA administrator began his lecture before three-dozen space crew retirees seated in the large auditorium. Their clothing was casual, but their faces were tense, waiting to hear why they were there. Although it was early March, the weather was warm; the air conditioning hummed softly.

The giant auditorium in Johnson Space Center had a big movie screen behind the podium and its lecturer.

Among the attendees, John looked around and couldn't believe his eyes. Astronauts from his past missions sat with him in the same room, just like in the old days when they were young and adventurous. *Only crazy people like us would do shit like this*, he thought.

The administrator adjusted the microphone, cleared his throat for attention, then said, "An errant missile launched from a British submarine was mistakenly directed to Florida."

A murmur flowed through the crowd.

"Is the cause known?" asked one man loudly over the rest of the commotion.

"Not sure yet, but we're investigating," the administrator said. "We are trying to rule out that the missile was hacked to a revised target."

"That would be a serious threat," added the same man. The rest nodded their heads, still whispering amongst themselves.

The Johnson Space Center had been used for many missions, including those of the legendary Apollo Shuttle era, which had been grounded a few years earlier.

Fifty glorious years of an aggressive, visionary space development had turned all eyes in the world toward America's bravery. The great American space era had ended with the last shuttle mission in 2011 that retired the fleet—as many would say, "Too early and too soon."

"My name is James Coolie, but many of you do not know me," the lecturer announced and rubbed his bald head with his palm. "I know you have many questions; I will tell you why we brought you all here out of hibernation." He smiled and exposed a perfect line of white teeth. The crowd cheered softly and politely, although some thought it was a bad joke.

Coolie confidently explained the global status from the White House administration's point of view. "The military is monitoring global threats all around the world, and I don't need to tell you that the picture is scary." He paused and took a deep breath. "The CIA, the FBI, and the NSA are all up to their necks in national security threats and dealing with issues twenty-four-seven without disclosing them to the media or public. These issues were offered minimal budgets, just like the space budget was. Just ignored and trimmed to the bone."

More chatter ensued.

"Why were we called here?" someone demanded.

"I'm getting to it. We are trying to connect the dots every time there is an event or incident, even if it is seemingly insignificant. We want to ensure we are not missing anything, and we are not exposing our back nor threatening our existence, especially when we are not prepared."

Coolie cleared his throat again and sipped from the glass of water on his podium. "Our military is investigating the

British missile, and we are treating it as a terror attack. We are unsure whether it was launched in error or someone hacked their control system."

He continued without slowing down; on the contrary, his voice was loud and clear, almost patriotic.

"*So*, this event has opened our eyes to a new era of cyber-security in the military arena. Cyber counterespionage in our country was a low priority for a long time. And then our adversaries progressed with it."

He checked his crowd's attention and then continued, "Other countries like China, Russia, Iran, and North Korea took the lead in this open niche and now almost equal us in military power...all due to the slowdown of our military buildup."

"No one on the watch!" shouted someone.

Coolie continued without acknowledgement. "At the time, the United States was watching China build with great concern. Military top brass had briefed the President. The mega Chinese military force built their jet fighters, their nuclear submarines, their aircraft carriers, and added one hundred thousand new marine troops to their combat force, but no one in Washington was concerned."

James took another sip of water but didn't wait for remarks before he continued. He was eager, like everyone else in the room, to complete this torturous lecture and take off his jacket to cool down.

"We suspect that China is operating undercover. The Chinese successfully launched a missile that destroyed one of their space satellites. In case of future conflict, the missile can be directed at our equipment in space. Also, they have completed hundreds of undisclosed rocket launches with unidentified payloads. We have no clue what they shoot to space."

John, who purposely avoided all media, had missed most of the world's tension and was caught by surprise. *It's overwhelming but obvious*, he thought. He would not want to be in Coolie's shoes.

"We at NASA are aware of a Chinese probe orbiting the moon that discovered traces of water just below the surface," Coolie said. "The signal tracing water was stronger toward the poles and showed evidence that the discovery could support a community, if that was China's goal. The discovery was deeply analyzed by our scientists at NASA and was kept top secret, until now."

Tired from constantly reading from his prepared agenda, Coolie took off his reading glasses, cleaned them with his handkerchief, and rubbed his eyes.

Questions regarding secrecy and protocol fired through the air, and Coolie dried sweat from his forehead with the same handkerchief, folded it, put it back in his jacket that hung on the chair, and rolled his sleeves.

Another question came from the back of the room. John recognized Milton, one of the crew members of SST-128, which launched in 2009. *A professional guy,* John reflected.

Milton had achieved the same career as most of the astronauts as an ex-Navy pilot; he sat beside Max, a stocky, semi-bald former specialist of four shuttle missions. Milton was built like an athlete. His entire six feet carried not a single gram of fat, despite his age.

"I'll get to your question, but first, we need you all to sign a confidentiality agreement if you wish to go further," Coolie explained. "Open the drawer of your desk, sign the form, and pass it up to me."

With a few eye rolls or smiles, the former astronauts opened the drawers and pulled out a single form donning the official NASA logo. Silence filled the auditorium as they read carefully.

In the interest of relieving some of the tension, Coolie said, "Folks, your signature does not mean that you agree to join our assignment. If you wish, you may resign after you hear why you are here. But this confidentiality agreement will remain in effect either way." He was a natural at his job—recruiting former NASA space crews, technicians, scientists, astronauts, and specialists.

Whispering and chattering once again charged the room with a spark. John read, signed, and passed the form forward. The others followed, and all the forms were sent to Coolie's podium. He examined some briefly and then looked back at his guests. He knocked on the microphone three times to regain their attention and continued his speech.

"As you know, the former administration eliminated the Constellation Program, claiming it was too expensive. This program intended to go back to the moon, establish a base, and from there, move on to Mars. Design and development for new shuttles and landing vehicles ceased, and all we had left was the ISS program. We couldn't even send supplies from the American base to the ISS or our own astronauts."

Coolie's voice bent with frustration as he spoke. He was very passionate about the subject, not without purpose; he was chosen to lead the revived space program, bringing with him his motivation to lift his country back to glory.

"Our new President, Robert Cole, is very concerned that we are using adversaries' facilities to keep our interest in space while letting our own equipment rust in museums. Also, using their equipment, fuel, and supplies has never been free. We always play the rich country and pay a hefty amount of money to keep up the appearance. I quote the President: 'To pay our share is humiliating.'"

John was not sure where Coolie was headed with his lecture. *"Humiliating" is just a false jab at former President Clayton,* John thought.

"No politics, Mr. Coolie," John said loudly, sternly, catching Coolie off guard.

The two men exchanged cold glances.

Coolie then swiftly slid past John's remark. "As adversaries were warming up and flexing their muscles, our defense secretary wondered whether the tensions would lead superpowers into—best-case scenario, a new Cold War; or, worst-case scenario, a nuclear war."

Coolie nodded for his assistant to bring him a bottle of Coke.

John seized the moment to inquire further. "What's ahead?" he asked as Coolie sipped his drink.

"Look," Coolie said through an exhale, "in a meeting with the President, he asked us point-blank, 'What do we need to make sure we are not behind?' And we said, 'Money.' We asked him to fund us, to help us reconquer and control space again. In my personal opinion, we are on the brink of a conflict."

As Coolie gazed out over his audience, he imagined them wearing space suits and helmets, walking without fear into the rockets filled with explosive gases and millions of pounds of thrust to shoot them into space. *These are not the same people,* he realized, tightening his lips.

The former astronauts were silent, still digesting the information being thrown at them. "It could be a good April Fool's joke," John mused to himself, glancing around at his former colleagues. He didn't fully grasp what NASA's target was. Reconquer space—really? What was Coolie not telling them?

Milton took the opportunity to speak up. "So, how are a bunch of seventy-year-old, retired astronauts going to save the world?"

He didn't lose his sense of humor, John thought with a smirk. Max punched Milton in the torso for calling them old. "Speak for yourself!"

"Would you go up there again?" asked Milton, raising his eyebrows and grinning.

Max instantly retorted, "Yes, I would, if the country called me for duty!"

"No one has called you yet!" John shouted jokingly.

Neither has changed at all, thought John. Milton had been the youngest astronaut in the Apollo fleet, the one who took his golf club on the last Apollo mission and almost killed himself swinging it on the surface of the moon. That famous club hung in his garage.

"I remember bringing that roast beef sandwich onto the ship," Milton mentioned to John. "I'm sure you do, too, John." Milton smiled and leveled his sharp old eyes. "Nothin' I wouldn't do today." John remembered Milton's breadcrumbs float about their heads in the capsule.

A few golf balls remained on the surface of the moon, and Milton's sandwich stunt put a veto on bread for future astronaut menus.

"We're probably rusty, Coolie!" laughed Max.

Coolie's face remained frozen, his thoughts churning. He reluctantly stretched a fake smile and said slowly, "John Glenn was seventy-seven when he went aboard the STS-95. A year older than you are today, Milton."

Most nodded, their eyes thoughtful. Coolie pressed a button on the podium, and the large screen dropped down from the ceiling. He pressed another button, and the light in the auditorium dimmed to total darkness. He grabbed a laser pointer as the video flashed onto the screen.

"These are our Twin Probes, two gravity-mapping ships that captured the Moon's dark side with a camera called MoonKAM. The spacecraft was mapping every shadow crater and valley for possible landing sites for a refuge and supply camp on the surface of the Moon. As you can see, the surface is scarred, a rugged landscape, which some of you orbited in the past."

Coolie pointed the laser as the video paused. "Here, at this point, we observed suspicious activity without immediate explanation. Our scientists from MIT and other astrophysicists from universities throughout the country were asked confidentially to investigate. Many theories were thrown on the table, but none were realistic."

The camera zoomed in on the Moon's landscape which seemed to glow even without the light of the sun.

Coolie explained that the MoonKAM project was aimed at schools so students could take part in exploring the Moon's terrain. New generations of space enthusiasts and future crews explored the surface of Mars after being inspired by this project.

Coolie sighed heavily, his shoulders beginning to slouch.

"One of the MIT students asked us to investigate this special site," Coolie pointed the red dot at it. "The student claimed that the geological activity in this area was not natural. It looked like power tools or machinery shaped it. When investigating the land, zooming frame by frame, they claimed that there were machine tracks in the dust, stuck like Neil Armstrong's first boot print on the moon."

The video lit the imaginations of the former astronauts.

"NASA, therefore, had to ask—is this legitimately unknown activity? If yes, by whom? For what purpose?" Coolie postulated to the audience. His voice rose. His laser pen moved quicker from side to side, until he eventually leaned on the podium, exhausted.

Sitting frozen in their chairs, digesting the information, the astronauts could only imagine what the media would do with this news.

The lights rose again, and they all examined each other's faces in silence. Coolie's round face had relaxed. His smooth, shiny head was still sweating. He wiped it again, drank some Coke, exhaled, and met eyes with his new potential colleagues.

"Welcome to the geriatric department of NASA," Milton exclaimed, breaking the silence. His hoarse voice and everyone's laughter melted the heaviness.

"And how do we fit into all of this?" John asked, doubt audible in his voice. John had always said, "When I look in the mirror, I ask, 'Who is that old man looking at me?'" and his wife had always replied, "You are the age you want to be."

Coolie didn't answer right away. He took his time and glanced at the entrance, as if expecting someone else to join the party.

Right on cue, General Bloomfield walked in and replaced Coolie at the podium, his chest still glinting with medals. He waited until Coolie took a seat in the front row before speaking.

"Gentlemen, glad you all could make it here—with my help, of course. The United States needs you!" Then, clearing his throat, the general's face fell serious. "We have not faced a situation wherein we needed to recruit professionals this aggressively since World War II. We have no one else to go to aside from you, unless you don't mind using cosmonauts for the job."

The general shared a laughed with his listeners.

"I had to drag some of you here personally," Bloomfield continued, and John audibly laughed from his seat in the crowd.

"We need to send astronauts back to the moon as soon as we can. We were the first there and should also be the second!"

The room went from lukewarm to hot again. The astronauts narrowed their eyes. The objective was now clear.

"We don't have the time to train new people or build new equipment. It might be a national security threat, so time is of the essence," the general said slowly, emphasizing his last words. "Therefore, we need you, our experienced astronauts, as well as our old—but refurbished—equipment. We need to send you up there. The sooner, the better!"

"Wow!" a few uttered.

Others chuckled as if he were joking, but he clearly wasn't. The general stared them down.

"You don't mean the old spaceships?" asked Milton, amazed.

"Yes, exactly that! It would take years to complete a new shuttle and landing module, not to mention it would cost a fortune that we don't have right now. The plan is to use a modified space shuttle for the four-day trip and fit in it a refurbished Eagle Lunar Module." Bloomfield clenched his teeth.

James Coolie turned around in his chair in the first row and announced, "POTUS wants us to be ready for launch in one year." Then he signaled to the general to continue.

General Bloomfield quickly regained his confident tone. "You didn't know this, but you are not the first group hearing this lecture. We are reaching out to all former Apollo astronauts who landed on the moon and have the experience piloting the Lunar Module. Your group is actually our second team. For now, this is an amicable volunteering request." The general then cleared his throat to raise his voice. "We need three fully operational spaceship teams and two LLM astronauts for this mission. We set up a schedule to launch two shuttles one year from today. One year!"

The general paused and looked around, trying to read the faces in front of him.

"Yes, Andy, I can tell that you have a question," Bloomfield said as he directed his gaze toward a tall, skinny man dressed in blue jeans and a striped shirt. His eyeglasses drooped on the bridge of his nose.

"Yes, General, a great plan," Andy began, "I mean, you must've thought about it for some time, perhaps a couple of years. But isn't it better to wait for the new equipment to replace the old shuttles? I assume you want us to get there and return in one piece, right?"

Such honesty drew murmurs from the crowd.

General Bloomfield offered a grim look and retorted, "As I already said, we have no time to develop new equipment, nor do we have the time to train new crews. We are bringing two ships back from retirement—Discovery, which is in the Smithsonian Air and Space Museum in Virginia, and Atlantis, which is on display in Merit Island, Florida. Enterprise will be on standby, and we will refurbish them within the timeframe POTUS requires—about a year. The currently intact Eagle, a twin to the one that landed on the Moon, is in the Smithsonian in D.C. We will bring them back from retirement and equip them with new, powerful computer software, state-of-the-art robotics, and avionics to make your trip a walk in the park compared to your last missions." It was a tough sell but something the Pentagon thought must be done.

"How is this all financed?" asked Andy.

"We just received a twenty billion down-payment from POTUS."

"The President bought your shtick?" scoffed Milton, stirring laughter from the group.

"It clearly didn't take much, as you can see by the President's deadline and financial support," Bloomfield snapped.

Chatter broke out once more. The general let them vent to each other. The mood of the auditorium conveyed he could start getting results. *Maybe we really can rekindle their adventurous spirits,* Bloomfield thought.

"What about the booster rockets and other equipment not held in museums?" John asked loudly.

"We have in storage five boosters and two main fuel tanks that have never been used," the general responded, maintaining his determination.

Coolie turned to his guests once more and asserted, "We are very confident that the plan will succeed. Have faith in your NASA engineers and scientists. Your mission will be a success, and we will bring you back home, just like last time. Remember Apollo 13?"

An understanding, nostalgic hum filled the auditorium. Coolie and the astronauts held knowing, still gazes.

CHAPTER SIX

4:50 p.m., November 17th, Last Year

The destroyed launch pad was immediately sealed off from anyone without a special security clearance. There was nothing left to save. The emergency fire department stood across the field and could do nothing but watch the fire consume the remains. Approaching the launch area without risking the lives of the firefighters was not possible; it had to wait.

The launch pad was pitch black, and only fire trucks provided random light around it, other than a few flames still burning. The firefighters sat in their warm truck cabins, waiting for instructions from the authorities. They were not eager to get out in the cold.

Concerns regarding additional explosions due to heptyl, amyl, and kerosene fuel, which had evaporated in the air, prevented them from going closer, even though they wore protective gear and masks. They would have to wait for a long time until it would be safe.

Greco and Dan got into their room, chatting about the unbelievable event. Now they flipped the switches in their heads to a different mode: intelligence security for the Mossad.

"Something stinks," said Greco, opening Spotify on his cell phone to play The Beatles' "Back in the USSR." They both enjoyed the irony.

"Very appropriate, even though someone might be listening. The walls have ears, too," Greco whispered.

They scooted closer together to speak in hushed tones.

"Although M. is retiring in a month and G. is supposed to take over, M. is still the boss," whispered Greco as he hunched his shoulders.

Dan furrowed his brow, questioning.

"M. wants us to nibble on the crash site before evidence is contaminated or 'magically' vanishes," Greco added.

"We do not have the proper gear and equipment for an excursion like this. I suggest that you stay behind to cover for me," Dan said, his anxiety contained in his even tone. This request was daring and unexpected, but as an agent, he was ready for any call, anytime, without questions asked.

Greco himself had participated in many missions behind enemy lines and knew well the feeling of adrenaline rushing through his veins.

They synchronized their watches, and Greco said, "It's 5:03, and we don't have all night. Be back within an hour or so. I will have the Samson cargo plane ready for takeoff when you arrive. But remember: if you get caught, we can't rescue you from here—so you are on your own. We will communicate via Rina app only."

"Roger that," Dan said with a nod. He narrowed his thoughts on his assignment. He never knew where destiny would lead him, but he usually could handle poking around in secret, considering his extensive training. As M. used to tell him from time to time, "Go, seek, and you shall find it!" It reminded him of when his wife shopped, hitting store after store in the local mall as the clerks asked her, "Are you looking for anything special?" She always answered, "I will let you know when I find it." Thoughts of his wife and children sprouted warmth in his chest.

Dan opened his diplomatic bag and pulled out his night gear, mask, infrared binoculars, and warm black clothes, and he changed quickly. He checked his equipment, mainly communication devices and a GoPro with infrared capability and satellite-connectivity. Then he disappeared into the night.

In the distance, he saw the lights of the vehicles and small fires still around the pad. He headed in that direction, taking advantage of the shadows for cover.

No one was outside. Dan maneuvered stealthily, using buildings and other structures to keep out of view. *A mile is a fifteen-minute walk on a treadmill,* he thought. The reality was different, though, and it could take half hour or more to close the gap in the dark. Dan was not ready to end his career in a Siberian basement, Gulag, or by getting shot on the grassland around the demolished launch pad.

The destroyed Proton rocket launch pad was to the northwest of the vast Cosmodrome city, close to Ashubulak Lake. The Yunileinty airport, where the Israeli Air Force's Hercules C-130J aircraft was parked on the tarmac, was some six miles east of the launch pad. He kept this info in mind for his escape route.

A few other launch pads were in between, and Dan took notice. The residents' building, known as Site Number 95, was a little over a mile southeast from the pad, comprised of a few buildings and barracks that also housed the teams that worked on the Proton rocket program. The barracks were away from the Proton launch pads, just a series of buildings offered to guests there to monitor the operations. The remaining distance was wide open once Dan passed the few facilities and low buildings.

Grass and sand covered his route, but since there were no facilities producing light, he could blend in with the dark, watching for emergency vehicles potentially using the same road. He used his night goggles to walk in and out of small trenches and ditches.

The headlights of two trucks shone behind him on the road. He quickly took cover in a ditch, lying flat and still. They passed by slowly, their powerful diesel engines gasping for air.

At first, he moved rapidly, remaining in the shadows as much as he could. In the open, there wasn't much to hide behind other than bushes and shrubs. As he got closer, he needed to sporadically crawl to safely move through the grassland. As usual, his GoPro camera sent live images of his mission directly to the Mossad control room that disclosed his location and communicated warning signals via satellite in the event of danger. The night goggles enhancing his vision were something he had used in his military service behind enemy lines many times in previous years. It was how he earned his reputation as one of the most daring soldiers in the Israeli armed forces.

His encrypted Rina app buzzed on his smartwatch. He pressed the button on the watch and listened through his earbuds.

"Test. What's your position?" asked Greco from his barracks.

"Close," Dan quipped.

"A lot of activity around the pad; there are armed soldiers," a voice warned through the app, and Dan recognized it to be that of his boss in Tel Aviv. "They are probably watching the area via diverted satellite instant imaging, using a high-resolution night camera in low orbit."

It was bitingly cold, and the northeast wind was an inconvenience for Dan. Winter temperatures there lingered between negative sixty and four degrees Fahrenheit at night. Dan felt lucky that evening, as it was one degree above freezing. He hoped the battery that was warming his overalls would last the trip; his face was cold, even with his mask. He tried to ignore it and move as close as possible to the pad. Initially, he found nothing of interest. The road he walked on was the only one leading to the pad. There was only one paved utility road leading to the runway, as well. This was the same airport near the Cosmodrome, which was used to load and unload space equipment from planes that landed from countries connected to the global partnership of the ISS program or private entities.

The fire trucks, parked at a safe distance, planned to be there until the area cooled down from the explosion.

The odor of burned metal mixed with other rocket materials joined the fuel fumes, and Dan readjusted his mask to cover his nostrils. Some shrubs had caught fire and were extinguished quickly by the firefighters.

Getting even closer, Dan noticed the military trucks that had passed him earlier on the road, recognizing them as the new Kamaz 63969 Typhoon armored vehicles used for reconnaissance and surveillance during nuclear, biological, or chemical warfare. This is what his agency had warned him about. It could carry up to sixteen troops, fully equipped, and Dan expected to see them deployed all around the burned launch pad. Each vehicle had a crew of two in addition to the sixteen, all carrying assault weapons. *Obviously protecting a secret*, Dan thought.

The picture was not pretty as well as unexpected. But that was the way it usually went. "Expect the unexpected; don't be surprised—handle it!" M. used to say to his graduates in training camps.

Through his infrared binoculars, synchronized with his smart watch and GoPro, Dan could take photos and videos to send via an encrypted satellite connection. The gadget could see images up to five hundred feet away in total darkness. Delicate sensors could detect heat and hazardous materials that might affect humans in a hostile area. It was like the Mossad had anticipated the catastrophe in advance and packed all his special equipment in his bag for him.

This could end badly, Dan thought as he watched the soldiers getting off the trucks, spreading themselves over the ground. He could not identify if they were Russian, Kazakh, or Chinese soldiers. But it didn't matter. They were a threat. No one was supposed to be anywhere around the exploded rocket without clearance. He pointed his binoculars toward the airport and saw his plane on the tarmac, exactly where he'd parked it when they'd arrived a few days earlier. He was relieved. The path home was open. He smiled.

Dan carried no weapon. In the event of a confrontation, he needed to use his hands, legs, and whatever he could find on the ground. Fighting a human face-to-face was not a problem. He was a master of Krav-Maga, the Israeli military's martial art—a combination of Judo, Aikido, and other forms of Asian combat and self-defense techniques. He hoped he would not have to use his skills; it was too cold to enjoy a good fight.

A safe distance away from the truck and keeping an eye on the troopers, he saw a few of them congregate in one spot on the pavement, receiving instructions from their leader. Dan was about five hundred feet from them and could hear their chatter. They seemed confident that no one else was in the vicinity as their leader barked his orders. He thought he heard Russian.

Dan saw nothing to report so far, no clues, no hint that might point to a breakthrough.

The soldiers acted as if they were searching for something, but he had no idea what that would've been. He decided to head back; there was nothing more for him to safely do.

The twisted metal and unrecognizable parts of the rocket were the only remaining evidence of any secret or story to uncover. Dan could hardly believe they used to be pieces of a proud, incredible, and advanced technological machine only two hours earlier.

Back in the residence building, Greco prepared his small delegation of assistants and technicians for transfer to the IAF plane, which was fueled and ready for departure. The security forces refused to let them go before receiving a quick "clearance" from the authority—which meant questioning. Greco delayed the departure without disclosing the reason to the rest of his delegation. *The less they know, the better,* he thought. He asked them to stay in the room and not ask or answer any questions.

Two short beeps in his earpiece alerted Dan and reminded him that someone was watching him from the skies. He smiled to himself nervously. He pressed himself firmly against the frozen ground when he heard a twig snap just behind him. Dan turned his head and saw a huge man aiming an AK-47 directly at his chest. The man was over six feet tall with a flashlight fixed to his helmet; he wore full gear, insulated winter overalls, and winter boots. *The Russians know how to dress their soldiers,* Dan thought, straining for a quick exit strategy. The man's body language didn't transmit a friendly signal—and he was threatening enough even without the gun. Dan had to act fast. Any second could be his last, and in this scenario, it looked like one of them was going to die. And shortly.

"*Kto ty?*" the soldier barked. Dan recognized the Russian— "Who are you?"

Dan interpreted the soldier's communication as an attempt to resolve their meeting peacefully without alerting his comrades. Dan didn't answer. Instead, he swung a kick at the trooper's heels, sending him straight to the ground with a heavy thud. Immediately, Dan leapt and held the soldier's gun barrel with one hand, deflecting it away from his torso. He kicked the soldier hard in the testicles. A loud groan escaped from the man's lungs, followed by quick gasps. Dan didn't stop as the giant Russian showed signs of a quick recovery, and he used his heel to hit the soldier with enough force to crack a cinder block.

A single shot pierced the darkness as the Russian crumpled in pain, and Dan, still holding the barrel away, was ready to kick him in the head, but the soldier locked his hands around Dan's feet, grabbed them tightly, and pulled back. Dan crashed to the ground just like his opponent had and let out a groan. *It's getting ugly,* Dan thought. *That gun is becoming a problem.* Dan scoured his mind for solutions. This fight needed to end. Fast.

The shot was heard by others, and Dan was sure that troopers would storm the area immediately. The rifle was out of reach as they both lay on the ground, groaning and struggling to get an advantage.

The soldier seemed determined to handle Dan by himself, and he didn't call out for backup.

The other soldiers in the distance had apparently thought the shot was a random, small explosion from the shattered rocket material.

"Dimitri," someone called.

The soldier spun his torso and easily gained control over Dan. Dimitri started to choke Dan with his bare hands, utilizing his enormous weight to crack his neck. With nothing to help Dan to win this fight, he feared he was taking his last breath on earth.

With potentially only seconds to live, he had to do something before he lost consciousness and slipped away. If he couldn't find a way out of this situation, he would be buried without a tombstone in the nearby marsh forever. His throat locked. His eyes began uncontrollably tearing. With the last bit of energy left in his body, he searched for the rifle or something else on the ground to use as a weapon to defend himself—rock, stick, anything...

Still groping with his hands, Dan felt an unusually hard object. Whatever it was, he lifted it and struck the man on his head furiously several times. The trooper released his grip, holding instead his injured head.

Dan didn't stop until the man was silent and immobile on top of him. With the first air Dan inhaled, he smelled alcohol on the soldier's breath. "Damn cheap vodka," he growled and cracked Dimitri's head open with the foreign object in his hand.

Dimitri went entirely limp. Dan felt terrible—this soldier probably had parents or perhaps children. But Dan didn't have the luxury of time to mourn. He checked for a pulse to make sure Dimitri was neutralized and with his ancestors in heaven. Blood poured down onto Dan from the soldier's cracked temple.

Dan rolled the dead body to the side and felt relief. He sat quietly for a brief second to evaluate his situation and regain his balance. He caressed his throat, which ached from where the man's nails had cut deep into his skin.

"Are you okay?" Greco asked, pleased to hear that Dan was victorious and breathing again.

"Yes; it was close," Dan whispered back.

"Okay, disconnect immediately, getting active."

"Roger."

Dan left the AK-47 close to the dead body, hoping it would appear that the soldier had accidentally shot himself. It wasn't safe to discharge the weapon again to make the scene more believable.

Dan checked his gear. He could not leave any trace behind that would instigate an international assassination frenzy among the spy agencies. He was not supposed to be there.

"Dimitri!" a call came from the distance, again.

Dan jerked from his thoughts and saw beams of flashlights searching in the dark.

With the little Russian language he possessed, he realized that the soldier's name was Dimitri. *"Da!"* he called back, lowering his voice slightly.

"Vse normal'no?"

Dan understood they were asking him if everything was okay, and he responded laconically, *"Da, ladno."* He hoped he'd won himself a few extra minutes to escape and vanish back to his residence building without leaving traces.

Preparing to leave the scene, he moved Dimitri's watch backward about fifteen minutes and slammed it on the ground. The watch stopped at exactly 5:21:23 p.m. Dan disappeared as fast as he could from the area, leaving the dead man behind in the cold.

Still holding the object that killed the Russian and saved his own life, Dan walked back as fast as he could. The object felt odd, invisible in his hand in the dark, a twisted metal or alloy of some kind. He decided to keep it and examine it later. After all, he owed his life to it. He knew that he was on borrowed time until they discovered the body of the soldier, and it was unlikely they'd buy that Dimitri shot himself—especially with head wounds from blunt force trauma. Dan had to escape the Cosmodrome, but he was not alone. His entire delegation was waiting for him and in danger, too.

As he hurried, he realized that he'd lost his left earpiece during the fight, and the communication with the agency via satellite was lost, as well. It was like losing eyesight and hearing at the same time, and he had to manage without them. The way back felt much longer. Making sure to avoid anyone nearby, he finally made it to his residence building. He looked like hell when tapping on Greco's door with the usual Mossad knock, like SOS in Morse code.

Greco anxiously locked the door behind them. He noticed the bloodstains covering Dan's clothing and the deep scratches visible on both sides of his neck. Immediately, Greco treated Dan's injuries.

"So, what the hell happened?" Greco questioned, his eyes wide. Dan showed him the bloody object he'd brought with him from the site as if it was a great archeological discovery he'd unearthed.

"What's this?" Greco asked.

"I had to kill a Cosmodrome guard who surprised me," Dan said as he took off all his gear and clothes. "Are we ready to leave?" he then asked.

"No. I was waiting for your return, and then we were asked to stay in our rooms—but the pilots are ready for departure."

Dan sighed and watched Greco.

"If they find the dead man, it's all over. We'll be stranded here, and hopefully, maybe they'll keep us alive. We need to get rid of all the evidence we have here," said Greco gravely.

Dan nodded his head in agreement. It was up to them to smuggle themselves onto the plane and take off without permission—and not for the first time.

"Greco. It's suicide either way; if we escape, it will be proof that we have something to hide, and when they find the dead soldier, they'll find my earpiece and comms near him," said Dan nervously.

"Well, everyone is a suspect—all the time," Greco said and cleared his throat. He shoved all Dan's bloody clothing and gear into the diplomatic pouch, which was the size of a personal military bag, and sealed it. In the event of a comprehensive investigation, he knew that hiding behind the diplomatic pouch probably would not help them much.

"I think we need to smuggle this to our labs for closer examination," Dan said, gazing at the foreign object in his hand. "I took photos of it and sent them to M."

Greco looked at the twisted, blackened object and shoved it in the bag, making sure he sealed it right the second time.

A knock on the door shook them out of their focused conversation.

"Shit," Greco whispered.

"Who is it?" asked Dan.

"Cosmodrome police," the voices behind the door shouted in Russian accents.

Quickly, Dan put a scarf around his neck to hide the scratches, and they both made sure that there was no evidence still lying around.

Greco opened the door, smiling, showing off the medals on his uniformed chest. Dan put on his delegation coat to show he was ready to leave, his scarf part of the warm outfit.

"Greetings," welcomed Dan. The two officers in full gear, ready for execution, had cold faces. When one of them forced a smile, Dan saw a golden tooth.

"*Poshli s nami*," they said and pointed their AK-47s in the direction they wanted Greco and Dan to go with them.

"*Khorosho, khorosho*," Dan said—meaning "good." Then he asked, "*Kuda my idem?*" (Where are we going?)

"*Avtobus*," replied one of the officers gruffly.

"Can we take our belongings on the bus?" asked Dan, and the officers nodded their heads.

"I assume we are safe," murmured Greco in relief.

"Let's hope so!"

Dan loaded his stuff on his back, hoping the guards would not change their minds.

They grabbed their personal and diplomatic bags and followed the two officers down the corridor, to the ground floor, and outside to the parking area.

When they walked out, they saw the two engineers standing there with their suitcases and two other police officers escorting them.

"Where is our scientist, Ezra?" asked Greco.

"He left for the plane with the cockpit crew," answered one of the engineers.

"It looks like the crew went to preflight the plane, and Ezra took off with them," said the other engineer.

Greco was puzzled. "We are in deep shit!" he whispered, concerned.

"Calm down, and don't show any sign of distress," replied Dan through a smile.

Only one Russian officer spoke some broken English, and he asked them to wait in front of the microbus while they searched the other rooms to ensure they were clear of people or anything suspicious.

They signaled to their leader that everything was good, and they let the Israeli delegation board the vehicle.

They didn't offer any details on their destination. Greco was still nervous, and Dan calmed him down. "They have nothing on us," Dan whispered assuredly.

"Should I ask them where they are taking us?" whispered Greco.

"Let's wait..." Dan replied as quietly as possible, his eyes on the officers. "If necessary, we'll take over the bus, keep the police officers as hostages, and direct the driver to the plane and then get the hell out of here."

The two engineers were unaware of the drama unfolding and just smiled, assuming everything was fine. One of the engineers had been born in Russia, though, before immigrating to Israel. He still spoke fluent Russian. He started a conversation with the police officer next to him. The conversation sounded like that of two old buddies, smiling and waving their hands in the air.

Dan inhaled deeply and exhaled slowly.

"This is the way to the airport," said the engineer calmly.

"Yes, that's the only road. We can see the planes in the distance," replied Dan in relief.

A mile away from the tarmac, the Hercules was flooded with lights for security purposes. A few police officers surrounded it. It was still unclear what the commotion was all about.

Greco signaled the engineer who was engaged in conversation to see if he could ask what was going on. The police officer explained that he had no idea; all they were asked to do was take them to the plane and wait there.

The microbus stopped short of the plane, and they were asked to board it quickly. The delegation greeted the police officers with mixed feelings, thanking some and ignoring others. Something wasn't right, but the delegation was just happy to be on board the plane; it was their home away from home.

Greco went straight to the cockpit and asked the pilot, Major Ilan, about the flight status. His copilot was flipping switches and frequencies, listening to the ATIS, and communicating with the control tower.

Greco, standing behind the captain, looked outside from the cockpit's side window and saw the police surrounding their aircraft's fuselage with machine guns aimed.

"What the hell is going on?" Greco asked the captain.

"The tower asked us to hold...a car is approaching the plane," the captain said calmly.

The car searchlight moved side to side as the vehicle made its way to the tarmac. At the same time, the copilot signaled that the tower was communicating with them.

The approaching car stopped, and the driver stepped out and spoke briefly with the police commander. Shortly after, the police guard boarded a military patrol vehicle and left them without explanation.

Greco sat in the cockpit behind the captain. He looked around, expecting the police to change their minds and storm the plane at any minute. His adrenaline sharpened his vision; his heart raced. Dan and the others were a little calmer in the main cabin, hoping it was all over.

Greco could not figure out why this episode had happened the way it did. It only seemed to confirm some political or security reasoning connected to the explosion.

"4 X-ray Juliet, Tango, Bravo, you are clear to taxi to runway seven zero."

There were only two choices: southwest or northeast heading, and the copilot, with his crisp English accent replied, "Juliet, Tango, Bravo with you; will depart using runway two five, heading west."

"Juliet, Tango, Bravo: variable wind, barometric pressure at 29.92. Taxi to runway two five for departure."

The majestic cargo plane roared and rolled to the runway.

Greco's smartwatch received an encrypted text message: "Are you airborne yet?"

"On the runway," replied Greco as the pilot aligned the Hercules on the centerline, pushing the throttles all the way to achieve maximum thrust.

"We had an unexpected situation," texted Greco.

"I know; I told airport authorities that our delegation got a bomb threat from a Chechnyan mafia group demanding ransom. I asked that they let you depart immediately with a heavily escorted guard."

As Greco read that text, his brow furrowed. "The plane was under our security watch the whole time?" he replied.

Dan walked into the cockpit, bracing his hands against the paneling as the plane rose. "What's up?" he asked Greco.

"M. was helping our situation from afar, as always," smiled Greco.

"That's him. His twisted mind is always working," chuckled Dan.

Greco turned to leave the cockpit and lay down on a stretcher, but then he suddenly walked about the entire aircraft, his eyes searching among the cargo and few passengers.

Greco returned to the cockpit. "Where is Ezra?"

"Didn't the engineer say he got on the airplane before us? I bet he's somewhere in the cabin." Dan said, glancing around.

Greco closed his eyes, rubbed the back of his neck, and released a ragged, exhausted breath: "I just came from the cabin."

CHAPTER SEVEN

6:55 p.m., January 3rd, Current Year

It's been forty-seven days since the rocket explosion, Chang-Jin lit a cigarette, one of the sixty he usually smoked during his workday. He sighed heavily; his face was crumpled, gloomy, and tired, clearly showing signs of distress.

The Head of the Chinese intelligence agency, known as The Ministry of State Security of the Republic of China (and its notorious Chinese Security Services department, or the CSIS), informed his superiors immediately of the catastrophic event and total loss of the Proton rocket and its payload. It was a significant setback for the Chinese space program.

Chang, reporting directly to the State Council, the raw administrative authority, had achieved victory in the previous few years for catching CIA spies roaming his country. One American agent was found guilty in a speedy espionage trial and was executed by a firing squad, despite pleas from the international community. The execution transpired in front of his colleagues, who were also caught after a coordinated sting operation. This execution was to intimidate the agents into talking. The CIA and the FBI could not figure out who'd set up dozens of CIA agents or how, with their strict training, they were caught. One theory was that they met with their connection agent at the same time and places instead of changing up their secret rendezvous locations—as they'd been trained. It could've been set up by a mole in the CIA or FBI system, but Chang kept it to himself. The last theory was that the CIA and FBI computers were hacked, disclosing all the spies in China and Far East Asia, but neither group would admit to that idea.

"It's devastating!" exclaimed the State Council. "What are your plans going forward, Chang?"

"We are investigating, your honor; I claim it was not an accident," Chang said with confidence.

"What evidence do you have?"

"The aerodrome authority found a Russian military policeman who'd died in a mysterious way. Something hit him," said Chang.

"Really?"

"Yes, the corpse is being examined by their pathologist under heavy supervision by the Russian intelligence medical examiner," explained Chang, hoping to be encouraged to proceed with his finding.

"Do you suspect anyone?"

"Yes—the CIA," Chang replied decisively.

Chang was concerned that the confidential launching of cosmonauts would be leaked somehow to foreign agencies.

"Cheating the world, Chang, takes superb confidentiality in our business," said the Council with authority, but without reprimanding their top spy. "You eliminated the foreign agents, cleaned up our county...that kind of information alone would turn the world intelligence community against the Chinese republic."

"True, your honor, Council," replied Chang, who considered the explosion of the Proton rocket his personal failure.

"The more this program is hidden under a blanket of secrecy, the better. It wasn't like North Korea, which displayed its nuclear capability left and right," continued the Council.

"Would Russia have done it? They are the only ones to gain. I ruled out the Israelis and..."

"What about the Americans?" asked the Council.

"Not sure. Perhaps. Russia followed the same strategy when launching 'killer satellites' about three years ago, which were found to be lethargic and non-operational—"

"Perhaps waiting for D-day when needed," the Council interrupted. "Russia launched and reported them as weather and communication satellites. However, the CIA reported that recently they had come alive and were maneuvering about one mile away from the Chinese space station. The threat was real, and we in the cabinet wanted to be prepared."

Chang lit another cigarette and said as he exhaled the smoke from his nostrils, "We learned from Iran how to manipulate and cheat the world during their quest to acquire the bomb. Agents on the ground and spy satellites were used to uncover the scheme. The eyes in the skies were always a problem for me. I know that I need to weigh every step to make myself look innocent, as multiple entities are constantly watching us. How we move our cosmonauts in capsules to the Proton confidentially will be studied in school as a principle of manipulation. The same way we installed a mega space station, piece by piece, over the last decade under the watchful eyes of the international community."

"No doubt that you are the best for this task," the Council assured Chang.

Chang, like his boss, was concerned about the loss of life, even if they had a full stock of cosmonauts in their possession. The concern stemmed from whether the explosion had disclosed the purpose and secret ambitions of the Chinese launch. No one knew at that point if the Chinese capsules were manned or not.

"I asked to seal off the site immediately and used our soldiers as part of the launch security agreement," Chang said. "As long as the money was paid, Kazakhstan and Russia didn't mind. They knew it was just a matter of time until we would use their Cosmodrome with their confidentiality and tight security. We sent one truck, and the Russians had a second truck."

"And better that they lost a soldier than us," the State Council said coldly. "The international community is following the United States and soon-to-be former President Clayton's footsteps in dealing with the global issues and have redirected funds from defense to social programs. We have a different priority; the people of our republic must invest and tolerate our political decisions for a better future. Our open market communism works; our social programs are better than during Mao's reign."

"Yes, your honor," Chang replied graciously. "Dimitri, the dead Russian soldier, was discovered with a crushed skull after he was reported missing by his commander. I want to know who killed him and retaliate. An eye for an eye. Most importantly, our intelligence must know if any security was breached during the launch."

"That's a Russian issue, isn't it?"

"Not entirely, your honor; breach of security is my primary concern, and secondly, Dimitri was half Chinese," Chang explained and opened Dimitri's folder, which had been emailed to him. Chang read aloud for the Council: "'Dimitri was born in a small Chinese community north of Moscow and spoke fluent Russian and Mandarin. He immigrated with his parents back to his homeland and joined the Chinese People's Liberation Army as a guard of the Rocket Force Division. His unit was deployed a few times to guard the Chinese rocket launches, sometimes joining the Russian troops, and he was very proud of his job.' His death marks the start of a countdown; I know that clashing with the most influential intelligence agencies in the world was just a question of time. Meanwhile, Dimitri's death is confidential for obvious reasons; we don't need anyone nibbling at the leftovers."

"Makes sense, Chang. A Russian-Chinese hybrid. Remarkably interesting."

"I must find out how and by whose hand Dimitri was terminated. Moreover, we must definitively know if the rocket explosion was sabotage or an accident. I dispatched our secret police to round up all of our technicians and scientists involved with the Proton to fly them to a secure location, a secret Army camp in northern China, to start an ironclad investigation."

"Was that necessary? These are our own people, Chang," reprimanded the Council.

"Well, the United States rounded up all their own American Japanese in World War II," Chang countered swiftly. "Also needing mention is that the Israeli Mossad Chief called me and asked for the immediate release of the Israeli delegation. If the Mossad knew something I didn't know, it could've been a trick."

"The Israeli intelligence community is considered our ally," commented the Council.

"Yes, they are considered an ally in many areas, but you never know...They spied on their best ally—the Americans," Chang said hoarsely through his cloud of smoke.

"Ah, had Dimitri intercepted the man that sabotaged the rocket?" the Council thought aloud.

"I scrutinized every second leading to the event after the explosion to find clues or a thread of information leading to a conclusion. I don't have any doubt that relationship and collaboration with Israel's technological division is advantageous. Where else could we find top technological breakthroughs for ridiculous prices? Our entire military buildup is based on other nations' startups and tech, pillaging their industrial communities."

"Our president would not allow me to jeopardize the relationship with this investigation. You walk a thin line between failure or success," warned the Council.

Since the explosion, Chang had figured out that his equation didn't work. *I'm missing parameters*, he thought. Letting the Israeli delegation leave without interrogation or search of their personal belongings was a mistake, even though they had lost a satellite in the explosion, as well. Wouldn't they too want to know what happened to the rocket that destroyed their satellite? There was not an official request to share information, although they'd asked to assist in the investigation and were declined. Perhaps it was too early, and agencies were licking their wounds first and waiting for the dust to settle. Chang's mind raced. "Too many unanswered questions," he whispered to himself as he looked up at his office whiteboard.

The large board displayed the timing of each event in front of him as he tried to imagine the exact chain of events. Chang read each aloud for the Council: "4:26:55, Engine T-minus five seconds. 4:27:00 p.m., T-time. 4:27:01, leak announcement, abort mission. 4:27:06, explosion. 4:50:00, emergency team dispatched. 4:57:00, first microbus transfers the Israeli delegation to their guestrooms from the control room. 5:03:00, assumption of someone's potential walk from the guest housing to where Dimitri's dead body was ultimately found, assumption of the deadly encounter to be between 5:18:00 to 5:25:00. If the person in question presumably walks back to the guest housing, it would be between 5:38:00 and 5:45:00 back in the room, not later than 5:55:00.

If the watch stopped with the first blow...or three minutes prior to his watch stopping, it's 5:39:12 to 5:42:12. IAF plane take-off registered at 6:05:17, that leaves you with twenty-three minutes to walk to the pad at night, kill Dimitri, return to the guest housing, drive to the plane, and take-off."

"Only a fictional superhero could assassinate Dimitri in such record time." The council was convinced, Chang concluded the same and explained to the council that fifteen to seventeen minutes were missing. So, either the watch was moved backward, or the watch was not synchronized in real-time. The investigators had searched for what smashed the watch but found nothing hard onsite. That convinced Chang that Dimitri was murdered, and the killer was at large. *We need to wait for the investigation to complete,* Chang thought.

"It is worth it to find more information on the Israeli delegation members. An interrogation request was made via the diplomatic channels," Chang told the State Council. The State Council asked to keep the situation confidential and not openly interrogate; rather, investigate quietly so no one would be suspicious as Chang spied on them.

Chang thought it was a good idea but wanted to ask the Israelis questions, not as suspects, but as witnesses. Chang respectfully ended his call with the Council and eased back into his thoughts.

Chang was informed that Dimitri had allegedly communicated with his commander and said all was okay, but that was right after the shot was heard and perhaps someone else answered the call in Russian. That was at 5:25:38 p.m. It did not make any sense; Dimitri did not die fifteen to twenty minutes after the time of their arrival to the scene. "Someone moved his watch forward, and if so, someone who speaks Russian was the murderer," Chang thought out loud.

No one else would want to know what was going on other than the Israelis. *Again, it was in their interest to know; otherwise they're primary suspects,* Chang thought.

Chang assumed that the Israeli delegation would have a Mossad field operative within, disguised as a scientist or technician, perhaps one of the security guards protecting the IAF airplane?...the engineers?

Chang chose to ignore the lapse of time and decided to act on his own without consulting his State Council further. If it was an Israeli who killed Dimitri, they must have been a very skilled and fit agent. Chang reviewed the Israeli delegation's names again and stuck their photos on his whiteboard next to Dimitri's smiling portrait.

Chang knew Greco from previous collaborations between their two countries. He didn't look like a man who would be able to handle such a task—at least to Chang. The other one, Oren Langer, was an enigma. Nothing much was known about him, and Chang knew that needed to change.

He scratched his temple, sank deeper into his chair, lit another cigarette, and watched the time displayed on the wall, which was his daily obsession. The two Israeli scientists he knew from their working meetings had coordinated the mutual launch.

The third one, the scientist, Ezra Maman, was a new face.

Oren Langer... Chang mused to himself. *His agency security cleared him, but he was the only new man on the scene,* he thought.

That same night, Chang was on the phone with the medical physician who'd witnessed Dimitri's body's forensic examination. The autopsy revealed that he died from multiple injuries, loss of blood, and a fractured skull. The most important thing revealed during the autopsy was that

Dimitri died during a struggle, and the killer's DNA was extracted from Dimitri's fingernails. They had the smoking gun.

Chang decided to reshuffle the cards and get his intelligence community and spy network to answer the questions which would satisfy his agenda and provide answers to his State Council in Beijing—who was less interested in who killed Dimitri—he wanted to know if the confidential space agenda was compromised.

CHAPTER EIGHT

M. carried a grim and tired expression when Dan and Greco stepped into his office early the next morning after the explosion. The traumatic event was fresh in their memories. Both agents were worn, having flown overnight from Baikonur to Tel Aviv; the military flight had been far from luxurious.

The Mossad headquarters in Tel Aviv was still asleep. People drank coffee, starting the day in low gear; it was Sunday, after all. Data analysts, behavioral scientists, psychiatrists, and spies would later mingle in the cafeteria to chat, but they never exchanged details about what they were involved in.

Dan—calm, as usual—carried his bag tightly against his body. A couple bandages covered his scratches, but the wounds were still very noticeable.

Most of the people in the office listened to news briefings with their first cup of coffee, and Dan grabbed a cup to jump-start his own brain.

The news anchors in Israel were always dead serious while reading their notes, which primarily covered security issues and tensions along the borders with neighboring countries. The constant pressure and boiling Middle East conflicts kept the Israelis glued to radios and televisions, as every day was unpredictably different.

There was always a security incident or terror attack, a car ramming pedestrians or knife-wielding Jihadist attacking random people on the street. The Israeli interior counter-terrorism unit, Shabak, oversaw the homeland's general security services and never had a day off. On the other hand, the Mossad had its long arms around the world as another means of force.

The humble, simply decorated head of the Mossad sat across from his two men with raised eyebrows and questioning eyes. He managed to put on a tired smirk to show his dissatisfaction with the situation. Dan and Greco sat down, moving some of the disheveled files across the desktop so they could see M. An overflowing ashtray sat waiting for a janitor.

M. put both hands on his desk, exposing his nicotinc-stained fingers, then flipped them palms up, as if to ask, "What happened?"

Dan set the bag on his boss's desk and opened it slowly. The object he'd taken from the site was covered by his scarf, which now had bloodspots soaked through it.

Black soot covered the object, keeping it unidentifiable. Dan tried to clean it with the scarf, but M. stopped him.

"Leave this to the lab!" exclaimed M. He paused for a second. "We should send it immediately for analysis."

Dan repacked it into his bag, and M. called his assistant and gave her a few quick instructions. She took the bag away and closed the door behind her.

"Well," M. exhaled with frustration, "the foreign ministry office in Jerusalem received a formal request from China to question both of you regarding the dead Chinese soldier. It's for assistance and not as suspects; by the same token, the Foreign Minister asked if there was any way we could assist with the investigation going forward."

"He was a Russian soldier," Dan claimed.

"How did you determine that?" M. demanded and pulled a cigarette from his almost-empty pack.

"He spoke Russian," said Dan. "He asked me, 'Who are you?' in Russian."

"He might have mistaken you for a comrade?"

"I speak some Russian, and this guy had no accent."

M. changed the subject and said, "We are trying to locate Ezra Maman. We could not trace him and have no idea if he was kidnapped, killed, or crossed the line. I asked the IDF to have our missing-persons 5701 unit help. This investigation might hold up our Orbixeye program by quite a bit."

"5701 are only doing that for the Air Force's pilots missing in action," Greco said.

"They have the tools; I need you both to describe the event, everything you saw, even unconsciously, to the individual assigned to the investigation."

Both Greco and Dan nodded their heads in agreement. Losing someone on their watch was tough. *Locating Ezra won't be easy under these circumstances*, Dan thought.

M. inhaled the smoke and scrutinized his agents. "So far, no one has come forward with any ransom demands or informed us of his captivity."

"He was a major figure; he invented the Orbixeye," Greco said anxiously.

"I know," replied M. calmly. "I asked the Foreign Ministry to send an official request to Kazakhstan to provide all the information they might have regarding his disappearance."

"They are a step ahead of us," uttered Greco, worried that Ezra's disappearance was, in part, his responsibility.

"Anyway, we tried to hack the Chinese satellite orbiting the launch area, perhaps to find any clue of his whereabouts. Not sure it worked," added M. as he extinguished his cigarette, making his desk even sloppier.

"It will only confuse them for a bit," replied Greco. "Dan moved the dead man's watch backward by fifteen minutes." His voice was deep and tired as his gray eyes crossed M.'s gaze briefly.

"This may play against us, but what's done is done. Everything is suspicious, and everyone is a suspect. Let's analyze a bit. We had a satellite in there, so why would we want to sabotage the mission? The Chinese had secret astronauts in there, I bet—so why would they want to kill them? Only the superpowers, America and Russia, could have an interest in stopping the launch, right?" M. was visibly excited.

"Playing devil's advocate, M.?" Greco asked.

M. attempted another tired smile. "There are things you don't know that we discovered just before the launch," he whispered as if someone was listening. "China, the United States, and Russia don't know what we know, which is that the rocket exploded thanks to our self-destruct system activation. The CIA and our agency confirmed that the Chinese intentions were to hijack our satellite and steal our Orbixeye plans."

M. paused so his agents could swallow the information.

"But what does that mean?" Greco asked, surprised. "We blew up the damn thing?"

"The CIA," replied M.

"How does the CIA or any agency know about Orbixeye at all?" Dan inquired.

M. shrugged. "We don't know yet how it was discovered— perhaps by hacking into our computer systems." He pulled the last cigarette from the box labeled "Dubek" and lit it. He was too tense. "We installed the system on our satellite at the last minute without disclosing it to anyone. A handful of people knew about it; it was a mechanism that would prevent anyone from tampering with the satellite in orbit."

"Wow," Dan exclaimed. "That explains a little more than what we knew...was Maman in the secret circle?"

"Yes, he was, but he was not a factor at that time," M. replied.

Greco started, "Could the Chinese perhaps have kno—"

"That's for both of you to find out!" M. snapped. "And another thing: don't forget that China has submitted an official request to interrogate both of you."

"And where do they expect us to report for questioning?" Greco asked, even though he already knew the answer.

"Beijing," M. replied curtly and continued smoking.

"Better there than Russia," scoffed Dan. Then he thought, *They're both bad, though...*

"I recommended that the Prime Minister put a hold on any technology sharing or equipment or company selling to any foreign country for security reasons," added M.

"Where are we going from here?" asked Greco, biting his lip. He knew he was not actually going to Beijing for questioning.

"I don't know; there are more unknowns than knowns... and the foreign ministry has ignored my request," M. grunted. "And you, Dan, have to go underground while we make arrangements. Your temporary identity as Oren Langer was hacked already. We left an obituary for Langer on the web. Our next satellite is scheduled for launch from Cape Canaveral next month. Dan—shave your beard, change your appearance. You're getting a new identity. You will depart for the United States to meet with the new Miami consulate security officer and watch the launch for security reasons. I am sure many curious eyes will be wanting to know what we are launching now."

Greco pulled a cigarette from M.'s new pack and inhaled the bluish smoke deep into his lungs with a whistle and exhaled slowly. Dan was not happy with the additional smoke in the room and moved his chair back a little.

The phone rang, and M. picked it up. M. listened and nodded his head. The metallic voice on the other end was obviously giving orders. "Okay, we will talk about it tonight," M. said and hung up.

He glanced back to Greco and Dan. "The Prime Minister has asked me to stay at my post for an additional year or until the tensions are over, due to the new developments. You will have to suffer under my command a little longer—but don't worry; I won't forget to resign when the time comes!"

Greco rubbed his temple while Dan looked down at his feet. Their boss smirked behind a plume of smoke.

CHAPTER NINE

7:00 p.m., November 20th, Last Year
The White House Roosevelt Room

President Clayton walked into the room with his team and shook cold hands with the man who would take his place in nine weeks. After short greetings and forced smiles, they sat around the long conference table, which was prepared for dinner's arrival later that evening. Clayton, who'd naturally taken his place at the head of the table, looked at his Chief of Staff and barked a few instructions about the next meeting in the Oval Office with his party's leaders.

The Chief of Staff left the room, closing the door behind him.

Clayton anticipated that this transition meeting would be short, somewhat friendly, and sweet. *Reality doesn't match your dreams all the time,* he thought and forced an artificial smile, as a polished politician does.

The President observed his successor's garments and noticed the high-priced designer suit, red tie, white shirt with monogrammed initials, and gold watch. Clayton himself wore a two-piece navy suit, light blue tie, and white shirt.

After congratulating President-Elect Cole in person on his stunning victory against all the odds, Clayton signaled to quiet down the small talk among the teams and clamped his lips tightly, his eyes serious.

Robert Cole was silent. He stared at the man who'd led the world for the previous eight years and felt a little compassion for him. *He had pitch-black hair when he started; now it's almost all white*, thought Cole.

Cole had brought a shortlist to this meeting from his campaign staff. The list included his proposed Chief of Staff, who was his former campaign manager; the future Defense Secretary, who was his military campaign consultant; and the political consultant, a former governor of New Jersey, who probably would be the future UN Ambassador.

Clayton seemed like a fraction of the man he used to be during his first presidential campaign, but he didn't try to salvage his ego. He looked worn down, tired, somehow malfunctioning. *Where is the energy, the stamina, the strength he displayed at the beginning of the first campaign, or the first year of his presidency?* Cole asked himself.

Clayton seemed like he wanted to get through things quickly and escape an uncomfortable situation. Transferring the reins to a successor was never recorded, as far as he knew. Soon, Cole would take the global stage, and Clayton, as a former president, would be analyzed and scrutinized by scholars making lists of the top presidents. Clayton hoped to be in a good place in the middle of the list, just after President Cleveland or before President Ford. His legacy, or whatever would be left of it, was dependent on the future actions President Cole would take.

He could hardly wait to go back to his home in Milwaukee, get out his easel and paint his favorite landscapes along the shore of Lake Michigan.

Cole had promised in his campaign that he would restore the military and cut taxes, which would reverse everything Clayton had proudly accomplished. The man who'd opposed and disdained him now sat before him, one breath away.

Clayton's party's candidate, his Vice President Henry Thomas, was openly gay. Thomas had vowed to continue Clayton's policies. Clayton, a liberal man, knew Thomas was gay, although he was married with children. He came out of the closet before the election that would denote Clayton's successor, and the voters were split down the middle. Thomas lost to a charismatic man without a stigmatized personal life.

The President-Elect was a nonconformist, which would reshuffle the political protocols and the status quo in Washington, worrying many Americans and the country's adversaries equally. His reputation sometimes was misinformed; after all, in business, you had to be profitable, and aggression was one method to achieve that. Politicians knew how to campaign and throw slogans here and there to be elected, but the real test was going live and to run the office by the platforms they were elected upon.

The result of the upset election was a punishing response to Clayton's foreign policies. The voters had carried with them long batons to the voting booths, promising to change the streets of Washington and replace the tenants who lived in the White House.

Everyone anxiously waited for Clayton to begin.

"We wanted to start the first transition meeting earlier than expected due to some serious global events recently. I'll have Tim brief you first," Clayton said and looked at his National Security Advisor.

Tim, tall and thin with thick prescription glasses, a long sharp nose, and small mouth like an eagle's beak, always looked angry. *Looks more like an IRS agent to me*, thought Cole, amusing himself.

Tim, the NSA chief for the previous fourteen months, took office after the surprise resignation of the former chief due to personal reasons that were never disclosed...even though everyone knew about his sex scandal.

Tim wore a wrinkled blue suit (with too-short hems that showed his black socks) and a long red tie that hung below his belt. He cleared his throat and directed his eyes to the incoming Commander-in-Chief, hoping to get through what he needed to say without being butchered by those staring him down.

"We have undeniable evidence that there is a situation needing serious attention. The explosion in Kazakhstan was not an accident. Someone didn't want this rocket to take off, and the CIA is investigating it. The Mossad contacted us and provided a piece of very valuable information that could change the rules of engagement."

Tim paused and waited for a reaction. Cole and his team were tense but didn't show it.

What the hell is he talking about? What a great way to start a new administration, Cole thought, stopping a curse on the back of his tongue.

"Also, just a few days ago, our Barium 31, a low-orbit satellite, and a Russian Cosmos 1350 experienced a hypervelocity collision. It was a Russian communication satellite, or at least that's what the Russians reported; a private corporation owned Barium 31. Russia immediately blamed us for the incident. We suspect it could be a weapons test, but we don't know."

"Not surprising!" growled Cole, learning quickly how the world under the carpet really looked.

Overlapping chatter and whispers from both teams stopped when Cole raised his hands. "Go on!" his voice thundered, and he readjusted in his chair.

"Well, we weren't responsible, and we believe the Russians weren't either; it could be the Chi—" Tim attempted.

"We don't know who is fighting whom here?" scolded Cole. "What is this, a prom party?" He looked at his future cabinet and chuckled. "First, who owned Barium? Second, is there a possibility that the satellite was hacked? Third, what information have you obtained from the Israelis?" Cole's face was red; his eyes held fire.

Tim nodded his head and looked to the CIA Director, Gene Bennett, to clarify the questions.

Gene clenched his teeth, tightened his lips, looked straight into Cole's eyes, and answered politely, "They can hack our satellites only once they break the codes. The old satellites were not tightly encrypted, and cybersecurity updates are not available for old equipment, so they could be easy to hack. To answer your question about Barium: it's a net of sixty-six communication satellites in low orbit owned by..."

"Wait a second," Cole jumped in. "So, how can we secure our space equipment?"

"Please, let me finish," growled the CIA Director. "We asked the Israelis about a new device they are developing, which will be used in space—a device that could make a difference if utilized for military attacks."

Tim and Clayton exchanged glances, both sharing the sentiment that the President-Elect needed to be lectured on how to identify a global threat without such dramatic commotion.

"The Pentagon is using the Barium for its purposes as well, Mr. Cole," added Tim, trying to be significant in the conversation.

Gene was a little firmer after visual encouragement from President Clayton and continued, "The problem is that they are not secured. The codes can be broken by a teenage hacker. Satellite hacking is not new, and it will get much worse. In the past, the British Skynet satellite grid system was attacked by a student from his personal computer. No damage was done, the frequencies and channels of the spacecraft were changed, and when he tried to change the orbit, he just couldn't do it. This event doesn't mean that it can't be done with advanced technological development in time."

Cole now listened intently and tried to grasp what he was hearing, despite his lack of technical education and experience with military matters.

Tim cut in again to support Gene: "That does not mean that an organized cyber team backed by a country couldn't launch a sophisticated attack on our satellites, grind them to pieces, or just shut them down."

"Cyber-attack programs to change orbits toward collisions are a matter of time, and the threat is real," continued Gene. "The Israeli Orbixeye can make it worse or help, dependent upon who is using it."

Cole was amazed by what he had to deal with right off the bat, even though he'd already decided to surround himself with a top military administrative team to show the world that America was back in business. It seemed as if the previous administration was expecting someone to come, take over, pick up the pieces, and start defending the country from scratch. Cole could almost hear Clayton's sigh of relief, happy to leave the issues in someone else's lap.

"So, in space, hypothetically speaking, do we know who is fighting whom?" asked Cole sarcastically. The idea of glamorous fun during his administration was gone, like dust in the wind. President Kennedy's Cuban missile crisis and resolution came to mind, his saving the world from a nuclear holocaust; Cole put himself in the same seat now while examining this surreal event. Perhaps JFK even made his decisions in the very room Cole sat in; that thought made him shiver.

What had just been disclosed to him was the first step. Cole hoped he had enough time to respond the right way. The next few weeks would require a deep dive, using the best military minds he could find. He thought of forming a think tank of the best minds to meet once a week in the White House to discuss threats and analyze possible reactions, like a wartime simulation game.

He was told that getting information from the intelligence departments was like pulling teeth; everything was twisted, sugar-coated, or missing the essential details.

"It's not *if* you asked the question; it's *how* you asked the question," Cole had always said in meetings addressing his employees and interns in the past. "You get different answers from the same question if asked differently every time."

He had already decided that he needed Gene Bennett on his side as quickly as possible for the transition. He liked the man's direct answers and professionalism. Bennett knew more than anyone else regarding what was going on, even though his intelligence department had taken a huge blow from adversaries when his entire team of spies in China was wiped out.

Cole decided that he needed to pick someone as a second-in-command for the CIA under Gene Bennett to avoid a grueling Senate confirmation...someone he trusted to brief him promptly, give him the truth without any political agenda, and be loyal to the new administration while working with Bennett.

Gene was still serious about answering Cole's question. "It's called a nonlinear war," he stated and waited for a reaction.

"Is that it? A 'nonlinear war'?" asked Cole, a wide smile stretching across his face. "What does that even mean?"

The group chuckled, sharing glances with each other, easing the thick tension.

Gene remained serious and thought to himself, *What the hell do these politicians know? They have no clue what's going on, really.*

However, with a calm tone of voice, he lectured his new leader as he would a difficult student in school; he explained nonlinear—or hybrid—war, using the Russian invasion of Crimea as an example.

"The soldiers appeared first in civilian clothing, and it looked like riots broke out. No one knew who was fighting whom or why. When it was all over and the dust settled, the world was informed that Russia conquered Crimea. There was no time for a response from the Western countries. No one had time to take any action to stop the Russians, either politically or militarily, either by counterattack or organizing aid for the Ukrainian army. That is the goal of a nonlinear war." Gene took a breath and set his clasped hands on the table. "Space is in the same situation; everyone would be blaming each other, everyone would be suspicious, no one would know whom to attack or whom to defend if a conflict broke out. The winner would be the one who instigated the others via disinformation and attacked using another country's equipment. It's an orchestrated chain of events with no one knowing how to stop it." Gene hoped everyone grasped what he was saying.

"Right now, since our spy network was eliminated in Asia, our intelligence information is poor. We depend on our allies," intervened Clayton. "Our CIA psychologists are trying to profile individuals in China to figure out what their intentions are, what motivates them, what are their goals, visions, political plans, religious beliefs, and so on. We assume an inkling of the Chinese and Russian intentions, but no one knows for sure, and we're not convinced the satellite incidents weren't deliberately performed."

Cole was not sure if Gene—or the others—were telling him everything. *Just a gut feeling,* he mused.

"The truth is, we simply wouldn't know who our enemy is," Gene concluded and leaned back in his chair. When he looked at Cole, it seemed as if the lecture was understood.

Discomforting silence engulfed the room.

"Well, we will need more information daily," asserted Cole.

"The Secret Service will duplicate all the information in the morning briefing," Gene said. "As a matter of fact, I think they've already started. Isn't that correct?"

"Yes," confirmed the would-be chief of staff.

"Okay, let's eat something. I'm starving," Cole muttered.

Clayton then decided to add another piece of information, even though he too was anxious to eat and move on from the topic. "There were a few other hacking incidents in the recent past; for your information, a group from Indonesia hacked a pirate satellite providing television services to other countries. It just shows that hackers are experimenting with new ideas all the time. Also, we are concerned that China could destroy a satellite with a missile from the surface of the Earth, using technology similar to what we used over thirty years ago."

"Perhaps they hacked us for the technology," groaned Cole, unamused.

Gene cut in confidently: "A satellite does not have to be destroyed by physical kinetic energy. It can be hacked by consumption of its computational bandwidth, disk space, or wasting its CPU time to cause a satellite malfunction."

Tim came to Gene's aid. "In other words, there are other methods of decrypting and configuring routing information; hackers can destroy satellites by loading up their disk space and crashing it."

Both clarifications were equally confusing for Cole, but he nodded his head and tried to look confident.

Cole didn't consider himself computer savvy; it was not his area of expertise. In fact, his grandchild could do more with a computer and cell phone than he could. The best he could do was Tweet and manage his private Facebook page. But he realized they were explaining that the United States was not prepared to protect itself from attacks in the event of a future global conflict.

"How long have you known about that type of hacking? How long has this been going on?" Cole asked loudly, shaking his head. He looked at Bennett and asked, "Was this technology recently used by China, destroying their own satellite, gained by hacking our defense contractors' computers?"

Tim interjected, "Our agents on the ground reported that China found that development and research would take years, so the hacking method was chosen. The high cost associated with missile development, productions, deployment, and maintenance is too great. On the other hand, they are developing new killer satellites and building a quantum supercomputer, which are all signals for a future war."

Cole's face went solemn when Clayton replied sarcastically, "Lovely exaggeration, Tim. Nice of you to throw the word 'war' around like that."

The rest of Cole's team was not amused by the information, either; their discomfort with Tim's statement and Clayton's dismissal was palpable.

Cole could not imagine the impact that his decisions would make on world events once he took office. He needed a technology guru in his think tank. He needed someone who could change the landscape of warfare. His head thundered with ideas yet simultaneously called for fresh air. Cole longed to get out of the room, but there was no feasible escape from his future responsibilities.

Cole had always felt that the American people were being betrayed by using financial resources that helped other countries. Cole always blamed those countries for their negligence and not having proper economies. Teaching was acceptable, but he deplored the government throwing money at them before they were able to continue on their own. Cole felt that other countries needed to contribute and pay for their own security and protection under the United States' nuclear umbrella. "No free lunch," was his mantra.

The political climate was complicated by animosity between the two major American political parties, as it had been for ages. Cole not only needed the best men, but also the most loyal and faithful men, those without political boundaries, to carry out his policies and commands. He felt a splitting headache setting in.

"Drink water," said Tim, seeing Cole's discomfort.

Cole poured a glass of water and drank all of it, realizing how dry his mouth was. With a new fresh breath of energy, Cole asked, "What is the immediate threat we are exposed to right now? Where exactly are we vulnerable? What are the priorities you prepared?" Cole narrowed his eyes on the President.

"We're working on it," said President Clayton. "Due to the recent events, I asked Congress to approve an emergency budget to deal with the new threats."

"Ah, I got it," exclaimed Cole bitterly. "We let China get ahead of us with cyber technology, and now they are equal to us in the space program, as well?"

"We don't have a space program anymore," Clayton snapped. His team was silent for a moment; then Clayton cleared his throat and muttered sarcastically, "We are dealing with threats, we are not sitting on our..."

Cole looked raised his eyebrows, eyed those around the table, and growled over the voice of the President, "I guess the new secretary of Homeland Security, National Security Advisor, and you, Bennett, have quite a bit to do to protect this country from a cyberattack before I take office, don't you?"

Tim and Gene nodded and looked at President Clayton, but then Gene changed the subject. He bent below the conference table and lifted a cardboard box. He opened it carefully and pulled out an object wrapped in a plastic bag and topped with a white cotton cloth. Gene uncovered a strange piece of twisted, blackened metal.

"What in God's name is that?" asked Cole dryly. Apparently, the meeting wasn't close to done.

"It came via a direct flight from the Israeli Air Force early this morning," said Gene. "They asked us to analyze it in our forensic labs." He cleared his throat and continued, "This is a piece of the Proton that exploded in Kazakhstan. It was briefly checked by our scientists, who first confirmed it was a cosmonaut's helmet, and then they discovered two types of blood on it."

"Let me explain," Clayton jumped in to save Gene from being interrupted by Cole. "We have great ties with the Israeli Mossad. Their agent attended the Proton launch and found this piece on the ground."

"The Israeli team managed to fly out from the Cosmodrome without incident. But China is investigating the accident seriously," Gene said.

Tim exhaled loudly. "This piece exposed the Chinese's purpose for the launch."

"The helmet?" asked Cole.

"Yes," Gene confirmed. "We suspect that China is sending cosmonauts into space in higher numbers than they admit."

Joe Wezniak, Cole's candidate for Secretary of Defense, finally cut into the conversation: "What do you mean? Do you suspect that China has more than one space station in orbit?"

"No, it's not that," answered Tim. "We suspect that they are colonizing their cosmonauts somewhere."

"Wow! That's new," said Joe, surprised. "How did they manage to do something like that without us knowing? And if that's what you suspect, it didn't start yesterday. It takes years of preparations, development, funding."

"Look, we just compiled all the events and information from the last few weeks and are weighing our steps," said President Clayton.

"I am sorry, and I'm not trying to be rude, but you were all sleeping on your watch," Joe answered bluntly. "This is a matter of goddamn national security."

Joe, a tough former Marine officer and previous commander of the NATO Alliance, was an extreme hardliner who was always ready for combat. He was of medium build, but due to his height, he looked like a gorilla with long hands and huge palms.

"Let me ask you a question you've conveniently avoided answering all evening," Cole said and stood up from his chair. "How long has this been going on? What steps, if any, did your administration take? Where do we stand?"

Clayton, still the President, popped his chin and hollered, "It's irrelevant, and this is not what we're here for!"

Joe, fuming, first looked at Cole and back at Clayton without intimidation. "Okay, the Constellation program you scrapped for a cyber department is still in its diapers stuck in its crib. China is testing new electromagnetic space weapons, has launched attacks on satellites, and is secretly launching cosmonauts in alarming numbers to another space colony. This information is not *worrisome* to you?" Joe breathed heavily. His heart raced and his shoulders shook.

Cole grabbed his arm and pulled him back down to his seat. "Relax, Joe!" he said calmly. "We will handle this."

"Let's calm down," Clayton warned, eyeing everyone around the table.

"Relax, everyone," Cole added, raising a steady hand.

Clayton was surprised by the bold attack. Politely, without raising his voice, he tried to explain: "We are not sitting helplessly. We took steps and started procuring and expanding our cybersecurity department; it's your call how you want to proceed after January 20th. This meeting was to give you a heads-up. I will continue with my plans until then, and as long as I am the President, you will be promptly informed."

Gene, charged with having to appease both the President and President-Elect, offered his calm voice. "The Air Force has a team of airmen in Vandenberg, California, monitoring and observing all space activities. Our Air Force space command is in control of the situation, and we have the best generals employed there. We started developing new satellites with lasers and EM bomb technologies. This was in response to the aggression we were witnessing in space. We try diligently to counterbalance the situation and protect our military satellites and space equipment in orbit. Russia and China are using geosynchronous orbits, which means they are stationary points not circling the Earth and, therefore, can be a threat if they are positioned above our heads."

Cole's mental thunder had not calmed. *How the hell have we gotten into this situation? This miserable peace puppet, the leader of the free world...* He just hoped he could do better. *Much better!*

"This is a catastrophe waiting to happen—if it's not doomed us already," spat Cole.

Secretly, Gene Bennett hoped Cole would reverse some of the bad decisions that had prevented his agency from doing their jobs. Bennett came from a military background and understood when there was a need for mission. Four things needed to happen for a new mission: identify the mission, select the commander, budget the mission, and establish a schedule and deadline. If the administration was putting their political agenda over the country's needs, it was a formula for disaster.

Cole had already decided that one of his first executive orders would be to take back control of space. Fund and power the space agency, which would give birth to a new program to defend the country.

The President-Elect now had a clear understanding of what the next global conflict would probably look like. Robotic soldiers would run the next war arena alongside drones and search-and-destroy vehicles, all independently controlled and communicating with each other via a control room filled with nerds like his grandson, treating the event like a computer game. The winner would be the one best prepared with the most advanced technology and minds.

"Right now, it looks to me that we're already losing the next battle," sighed Cole.

Gene even admitted that with his department's deflation of funds, their adversaries were markedly, threateningly ahead.

Clayton said, "Let's concentrate and work together. We need a smooth transition. Let's curb the drama and stick to the protocols."

Cole leveled his gaze on the President. "Until I take office, I want to have a weekly meeting with my transition team, a full report on the state of our nation, info about everything you are working on, and everything that is started or stopped due to budget cuts. And as far as Russia, I'll take care of it myself."

As if adding to a conversation existing only in his own mind, Tim murmured, "It might be sabotage, plain and simple." His eyes were glued to the strange metallic object still resting on the table.

Clayton pointed to the object and said, "If you'd just let Tim speak, like he was doing before your outbursts, he has more to tell you about this piece of evidence."

Tim continued. "What's significant in this finding is that even though it seems that the Chinese have nothing to hide, this object blatantly proves the opposite. As we were saying. The helmet found in the Kazakhstan explosion also destroyed the Israeli satellite Amos 5 with its Orbixeye space GPS."

"You said that—" Cole started.

"We want Orbixeye," Tim said, holding his ground. "It's an essential platform to control the orbit, and the Israelis own it. Someone prevented it from being deployed to space."

"What exactly is Orbixeye?" asked Joe Wezniak.

"It's a device developed by the Israeli technological industries that monitors and maps all the objects in space, and it was supposed to be deployed in space with the Amos 5 satellite," Gene Bennett explained further.

"But now it's gone," Wezniak snipped.

"Well, yes," said Gene. "We intercepted the Israeli communication codes from our NSA intelligence base in Cyprus and hacked some of the plans to find out its purpose. We were concerned that this device would be hijacked by the Chinese and used as a platform for military purposes."

"Did our country hack into Orbixeye?" Wezniak countered.

"No, we couldn't; it's not a server-based device that you can hack. The Israelis are using computers from around the world and combining them to serve as the platform, so when they send a signal, you don't know where it comes from—or it gives you millions of addresses."

"It's years of investigations," said President Clayton. "It's only piling up now, so you understand that we're diving into this just as you're being informed, Mr. President-Elect."

Cole noticed that his proposed future Chief of Staff was silently taking extensive notes. Under these circumstances, Cole felt like they were playing soccer—without a goalie—against the best team on the planet.

As the upcoming Chief of Staff wrote down details, he also made a list of departments that needed new directors and assistants. That was a huge task to complete in just a little more than a month. The new administration needed to start with a big bang, no blinking, no hiccups, and let the world know that there was no downtime between administrations and positions.

Cole decided he had to immediately counter the clear and present threats. "Set up a meeting with our transition team tomorrow morning at seven o'clock in my apartment," Cole demanded of the group. Then he glanced directly at Gene and asked, "What else?"

"Now, we assume that this wasn't the first time the Chinese disguised space launches as satellites in order to send astronauts to Chinese space stations," Bennett said.

"Where are they putting them all?" asked Wezniak, living up to his nickname ("The Sledgehammer") that he'd gotten in the Iraq and Afghanistan theaters. Like the late Ronald Reagan, Wezniak also was not to take any prisoners.

President Clayton paused and looked around before he said to Cole, "It is for your administration to discover what the aim of the Chinese program in space is." Tim added that there was some progress, but for the most part, that would require further investigation by aggressive means and counterintelligence methods.

"Let me ask you another question," Cole shot at the tired President. "What would your administration do if you were President for the next four years?"

Clayton rolled his eyes and offered a nervous smile. "I can't *tell* you what I would do, but I can *ask* you what would you do."

"Tell me about the secret Constellation program you defunded eight years ago," Cole barked in irritation.

Clayton went silent. All eyes were on him. Even his own cabinet couldn't tell what he was thinking.

"The Constellation program was scrapped due to the high cost...two hundred and thirty billion...an unbelievable number, just to start..."

"So many other nonsense programs were funded with that kind of money. Now we no longer know what's lingering above our own heads," Cole yelled with frustration once again.

"We had already been to space, Mr. Cole. You can calm down. We didn't have to be in a new space race with the Russians or Chinese. We had many other programs that needed funding, and the Constellation just wasn't a priority at that time." Clayton remained steady.

The room was quiet. A buzzing fly would've sounded like a Sherman tank rolling into combat.

"China hacked NASA and the CIA numerous times and copied plans for most of our missions to the Moon and Mars. Plans for programs we were working to develop in recent years," Gene Bennet added, his voice lifted an octave.

"And what did you do about it?" snarled Cole.

"Nothing. We tried to upgrade our servers to prevent hacking; we were unprepared to deal with the threat," Bennett explained. "The President decided to ignore it because there was no logical reason that China would need dated Moon-landing programs. They were old news. But now, China is testing the next mass destruction weapon we developed in our Area 51 labs, the electromagnetic bomb, and new laser cannon technology. We assumed that China launched about fifty military satellites into orbit recently, and the Israeli Orbixeye system would disclose this to its allies."

"Bennett, you make us sound like we're just sitting helplessly!" exploded Clayton, tired of his CIA Director making him look impudent. No one came to Gene's aid.

"Clayton, did you not think those Chinese advancements were dangerous?" chuckled Cole mockingly; the rest of his transition team exchanged nervous smiles.

"Save it," grumbled Clayton.

The standing Chief of Staff handed Cole a folder labeled "Top Secret." Inside he found the transition protocols.

"One of the most important procedures in the protocol is to log into our secure email server when exchanging emails," Spinach explained.

"Oh, yeah, we definitely wouldn't want to make the same mistakes someone else made," Cole taunted.

Clayton and his team were silent.

Everyone opened the folders and flipped through the pages like they were examining a restaurant menu. Despite the room's heat, they looked bored.

"This piece that came from Kazakhstan," Gene started and pointed his finger to the object on the table. "It had two types of blood on it, like we said. One type is from the astronaut wearing the helmet during the explosion, obviously. The other is most likely from a Cosmodrome soldier guarding the accident site after the explosion. That Cosmodrome soldier was probably killed with this object by the same Israeli agent who kept it and helped it get here. A smart move."

"Holy shit, what a mess," said Cole through a sigh.

President Clayton tiredly rubbed the back of his neck, trying to stave off a headache by imagining the smell of the breeze coming off Lake Michigan, near his hometown.

Bennett eyed the soon-to-be cabinet and their impending leader. "The worst thing is that the Orbixeye's head scientist disappeared from the Cosmodrome in all the commotion after the Proton explosion, and no one knows where the hell he is."

CHAPTER TEN

7 a.m., January 27th, Current Year

China's top spy wasn't one to give up on an investigation. Too much was at stake, and he wouldn't slow down.

The military cyber department STD, under the Defense Department, hacked and stole development programs from other countries with a focus on the United States and European Union Space Agency. The stolen data was for the implementation of their own space program, which would then develop in half the time.

Chang realized whoever controlled space would control the world and beyond. Chinese technological departments used the new data to create their own electromagnetic bomb and satellite hijacking capabilities. Chang and his tech team supervised the first hijack on one of their satellites, which they brought back to Earth successfully. The world intelligence agencies were stunned.

"This advantage put us in the front seat and probably in direct competition with the United States, Russia, or both," said Chang in one of the meetings with his team.

Gene Bennett had taken notice of the hijacking and alerted President Clayton, who decided to resolve the issue via diplomatic means—but it was in vain. Gene didn't press the issue any further.

Frustrated, President Cole, who had taken the oval office a week before, needed to take the bull by the horns immediately and confront the burning global issues head-on.

Cole's first executive order was to fund NASA an additional fifty billion dollars to activate an improved and more significant Constellation program and land on the Moon within one year. The program that had sat gathering dust for more than a decade got a jump that would take time to ignite. The CIA was funded an additional five billion dollars to address immediate global threats on the ground and flood the world with spies and informers, especially to gather information about the Chinese intentions and how far they had gotten with their new program.

"So, how are we doing?" Cole asked in his first security cabinet meeting. "What fires do we need to put out?"

The Defense Secretary, Joe Wezniak, took the opportunity to start since the question was directed at him. He pushed his gray hair back and laconically said, "We are going to the Moon, Mr. President."

Cole scoffed at his top defenseman. Wezniak didn't sugarcoat anything and put it right on the table. His job was to give military personnel and consultants space to work, while the information went through him for a final decision. He would likely go along with their recommendations if convinced that it was the right direction, because no matter what, the President was responsible for the consequences.

"Brief me," said Cole.

"As you know, after the shutdown of the space program, money was funneled to social programs, environmental-protection agencies, and new parks, as well as programs that were not aiding our economy but instead promoting economic growth in Africa or funding foreign countries' political parties. Also, billions went to climate-change programs in underdeveloped countries without confirmation that the monies even went there, not to mention funding over twenty-five percent of the United Nations and NATO's annual budgets."

"Stop, stop, stop right there. I promised to stop that immediately; I want a full report by Monday of all of our expenditures affiliated with the UN bodies' financing," Cole scolded and glared at his Chief of Staff, who took the note and left. Then Cole growled to his Defense Secretary, "Continue!"

"For your information, the plan was to land on the Moon and create an intermediate transfer station to Mars. NASA started to develop a new spaceship and space vehicle to transfer the astronauts to Mars."

"So, what's the problem?" asked Cole impatiently.

"NASA developed only a mockup plan, and that's it. No more money." The Defense Secretary shrugged, waited for a second to see how his boss would react, and then continued. "We are concerned that over the last eight years—or, worst case scenario, sixteen years—our adversaries advanced radically in space exploration and developed weapons with new abilities to attack anyone in space, specifically us."

"We need to assess and act on this immediately; I want recommendations ASAP!" demanded the President and pointed a finger at his cabinet.

"We were shut down, period," Gene Bennett cut in, disappointed and embarrassed for not pushing to increase the budget with his old boss. Now it looked as if he'd contributed to the situation. Although the Director of the CIA was not a political appointee, he still owed someone a big thank you, and that was the American people.

Gene continued with his thoughts, "When we quit exploring space, it left a big void that was easily filled by others. Opportunities like that don't come often. Everyone in the world wanted to see us crippled. When our defense budget was cut, it showed weakness, a sign of indifference. China and Russia aggressively increased their space budgets, and we estimate that China invested close to a trillion dollars in space exploration and new weapons alone."

Cole cut in like he was still on the campaign trail: "With the help of our own money due to trade deficits and hacking of our defense programs." He shook his head and scoffed with a sad smile.

"So, we are going to the Moon to make sure no one else is there and prevent anyone else from coming in behind us," said the Defense Secretary, closing his opening argument.

"We can't allow it," added Bennett.

"You will get what you need to go to the moon—even to go to Mars!" exclaimed Cole, and that was exactly what the new administration was hoping to hear. The green light given, which they hoped would inspire the American people and change the political landscape of the world for years to come.

"What do we know about where China is now?" Cole asked and looked at Bennett, who had the most experience with the subject.

Bennett nodded and spoke. "China is closing the technological gap with us very quickly. They are developing electromagnetic bomb equipment and experimenting in their newly assembled space station in low orbit, called *Tiangong*, meaning heavenly palace. They are building the largest Cosmodrome on Earth with a sophisticated space command center. We think China aims to prevent other counties from using space-based assets in case of a conflict. They also aim to prevent other countries from exploring beyond the Moon for the same reason. It's scary."

"Okay, I've got the picture. We have to pick up where our program stopped and move forward—immediately," said POTUS as he leaned over the table to show his seriousness.

"After our program stopped, we had to beg the Russians to use their Proton rockets to send our astronauts to the space station and do it on Russian land," added Gene.

"Ridiculous!" Cole exclaimed. "We need to change this. Now!"

"NASA started putting together teams of astronauts, scientists, and technicians from the Apollo and the space shuttle programs to go to the Moon within a year, as per your inauguration speech."

"I don't get it, Bennett. Why Apollo? They're all about my age now," Cole chuckled.

"They have the most experience and best training and will cut the preparation time in half. Also, seeing as though we have no new equipment, the machines we do have are ones they're familiar with, especially the XB-25 Space Orbiter. We can use the old ships and the Apollo landing vehicles to inspect the Moon and, at the same time, continue with the development of our new, more-advanced equipment."

The President absorbed the complicated situation quickly and had to agree to let his professionals handle it. He knew time was not on their side and thinking out of the box was essential, but more importantly, while using the old equipment, it was necessary to continue developing and funding new machinery and strategies.

No one in the room wanted to think about what could happen if their catastrophic predictions came true, especially on their watch. No one would blame the previous administration now that they had the reins. The country's hibernation years caused security issues that were not easy to patch.

In this new era, the Defense Department, CIA, and NSA started to work nonstop in harmony together, but not before changing all the codes and bracing all firewalls to prevent further hacking.

Gene Bennett, the previous CIA Director under President Clayton, knew precisely the damages from the policies Clayton had employed. Regardless of how Bennett felt about said policies, resignation was never an option, and Clayton would not have accepted it, anyway.

Gene sometimes felt like a puppet. He worried that agency failures would be blamed on him, even though the CIA's hands had been tied, restraining him from performing his missions.

In truth, Bennett didn't mind working with the new President. He preferred a professional relationship rather than the friendship relationship he'd had with Clayton that had soured at the end of the previous administration. He felt that his valuable information, expertise, and experience in this chaotic world were assets to the President—and he knew that's why Cole had asked him to stay.

Joe Wezniak's first step had been to ask NASA to reactivate Area 51 and perform all their activities from the most secured area in the world. The second step was to revive the experimental Orion spacecraft, which had orbited the Earth twice before it was retired due to budget cuts. Although the Orion was designed to take astronauts to asteroids and Mars, it would be reassigned. The rocket that was designed to carry Orion to space had died with the Constellation program cancellation. NASA checked frantically to see if launching it with the same rocket boosters that launched the space shuttle would work. This would help house the Orion in the cargo bay in the future and cut time and cost.

In theory, it would work. It would bring all the historic defense contractors back to work, fabricating avionics from the old designs, with new thermal shingles to cover the space shuttle, making this concept the new reality.

The climate was the same as on the eve of World War II after the attack on Pearl Harbor. In that time, America's industry had awoken from a deep depression, built thousands of war machines, planes, ships, and trucks and, in the end, won the war. President Cole felt it was his fortune to handle a similar situation to what FDR had faced when his Navy Secretary burst into the Oval Office to announce the attack on Pearl Harbor.

America proved that when it decided to gear up, the entire country would chime in as they had in the past. It was the same plan now but on a smaller, different scale. America was at war without declaration and without waiting for a surprise attack. *Call it paranoia, but better safe than sorry...we'll see*, Cole thought, convinced that his country was already secretly under attack.

In the meantime, in another room in the CIA building, NASA image analyzers and scientists examined the photos sent to them from the experimental MoonKAM spaceship orbiting the Moon. The images were released on NASA's website, and tabloids immediately reported that aliens had landed on the Moon. Reporters wrote as if everything they claimed was backed by NASA, which was far from the truth. What they allegedly found was a nuclear station producing electricity for an alien camp, buildings, and roads. Another story was published claiming that the Moon had been conquered by aliens who were preparing to attack Earth.

"The country has gone mad," Joe Wezniak said on a morning TV show. "There is nothing on the moon—just rocks and dust."

"People want the President to announce it!" the anchor pressed, but Joe just moved on to another matter.

The tabloids printed whatever the readers wanted to read, igniting their imaginations about the upcoming alien invasion. They showed maps of precise locations where aliens had landed on the Moon. It created an Invasion Theory Club that protested in the streets to bring this to the attention of the American people. People walked about in alien costumes carrying banners reading, "Kill The Aliens," and, "Prepare For War." Others rioted, and the police needed to defuse the tensions and the craziest hoarder-built shelters, which accumulated food that could last for weeks.

Cole was furious with the tabloids and Tweeted to his twenty-two million followers that this was all "Fake News." The Tweets reached the media and were shared millions of times.

The pressure was on NASA to come up with answers and keep things under control.

The Secretary of Defense instructed NASA to refrain from giving information to the public and restrict their website. The CIA's challenge was to discover the truth about the igloo-shaped structures shown on the MoonKAM photos. Time was of the essence, and there were too many unanswered questions.

Throughout the public unrest and spectacle, the CIA and Defense Department continued secretly investigating the Chinese satellite hijacking program, moving closer and closer to finding their response. Over everything else, Orbixeye needed protection.

CHAPTER ELEVEN

11:12 a.m., January 27th, Current Year

Chang received the news they were waiting for—Oren Langer, the Israeli Military Attaché, had died in a mysterious car accident in Israel the same day he'd returned from Kazakhstan. Chang watched a clip of the news video showing how a pickup truck rammed into a bus station in the West Bank, but no victim identities were disclosed. The attacker, a Palestinian driver, was neutralized by soldiers at the same location, and the incident was reported and investigated as a terrorist attack.

"Great," Chang sighed. "What a coincidence—he murdered himself."

Greco's trip to Beijing, and even a video conference with Chang, was eventually declined due to continued conflicts. Chang was told that if he wanted to meet Greco, he needed to visit Israel; and besides, Oren was dead.

Chang focused on his whiteboard on the wall. He crossed Oren's name off and wrote underneath it, "To be determined/confirmed."

The State Council still needed to know who was involved in the incident and if it was sabotage. Chang could not do it alone. He needed to activate his spy network to investigate and then think of a counterattack in case his superiors ordered it. He knew that the existing and new relationships between the countries was on the line, and time was working against him.

He paced throughout his office, thinking of his next move. *A field information gathering should be the next step*, he thought. Frankly, he was not too concerned about the death of the Chinese Republic's soldier, Dimitri, but he *was* concerned about *why* he was killed and if any evidence was collected from the site that exposed the Chinese plans. It was time to activate his dormant agent at 222 Ben Yehuda Street in Tel Aviv, the Chinese Embassy.

The six-story embassy building was an old Art Deco building restored to its original design with round terraces. It sat on a bustling main artery of the congested cosmopolitan city of Tel Aviv, the business nerve center of Israel.

Chen Su Yong was working directly under Chang's intelligence machine disguised as a clerk in the embassy. The twenty-fifth anniversary of the Chinese-Israeli relationship was celebrated at a gala event filled with fake smiles, great Mediterranean food, and a deluge of alcohol, since the relationship was important for both countries.

Chen did not attend. He kept a low profile as an administrative assistant of consular services in the visa department. He was excited to start his new assignment. He had been trained, many years before, to be a covert field operator, a spy.

Chen, a six-foot-tall, fit, and lean man in his early thirties, was a former hacker who'd served in the 61398 unit based in Shanghai, which was responsible for many cyberattacks on the West, especially the United States. This cyber-espionage unit was responsible for stealing many documents and plans from NASA and other defense contractors involved in the Apollo and other programs.

During the previous administration, the Pentagon, by order of the Secretary of Defense, paid no attention to why

China was interested in building a lunar landing vehicle or how the space shuttles worked. They simply decided to ignore incursions, assuming it was just Chinese kids doing the hacking, and they foresaw no harm to the country.

The NSA and other defense agencies displayed this information freely with a sense of pride and without thinking of the consequences, which invited more and more attacks that displayed the vulnerability of America's defense systems and damaged its reputation.

Many cybersecurity companies in the United States watched as the world nibbled at their advanced and future defense programs due to the Pentagon's budget cuts.

Chen Su Yong didn't issue visas from the embassy. His real job was nonstop hacking of whomever and whatever he could. His superior instructed him what to look for, and he took it from there. His assignment was to search for the new laser gun developed by the United States, which the Navy had installed on an old American frigate serving in the gulf. The plans for this laser gun were hacked, and Chen hoped it served his country well. He saw that in one of the laser-gun experiments, it had demonstrated lethal destruction of a drone five miles away at the cost of one dollar a shot. He hoped that the greater Chinese plan would be to develop a laser gun far more powerful than the thirty-megawatt laser on the frigate.

The new assignment was to find the identity of Oren Langer, the dead Israeli Attaché of the Kazakhstan team. It was suspicious that he'd died the same day he was asked to go with Greco to the Chinese Embassy for questioning.

Chen prepared himself by obtaining as much information about Oren's death as possible. He found an obituary mentioning that Oren's funeral was the day after he allegedly came back from Kazakhstan. The obituary said that he was buried in Carmelite Cemetery, which was located in a small settlement town in the southern part of the West Bank, a short drive from Jerusalem. That was also the town where Oren Langer had supposedly lived.

Chen decided first to check the fresh grave and, if needed, identify the body by reopening the ground. He determined that he should drive through Be'er Sheva, the fourth-largest city in Israel, and not Jerusalem, to avoid Army checkpoints and even Palestinian roadblocks that would not distinguish between an Israeli and a foreigner. Also, to avoid other people seeing him, he decided to fill the gas tank and use an embassy vehicle.

It was a two-hour trip from his office over the rugged roads entering the West Bank. He learned the Biblical history of the town and its surroundings before his departure. Every clue could be significant.

The weather was good, and the traffic was light. Chen got there in the early afternoon with no issues other than passing some nervous Israeli drivers who honked at him, something he'd gotten used to in Tel Aviv. He entered the town of a few hundred people and immediately drew attention since everyone knew he wasn't a resident.

Chen stopped the car beside a woman strolling through the relatively warm day with her baby.

She gave him directions to the cemetery, which was a few miles away.

He stopped at the gate. No cars were in the small parking lot in front of the cemetery. He looked around at the surrounding hills. It was as quiet as death.

He opened the window, and a cool breeze blowing from the west gave him a chill. He zipped his jacket tight, put on his sunglasses, and sat in the car for a few more minutes. There was something creepy about the place. He wondered if sitting behind a computer screen wasn't a better thing to do. Chen was ready with a cover story if asked about his presence there.

He saw the main path leading uphill to the graves. On his right was a small, room-sized structure, though he was not sure what its purpose was. Just a little to the left, he saw a simple pavilion where mourners would spend a few final minutes with bodies before the final burials.

He started looking at the gravestones.

He could not read Hebrew and had no idea where Oren Langer would've been laid. He narrowed his search for a fresh grave.

Suddenly, a man appeared and asked him a question in Hebrew.

Chen was caught by surprise; he hadn't expected anyone. The parking lot was still empty, but he was not concerned— the man seemed friendly and looked eager to help.

"English?" asked Chen, tilting his head.

"Can I help you?" the man asked and slowly stepped closer to Chen.

"Yeah, I am looking for Oren Langer's grave," Chen replied politely with a sad smile.

The man examined Chen and nodded his head sadly. "The entire town was sad at his passing." He seemed genuinely emotional, as he'd probably known him.

"Can you show me his grave?"

"Sure, but you must wear a yarmulke," the man said while pulling one from his pocket. He reached out and put it on Chen's head. "It's a Jewish cemetery. Come, let me take you there; it's just around the corner."

Chen walked silently and again admired the quiet land with its rolling hills. The man spoke about the historical proof of many Biblical stories and towns flourishing during King David's reign. As he mentioned the Roman occupation of Judea and Samaria, they reached a fresh grave.

A small sign marked the name and position of the head of the deceased. Chen would not have known this if not for his unexpected guide, who was curious to know more about his relationship with Oren.

"What was he to you?"

"A friend, a good friend. When was he buried?" replied Chen.

"Yesterday," the man stated without hesitation. "It's a shame how he died...no family, just a couple of friends."

Chen decided to press the subject. "What happened to his family?"

"They were all killed in a terrorist attack in town, and he was heartbroken for years. In fact, his entire family—wife, son, and his two grandchildren—are all buried right there." The man pointed at a few graves sharing the same headstone.

"Yeah," Chen said. "In your town, a communal town, everyone has a duty, so why would Oren be living here?"

The short man in his early seventies wrinkled his face and squinted his eyes. "I don't understand what you mean. I am the Rabbi of these towns, and I purify the bodies, preparing them for the burial. Oren was a senior citizen who was one of the first settlers, a leader, and a high-ranking officer in the Army; he was the county secretary."

Chen could tell the Rabbi was more than willing to talk. He ignored the cold breeze and looked at the sun, trying to warm himself up in vain. "It's hard when someone dies so young from a car accident."

"He was my age," the Rabbi remarked, surprised. "I knew him for fifty years, since our service in the Nahal Brigade, and he died from complications of pneumonia."

Chen was stunned but kept his cool. Oren, the man he was after, was in his early forties or late thirties (hard to tell due to the beard), so this was not the same person.

The only explanation was that the Israelis had sent an attaché with a borrowed real name of an Israeli citizen. He was selected knowing that his days on earth were numbered. Chen remained silent but his thoughts were loud. *So, where is the man I'm looking for? What is his real name? What was he doing in Kazakhstan?*

Maintaining his outer composure, Chen commented, "Yeah, seventies are still young."

He turned his back and thanked the old man for his time. He offered to pay him for his service, but the man declined, stating, "You don't need to pay me, but in that little purity building, you will find a money box for donations."

Chen pulled out a few Israeli shekels and dropped them in the box. Then he took off his sunglasses and wiped them with his handkerchief in preparation for departure.

The old man looked back at Chen and exclaimed, "Oh, you're Asian!"

"*Gāisǐ de,*" (damn it) cursed Chen in Mandarin.

Chen closed himself safely into his vehicle, started driving, and called Chang's office.

Chen felt he'd failed the mission by exposing his face. He was not a killer and had dismissed the thought of neutralizing the Rabbi. *Perhaps the old man won't mention it to anyone*, he thought.

"Boss," Chen said, adjusting the volume in his car. "Can you hear me?"

"Go ahead, Chen," Chang replied through an audible exhale of smoke.

"We were fooled by the Mossad," Chen stated.

"Quick—what did you find?"

"Oren Langer was an old man, nothing resembling the man at the launch pad."

"Bingo," chirped Chang. "The Mossad is in for some interrogation."

"Sir, if this new suspect is the man that killed Dimitri, I personally want to put my hands around his neck."

Chang chuckled, but Chen was serious. Chen also hoped this gesture would erase any doubt that he was a serious agent, and if his ethnic identity giveaway would resurface somehow, Chang might forgive him.

"Damn it, why didn't I just keep my glasses on," Chen muttered to himself as he drove on.

CHAPTER TWELVE

Area 51

The photos from the dark side of the Moon were mysterious and strange, and some showed what clearly resembled a base.

General Bloomfield and NASA Administrator Coolie examined the progress of the new space equipment tested by the former astronauts.

"You should remove all MoonKAM photos and stop the operation altogether," said General Bloomfield.

Coolie nodded his head and replied, "We shall advertise only on a need-to-know basis."

John Fisher joined the pack in reviewing the progress. He said, "It was easy to believe activities on the surface of the Moon were real. Many obstacles prevented people from understanding the phenomena or analyzing it more accurately." He looked out the window, admiring an F-22 Raptor taking off.

"We're not clear if what we saw was geological activity on the surface or solar winds created those long igloo shapes," General Bloomfield said.

"Scientists were analyzing the photos coming in from all over the world and asked not to disclose what they saw. People took photos with their own telescopes without even understanding the area in question, especially when the dark side of the Moon was not facing the Earth," explained Coolie, scrunching his face.

"Ha, and those bloggers freaking out about the end of the world...did you read about those doomsday shelters some people built?" John said through a grin. "Someone even claimed to see a face, a tank, and an alien spaceship that had crashed, which looked amazingly similar to the Enterprise from *Star Trek*. Next, they'll say the face on the surface of the moon resembled Han Solo, Harrison Ford himself."

The three laughed out loud.

"Cole asked us to control information sharing that would increase the demonstrations. Those didn't make the administration happy. Countries around the world were looking at us," Bloomfield said calmly, watching the runway activity from beside John at the window. "I see a lot of progress to report to the President; the plans to reactivate the spaceships are taking shape nicely," he complimented Coolie and John.

"The various museums were notified by my officials and asked to keep this lunatic request confidential," Coolie replied. "The excuse was that NASA decided to refurbish the ships to display them in the glory they deserved—clean and shiny, with all the bells and whistles a museum piece required. That was John's idea." Coolie let out another laugh.

"Well, how could we tell the world that we're moving all the museum pieces back to Area 51 without some serious questions?" John scoffed and rolled his eyes.

"True, I agree. This had to be done with the utmost confidentiality," added the general, dusting off his sleeve.

Coolie added, "The delivery to Area 51 was a logistical challenge by itself but went without incident. Now everything's safely in the hands of our engineers. It was impossible to stop the party on social media about all of this, though. Did you read the article on the *Washington Daily Gazette*'s webpage? 'Refurbish to make room for more fast-food restaurants; money talks!'"

The three laughed again, and the general said sarcastically, "What would we do without reporters?"

"We got the Lunar Landing Module of Apollo 18, which was never used. It's amazing that all systems where operational after being displayed for fifty years in Long Island," Coolie said. "Honestly, all the arriving equipment is in amazingly great shape."

"I ordered the entirety of Area 51 to be sealed off," Bloomfield said as he adjusted his uniform. "All roads in and out were closed with roadblocks, and Army personnel patrolled the area by land and air, keeping anyone from coming close to the facilities or sniffing around."

"Base control tower reported that a Boeing 737 on its way to Las Vegas from Phoenix requested a diversion due to bad weather. Ten miles east of its route, it was intercepted by a pair of F-16s from the nearby Nellis Air Force Base that escorted it until the jet cleared the restricted airspace," said John.

"I expect more like that incident. Everyone's staring at us after the explosion in Kazakhstan," replied Bloomfield with concern.

"The ships and the LLMs were stored in the old hangars," interjected Coolie.

John added, "I worked on a ton of secret projects in that hangar."

The general and James Coolie looked at John with admiration.

"Perhaps your base witnessed the first alien to ever step foot on Earth. Who the hell knows, right?" the general chuckled, but they knew the secret.

Bloomfield, Coolie, and John exited the office building and walked to examine the museum pieces. The scientists and astronauts analyzed the space vehicles, and some even talked about memorable past moments with them. Others were visibly emotional.

Coolie and General Bloomfield walked among the steel sculptures that were once the symbols of American power and pride. They mingled with the astronauts, and then they took their seats in metal chairs beside an improvised desk to address the group.

The astronauts and scientists remained congregated near the food and beverages.

James Coolie stood up. "Thank you, all; please be seated," he said and examined the audience. Everyone present had passed a new security clearance and medical examination, as many of the old astronauts were not suited for the mission, even though they'd volunteered. Coolie started with a description of the program, once again detailing what NASA was looking to accomplish and how. "Remember Gene Kranz?" he asked. "Our legendary flight director of Apollo 13?" He paused and examined the faces in front of him. They already knew where Coolie was going with his speech, but he continued, regardless. "Kranz asked his scientists to create and attach a new square CO_2 filter to a circular opening, and they had to make it with only the material available to them within the Command Module in space. We are in the same situation but with a different type of equipment, right here on Earth. We must take the Lunar Landing Module and fit it into the ship's cargo bay. The spaceship will eliminate the need for a Command Module. We can also fly more cargo and men to assist."

At first, John thought the plan was crazy—but doable. He also understood the mission, up to a point: they would orbit the moon, which he could perform, but he had never landed on the moon; and if he would be trained to do that, what would follow? What did they expect? Those details were still a mystery.

Coolie was prepared for any questions that the old space folks could come up with. He mentioned how the Gemini astronaut, when examining the space capsule without a window, insisted on having one put in, despite the engineering team's resentment. In the end, they got their window. "Our engineering teams can tackle any challenge, and we trust them," he went on. "As you've already been told, our first mission to the Moon will be to explore the strange formations on its dark side."

"What do you expect us to find?" asked John. His colleagues widened their eyes and waited for the response.

"What if there are other...things, or beings there? How will we protect ourselves?" Milton jumped in, his tone skeptical.

The men mumbled amongst themselves.

Coolie adjusted his red tie and said, "We will explain all the elements of the operation in your advanced training. In the meantime, we are monitoring all the evidence and data from the Moon, including information coming to us from the Pentagon."

Without any further comments from his audience, Coolie continued with the plans. "We've started assembling a hybrid space vehicle involving the retired Shuttles Discovery, Enterprise, and Atlantis, all of which are with us here today. Some will be for parts, and some will be to fly."

John interjected, knowing NASA's original spacecraft design and purpose: "The Shuttles were not designed for a long trip in space. You'll need more room for fuel."

"True, and our scientists have covered that," Coolie said. He knew the astronauts were smarter than he when it came to the equipment; they'd operated it while risking their lives decades earlier. He was sure they would understand the upgrades in the space vehicles. "The extra fuel tanks were designed as drop tanks, just like in a jet fighter. They will be abandoned in lunar orbit to land on the surface of the moon once emptied. Our engineers are already working on the trajectories and additional thrust calculations."

"Crazy—but a good idea," murmured someone the audience.

"And I must announce that for this mission's commanding leadership, we have selected pilot Colonel John Fisher!"

CHAPTER THIRTEEN

April 17th, Current Year

After one hundred days in office, President Cole already despised his job. At least, that was what the media claimed. However, in truth, the issues he was dealing with in space and on the ground made his head spin like a whirlpool. Cole ignored the daily briefing, and his advisors ran after him down the White House corridors, reading the most important notes. He required the highlights only, as he never read the full briefs. His Chief of Staff mentioned meeting requests from administrators in vain. Cole was locked into his own world, shooting curses in all directions.

The media reported that President Cole had cut a deal to sell China eighty percent of the aluminum and steel from his scrap metal business—an obvious conflict of interest, considering his new station. Cole had then transferred the control of his company to a trustee and canceled the deal when he was inaugurated. The stock market reacted sharply in Asia, and the American market dropped significantly. Without the necessary raw material, China could not manufacture cheap products, and investors were worried about the outcome of Cole's actions.

Cole's premise was that China might use the material for its military ambitions and less for the cheap products to fuel the stock market and megastores.

Cole decided to split the issues between two different security cabinets that would brief and report to him on their progress in each of their special categories. One would be the Space Security Cabinet (SSC), and the other would be the Planet Security Cabinet (PSC).

Both cabinets were in tune with their objectives: to keep both space and their planet under control to prevent an unnecessary war. The head of the CIA, the Defense Secretary, and the Director of the NSA would participate in both. Splitting the responsibilities would alleviate the amount of pressure to accomplish tasks at a speedy pace and give the President time to react responsibly.

Cole was proud of his original idea, but since he was a successful businessman before he became the President, he would naturally use his organizational skills. It was evident that he knew well how to split the responsibilities among his administration and monitor their progress.

There was a connection between the current wars on the planet and the struggle to control the orbit. Conflicts in the Middle East, especially Syria and the Korean peninsula, were ready to ignite the first global nuclear war if leaders didn't show restraint.

The bottom line was always money and energy. Syria was a vital pipeline corridor, and the superpowers struggled to control it; some were for joining the conflict and some against it. In Korea, like Iran, the nuclear program was developed to protect the regimes, keep them in power, and expand their ideology, while, of course, controlling money and energy. So, instead of fighting on Earth, superpowers were taking the war to space—the last battlefield.

Cole knew all of this and more. He also knew how generals had convinced previous presidents to wage war by bringing fake evidence to the table, like the weapons of mass destruction in Iraq that were never found. Disinformation spread by other spy agencies was a factor, as well, and he hoped it wouldn't happen under his watch.

President Reagan had acknowledged the importance of controlling space when he'd announced his Star Wars program (a false statement, as the technology didn't exist then, and it was not in development mode). The announcement echoed around the world and toppled the Soviet Union and its allies. Technology in Cole's time was advanced compared to that of the 1980s. New breakthrough systems, ideas, and equipment were developed on the theory that one day it would be used for Star Wars programs by adversaries.

The SSC meeting had just begun as the President walked into the meeting room in his slippers and robe. It was six o'clock in the morning, and breakfast was served on the wooden conference table.

Tim Woodward, the new National Security Advisor, shoved a note in front of the President and sat down next to him. Cole looked at Tim's skeletal face sharply and read the piece of paper:

Space Satellite collision: Iridium 33 and Cosmos 2251; 776 kilometers high. Russia is accusing us of deliberately destroying their satellite. Cole looked at Tim then Joe Wezniak, his Secretary of Defense, and asked, "Do we have anything to do with it?"

Tim, with short brown hair compared to Wezniak's white strands, was younger and more energetic, but both managed to answer at the same time: "No."

"How can that happen?" asked the President.

"Mr. President," said Coolie, who was asked to attend the cabinet meeting as an NASA representative, "there are thousands of satellites in orbit, moving in every direction and every altitude. A collision might have taken place if one satellite was diverted from its orbit."

"Okay, I understand. Since we didn't do it, is there any possibility that someone else hacked our satellite and caused the collision?"

There was a long silence, as they all took time to think before they answered the simple question. Coolie volunteered again to explain: "Yes, the satellites in orbit are not safe or protected against hacking, especially old satellites. Today, we are making sure to secure the programs with encryption codes to make it impossible to break in."

"It could be Russia, China, Iran, North Korea, or Israel; they all have satellite-hacking abilities," Wezniak started.

Cole growled at him, waving his hand with such force he knocked over his mug, spilling coffee onto the tablecloth. "Stop listing capable countries; all I want to know is who has specific reason to do it."

Joe sank back into his chair.

"Would Russia possibly conduct an experiment and blame us?" asked Cole.

"Possibly, but Bennett might have a better answer for you," replied Woodward.

Gene Bennett cleared his throat. "Not sure...we will investigate," he said in a relaxed tone. "All we know is that Russia has no interest in fucking with us; if anything, I would suspect the Chinese, who are expanding their space programs and technologies at an alarming rate."

Early morning thunderstorms added to the oppressive mood in the Roosevelt Room. Lightning struck nearby and reminded Cole of issues he was constantly hit with. His desk was covered in heaps of files.

"This is one of the reasons why I signed an executive order to build up the military. Before we start a war in space, we need to win here on Earth," stated the President. "We need to keep a close eye on our adversaries. I'm meeting with the

Chinese and Russian Presidents next month in Malta, and I will discuss this with them. What's on the agenda for today?"

Tim Woodward took the initiative to explain the new developments and reasoning regarding the Kazakhstan incident. "The agenda is Orbixeye," he said. "As you know, Mr. President, the Israelis cut a deal with China to buy their satellite company that also developed the equipment that was destroyed in Kazakhstan."

"I've heard this before. Remind me again—what's Orbixeye?" asked Cole tiredly.

Bennett explained, "The previous POTUS was informed of the development of a new space GPS by an Israeli satellite company. The Israeli company's idea was to form an international club with membership fees. The fees were to pay for launching satellites into orbit to avoid collisions and communication interferences. Pay to play to use Orbixeye."

"What else can the human mind come up with to make money?" Cole chuckled.

Bennett continued, "We discovered through our agents that Orbixeye is a computer platform connected to radar that is capable of mapping all the satellites in space and disclosing the type and country of the equipment by intercepting the frequencies they use. In the event of a successful launch and deployment of Orbixeye into space, it will need protection."

"And what's the answer?" Cole asked his cabinet. The men murmured among themselves, and Wezniak said, "We can't let China have it. It goes both ways, Mr. President. It's good to have such a system in the right hands, but in the wrong hands, it's fatal, and space will never be the same."

The sun peeped through the window shades as the storm moved away, and the downpour stopped. The rays cast light and shadows on the tablecloth while POTUS thought deeply.

Cole never thought that he would have to deal with threats so beyond his comprehension. This type of situation was not on the radar when the previous administration was in power, nor had the media ever discussed it. He needed to study the events at a fast pace and not lean totally on his advisors. He trusted them, but he wanted to call the shots. Cole gave his military enough rope to make their own decisions when required, as long as they didn't start World War III while the United States was not prepared for it.

"I can call the Israeli Prime Minister...we have an excellent relationship..." Cole murmured.

"It's not necessary, sir," Gene Bennett said, internally acknowledging that the President was clueless about the real situation. He then added, "We hacked the Israeli satellite, and we found that they'd installed a self-destruct system. What we don't know is if Orbixeye can hack satellites in orbit. We could not wait to find out. The Israelis didn't know that China could hijack their satellite...and with all the transition issues between you and Clayton, I didn't have any choice when I found, before the rocket was launched, that the Israelis had installed their Orbixeye in Amos 5. My hacking department broke the code, and I remotely activated the self-destruction mechanism. The Mossad was informed."

It was like a bomb exploded in the room. Everyone was amazed by the bold decision and understood why Bennett had done it, but the President was not amused.

"You did what?" scolded Cole. "I was entirely available to discuss it with you."

"What would you have done if you were me?" asked Bennett, who then continued without waiting for an answer. "I ordered them to initiate the self-destruct sequence of Amos 5. I took charge of the situation without having the luxury of time to go through the official channels for the proper permission."

Tim and Wezniak nodded in support of Bennett.

"Sometimes, the soldier in the field—who knows the condition he is facing—is the commander in chief at that time," said Wezniak.

"Would you really have done any differently?" Gene Bennett asked again and stretched his arms wide. "You asked me to stay, so I am telling you this. You always have the option of firing me."

"I would blow the rocket out of the sky and leave no trace but *still* get permission first!" Cole shouted and slammed the table with his right hand.

Bennett was speechless. He'd thought POTUS was on his side.

"This is not the Wild West, and you are not cowboys. This is not the O.K. Corral; it's Washington!"

Cole was angrily astounded by the CIA Director's bold steps. These actions would make his diplomatic efforts to achieve a peaceful solution and avoid nuclear war far more difficult, but what was done was done. Perhaps this would show how serious the United States was about taking steps to tackle threats.

Now all traces that might have tied America to the rocket explosion would be hard to erase without spy work and sabotage. In the meantime, the new development the President didn't know was that China had launched a probe to find out what happened in Kazakhstan.

For a few minutes, they thought quietly while eating their breakfasts. Finally, the President raised his refilled coffee mug and said, "Start erasing all tracks on this. I'll get into the Orbixeye shit. Goddamn, the Israelis owe us big."

Bennett could tell the case was closed for the time being. This act of war was in the best interest of the United States.

But perhaps this is just the beginning, he thought. He also needed to make sure that Russia would not intervene in the process, since the rocket had been designed by them, and they probably wanted to know what caused the explosion.

The summary of the meeting was sent to Cyrus Bradford, the Secretary of State, as a top-secret file. All members of the cabinet signed a confidentiality form.

Cole delegated the sensitive job to his Secretary of State to ease the tensions and ensure that fingers weren't on any triggers. In a war, there were no winners or losers...only those who lost more.

CHAPTER FOURTEEN

Tel Aviv, Israel

"Damn!" M. spat to himself. He had reluctantly accepted his Prime Minister's request for his remaining as the head of the Mossad for another year. "It's a crazy time," the Head of State had told him. "And the state's existence always depends on its intelligence community's discovering crucial information."

The Prime Minister was also M.'s friend and used him as an advisor for sensitive issues that required experience and wisdom. His proposed successor, who was the second in command at the agency, had resigned his post in protest and started his own private security company. Later, this new company provided bodyguards for VIPs such as actors, politicians, and anyone who could afford the high fees for an Israeli bodyguard. A few times, he'd even secured famous Hollywood couples' weddings and honeymoons like military operations.

The elderly man in charge of the cemetery in Carmelite informed his county security officer of the mysterious foreign man who'd visited Oren Langer's grave. The officer then told the military governor of Judea and Samaria and M. It was an Israeli instinct to report suspicious behavior or anything odd.

A quick inquiry by the Mossad and the internal agency Shabak revealed that an agent from the Chinese Embassy was inquiring about Oren Langer's identity. Now the Chinese knew that the person in Kazakhstan was not the real Oren Langer. This discovery would intensify the investigation, and M. prepared the agency for that.

M. was ready for the challenge. He informed his Prime Minister in a quick visit to his residence in Jerusalem and disclosed the next steps to him.

"We know that China is confidentially sending astronauts to space. We know that they have the capability to hijack satellites, and we also know that they can shoot satellites down," Prime Minister Udi thought aloud. "How can we stop it?" Udi was famous for his impeccable annual speeches in the United States during the UN General Assembly.

M. had to come up with an answer to this million-dollar question, but Udi continued without waiting for an answer: "If we know that, our American friends definitely know that; any idea about how they are dealing with it?"

They sat in the living room without their usual staff members and consultants, as they regularly did before presenting something for a last-minute vote in the cabinet. They had often just gone ahead with a mission, only to inform the cabinet members when it was all over to avoid leaks from opposing members or the grueling media.

"What preparations would you make for the next rocket with the future satellite in Florida?" Udi inquired.

M. explained in a relaxed tone, "Dan Eyal would be sent to prepare the area for the upcoming launch. He would be in contact with the Miami Consulate, which is two hours from Cape Canaveral."

The idea was also to keep Dan out of the country so the Chinese agents would not trace him for retaliation to the Chinese-Russian soldier's death.

Dan had changed his appearance. He shaved his beard, cut his hair short, and dyed his locks back to their natural black color. He trusted the Mossad to erase any connections between him and the Oren Langer persona.

"I agree," the Prime Minister said. "Dan is the right choice for the task."

"We also need to clean the area; I am sure those who wanted our satellite intact will not rest until they get it or we drop from the race to space."

"It was confirmed that our friends destroyed the Proton?"

"They confirmed and I support their decision," answered M.

Dan concentrated on his next mission to secure the upcoming launch of the upgraded Amos 6 satellite, which was important for Israel, and he hoped it would go off without incident. Many companies were involved with this satellite's development, and it was supposed to replace the Amos 3. Keeping eyes on their enemies in the Middle East was Israel's top defense priority, no expenses spared. As was said before: "Information is worth more than oil."

A shelved option was to launch Orbixeye with its future satellite later using the IDF's own Jericho rocket. Due to time constraints, this idea was passed over, and the Mossad revised the plans accordingly.

M.'s administrative assistant came into his office without formalities, dropped a folder on his desk, and walked away grumpily.

"What's wrong with her today?" M. mumbled and pulled out a list of employees from the Chinese Embassy. The elderly man from the cemetery had been asked by his country's security officer to point out the man he met. Based on the information he'd disclosed, M. would find the man who sniffed around Langer's grave.

It was very easy to find him on basic descriptions and personal information alone. Also, his Bank of China credit card showed he bought a full tank of gas in Tel Aviv and drove an embassy vehicle with a diplomat license plate. *How unprofessional,* thought M. to himself. The man in question hadn't stopped anywhere else on his way, and there were no other people who could identify him. He could've used the car and never left Tel Aviv, but the obvious conclusion was that it was Chen.

"Hello, Mr. Chen," M. whispered. "I need to stop you before it's too late."

His office door opened; his assistant peeped in and rolled her eyes. "Who are you talking to?" she asked.

M. smiled and replied, "It's okay. You know I talk to myself sometimes."

She laughed and slammed the door behind her.

M. didn't like to take prisoners unless absolutely necessary. He decided to monitor the situation closely and started to plan new ideas in his head.

M. decided to send Dan under another fake identity in case the Chinese tried to track him down further. Dan's departure to America would be a test to see whether he was being followed by Chinese agents. Therefore, the operations officer and M. attached a shadow agent to Dan and an additional Mossad covert agent.

The intercom beeped, and a voice alerted M. to a person in the waiting room. M. looked at the camera and identified the individual. He pressed the intercom button and asked his assistant to let her in.

"Hi, Joan. How are you?" M. asked with a smile. "Have a seat please." He offered her a cigarette.

"Thanks, but I'm not smoking," she replied, waiting for the boss to explain why she'd been dispatched to see him on such short notice.

Joan Farrelly was a high school English teacher in her late thirties. She was a native New Yorker with a Brooklyn accent. She'd vowed to come back to Israel after visiting the country for the first time as a volunteer teenager in a Kibbutz. She'd immigrated to join the Israeli Defense Force after graduating from Baruch College in New York.

Her devotion and remarkable achievements in the military as a lieutenant officer had caught the eye of the Mossad. She'd once patrolled the Israeli-Sinai border with her Duvdevan commando team when they were attacked by ISIS militants. A rocket-propelled grenade hit the car in front and wounded the driver. Miraculously, she was not hurt, and the two Israeli soldiers in the back escaped and took shelter nearby. Joan immediately threw two grenades, one after the other, making contact with the enemy. She then surged forward and killed all three militants by herself. She saved her driver by providing him with first aid and calling for help.

Once she was caught in the Mossad web, there was no way out. She was trained, got a job, got married, and raised a six-year-old daughter without anyone knowing her secret agent life. Even her husband thought that the education department was sending his wife to other countries for continuing education programs. She received a fake diploma from fabricated programs to show her family proof of her excursions. Although most of her missions involved low-risk conditions, she was always on alert and ready for action, constantly challenging her boss to let her get involved in more complex missions.

Dan Eyal then walked into the office and was introduced to Joan for the first time. He was a few years her senior. Dan looked over her file briefly after M. handed it to him for review.

"Are you concerned that we might be stepping into some trouble in Florida?" asked Dan carefully, his mouth dry.

"I suspect a lot of commotion, Dan. Prepare as you would to meet your adversaries but hope it doesn't happen."

"Got it," replied Dan, and Joan nodded her head.

"I am concerned that your identity will be discovered by Chinese agents. While we play espionage games, the Chinese and our politicians are inviting each other to gala parties, taking photos, smiling like nothing is happening between our two intelligence agencies," M. said, lowering his head.

"What did you discover?" asked Dan. Joan leaned in to listen.

"They are after you. The Chinese don't yet know where to find you, but it's just a matter of time. Joan will be watching your back in Miami." M. looked at Joan and said, "You will communicate as trained. No one knows of your existence."

"I like that," Joan said, her blue eyes sparkling with excitement. She craved missions like oxygen, the chance to get away from the monotonous life as a wife and mother—although she wouldn't have traded her daughter or husband for anything.

"Don't get excited. I don't like people who get excited," M. complained.

Joan smiled to herself and sighed.

"Obviously, you both will depart under new identities in case the Chinese hack the airport passenger lists in search of your names. Especially yours, Dan," M. continued. "Your fake names are existing people's names, so if something goes wrong, you will disappear. And if we're asked for your names here, we'll say you never left the country. Understood?"

"This will reshuffle our cards," observed Dan.

"Sure, it will," M. remarked.

He then handed them their new Israeli passports, already stamped with the United States Embassy entry visa. They turned the pages, and Joan chuckled, "Wow, it shows all the real countries I've visited in the past. For pleasure, at least."

"True," stated M. "We marked only your private visits to avoid your getting questioned about past missions."

M. looked at his agents and waited for their questions. The intercom buzzed again, and he granted entry to his next guest.

"Sit, Ran," M. commanded without charm. "Ran is the commander of the mission and will monitor your steps for logistics from above. He will help with money, accommodations, weapons, and any other issues that may come up. You won't have to throw your identities around unnecessarily."

M.'s three guests all shook hands.

Dan was familiar with the rules and logistics in foreign countries. He preferred to work alone but also understood that he was in danger of elimination. *It looks like freaking Dimitri will haunt me for life*, he thought.

"We will keep you off the Chinese radar for questioning regarding the explosion, Dan. I guess they believe we did it," M. added.

"What about Greco?" Dan asked. "Did you let him be questioned?"

"No; we said he was classified and couldn't attend the deposition. We didn't take any chance that he might expose you or incriminate us by mistake. It's worth the disconnect and the diplomatic tensions."

Dan, drifting, thought for a second, then said, "They might be after him."

"We took that under consideration. Greco is underground in his IDF base unit," M. replied.

Ran Shomron was a broad-shouldered man in his late sixties with a square jaw and piercing eyes. He had short gray hair and a curled mustache above his thin lips. He'd immigrated to Israel thirty years before after serving as an officer in the United States Marines for five years. He was perfect for this mission that did not require physical strength. He was an asset to the Mossad with his quick field analyses that had saved agents' lives. Dan had heard about him but hadn't worked with him before.

"At this point, it's all open," claimed M. "We know about Chen. We need to assume that they know about Dan and Greco. All bets are basically off." He paused a moment, glancing down at his hands. "We just have to accept that he's on your trail. They will also send other agents from their arsenal to track you and Greco down—and all this while trying to protect our interests on American soil when launching our satellite. We've gotten many warnings that China is looking to retaliate, and we want to be sure of the safety of our equipment, launching Orbixeye safely."

The three focused intently. They all understood the burden they carried.

"There might be sabotage to harvest this piece of equipment. From the moment our satellite lands in Cape Canaveral via our Air Force cargo plane, we will have technicians watching it night and day. We'll also be monitoring the assembly of the Spax rocket, paid for by a private investor."

M. then looked at Dan and added, "The object you brought with you from the explosion site was sent in a diplomatic bag to the Miami Consulate. From Miami, you shall contact the CIA via our channels. They're better equipped to analyze it."

"What's that...?" asked Joan.

"It's on a need to know basis," replied M. bluntly.

"Any findings?" asked Dan.

"Yes and no. All that needs to be confirmed, so let the expert Americans come up with the answers. They have a lab in North Carolina, where the CIA and federal government are sending all suspicious samples for identification and analysis. They are specialized in the most complicated chemical and forensic samples. We don't want to speculate without a second look. We already communicated this to our allies, and they are waiting for the package."

An hour later, the team split up, preparing to leave the country at once to head to New York City. It was a few days later when Dan reported to the embassy and met with the security officer, Shimi Greenberg, a former officer for the IDF. They hadn't seen each other in over ten years, and they shared memories as all Israelis do when they meet. As always, the first question was, "What was your duty in the Army?" and from there, the conversation flowed swiftly.

Joan got to Miami a few hours later and moved into a motel in Cocoa Beach. After two tiring flights, she situated herself for the long haul and waited for further instructions.

Ran Shomron, or "Rani," as he was sometimes called, flew to America on a connection from Heathrow to Miami via British Airways. From there, he rented a room at a hotel in Cape Canaveral and ordered two tickets to tour the space center a couple of days later. Dan would meet him there.

Dan and Rani got clearance to visit the site through an embassy request. They would inspect the area where the satellite would be stored and watch over the technicians maintaining and preparing it for launch.

In the meantime, M. focused on throwing off Chen, who worked for NCNA, the undercover Chinese agency operating from the embassy that performed intelligence activities under the umbrella of Chang.

"Think like your enemy. But much quicker," M. had told his agents as they'd departed for their new mission.

CHAPTER FIFTEEN

The NASA astronauts' training center in Johnson Space Center was refurbished quickly to accept the former crews. The complex training process was an accelerated program, yet like a refresher course in dealing with the old equipment and learning the new and more advanced technological systems to be installed in the same vehicles they'd flown in the past.

Medical tests and physical training were performed twice a day, one session in the morning and one in the evening, ensuring consistency with their progress. Unfortunately, a few were eliminated due to physical and medical conditions, and John suggested that some could be valuable as consultants on the ground once the mission began.

During the day, they trained in extravehicular procedures and scenarios they might encounter on their voyage to the Moon. Of the twelve American astronauts who'd previously landed and walked on the Moon, no one was present other than two who'd orbited the Moon and piloted the Command Modules from Apollo 14 and Apollo 17. Colonel Clifton "Cliff" Taylor and Colonel Isaac Holmes, AKA Shiké (derived from his middle name, Joshua), both had the experience to pilot the Lunar Landing Module with which they were already familiar.

Two other astronauts that NASA brought aboard had trained for the Apollo mission but had never flown; they'd been on the standby team in case Cliff or Shiké could not make it. A few astronauts had died years earlier due to car accidents or NASA jet plane crashes, and the veterans shared their memories. Out of more than three hundred and thirty original astronauts, two hundred and forty-one were accepted—a few would make it to space while others were not physically able to fly. At that point, all NASA astronauts who'd trained to work on the ISS were not pilots. They did not have the required ability to operate the old equipment or complex ships. NASA put them into teams and let each mission commander select his crew, and they all trained together.

When someone dropped out due to a medical or physical reason, he was replaced with another to fill the gap. General Bloomfield and Coolie still needed two fully operational and mission-prepared crews to man the shuttles.

Each shuttle would fly one Lunar Landing Module to the Moon with its appointed crew. Each mission specialist would deploy the LLM from the cargo bay into space using the Canadarm robotic limb, precisely at the right height and position to land on the Moon.

Four astronauts would land on the Moon while the spaceship orbited and then rendezvoused with them on return from their mission.

These four astronauts trained in a confidential structure in addition to the other facilities with the rest of the astronauts. Any attempt by their colleagues to find out what it was that they were experiencing was met with frozen faces and sealed mouths.

The two full crews of the LLM were split into two: LLM-1 and LLM-2, with LLM-3 as a standby and problem diffuser; in other words, they were assigned to find solutions to any issues that might have come up during a flight, based on the experience from the Apollo 13 mission.

General Bradley Bloomfield oversaw the four landing astronauts' programs, and the rest were under the command of Coolie, who stood in front of the entire space battalion with a PowerPoint presentation on the screen behind him.

On the screen were the crew members' names. Each name was assigned a duty next to the space vehicle he manned.

Excited chatter gave Coolie an opportunity to exchange notes with Bloomfield, and then he raised his hands to cool the crews down. He stated with composure, "Each shuttle crew includes a mission commander, copilot, and mission specialist. The Command Service Module was not required and scrapped from this program. The spacecraft fulfilled the CSM's duty and that of the Saturn 5 rocket." Coolie looked at General Bloomfield, who grabbed the microphone.

Bloomfield announced, "Cape Canaveral will be closed for the duration of the final assembly until they are ready for the mission. It will be the first time that the ship is launched in years—and also the first time that two shuttles will be launched simultaneously, within mere minutes of each other."

The room exploded in applause and praise: "Unbelievable!" "This is history, boys!"

CHAPTER SIXTEEN

The activity in Area 51 drew the Russian and Chinese counterintelligence agencies' attention, and they poked their noses into the murky situation.

Tupolev Tu-160 bombers, nicknamed Blackjacks and revived from the Soviet era, started flying from Alaska to Southern California on intelligence missions. Although they flew about twenty-five miles off the territorial waters of the United States, the USAF dispatched a formation of four F-22 Raptors to intercept and confront the aggression.

"Sniffers!" hissed General Bloomfield to his aides in the office.

"China just introduced their new H-6K long-range bomber, a replica of the Russian Tu-16 Badger," said Coolie.

"More sniffers," grimaced the general. "They're all dying to know what we're doing these days."

"The defense department is in total panic after seeing these in the sky," mentioned John.

"I can only imagine the chaos in the White House and the headache for the CIA. Very little is known about the planes' capabilities," Bloomfield muttered.

"You said that the Pentagon demanded all activities to be confidential," John said, eyeing the general seated behind his desk. "How do you keep this confidential? It's practically impossible. I'm sure that they will know one way or another that we are on the way to the Moon. Then what?"

General Bloomfield tried to offer more information. "Gene Bennett informed me that many spies roam our land these days. I'm sure that covert agents from around the world have reported that the Johnson Space Center was reactivated and is holding space-mission activities. I doubt anyone took the bait that we're supposedly planning to 'fly to Mars' without our showing any new equipment that would actually get us there. So, then the CIA started spreading disinformation showing new spacecraft and a 'final plan,' claiming it would take about five to ten years." Bloomfield inhaled deeply, his face stone.

"Impressive," admitted John.

"We just need to make sure that no one is slowing us down. Expect the unexpected," concluded the general as his face melted from ice to a victorious smile.

The CIA had sabotaged the traces that NASA left behind. They planned to build quick replicas of the new-era space orbiters and display them publicly alongside the NASA administration on prime-time television. This plan would probably reignite the old conspiracy theory that the Moon landing was orchestrated in Hollywood and hadn't actually happened. "Let them believe we are incapable," Bennett used to say in every planning meeting.

A public statement came from the Smithsonian stating that the space equipment displayed had to go through resizing to fit into the new designated room in the museum. NASA stated on national television that President Cole had signed a new executive order to explore Mars and land on the red planet by the year 2030.

"Not sure it's enough misinformation," Gene Bennett had claimed as he incessantly searched for ways to keep his adversaries asleep.

The Smithsonian statements didn't convince Chang and his Russian counterparts, as both agencies had collaborated for many years under a confidential agreement signed in Moscow during the Soviet era. Chen had resumed normal operations at his embassy in Tel Aviv after the cemetery visit and decided, upon his superior's orders, to continue his manhunt. Images of Dan in Kazakhstan were Photoshopped to show how he would look without a beard and compared to pictures of past IDF officers.

"It's like trying to find a needle in a haystack," murmured Chen.

Hundreds of name-labeled photos were printed and compared to other faces. After obsessive hours of nonstop labor with a few assistants, they came across a couple of pictures that could match the man they wanted.

Chen studied the photos and checked every detail: hair, cheekbones, eyes, ears—he missed nothing. The name under one potential match was Dan Eyal, a retired colonel from the IDF. Chen searched for more information about the man but found nothing. He created a new image entry and sent it to the main office in Beijing.

Chang was satisfied with his agent's work. He ordered Chen to immediately track Eyal down, verify his connection to the explosion, prove that he killed Dimitri, and, finally, eliminate him. Chen sent his spies to cover Tel Aviv and the international airport. They had no clue where to start, so they spied on IDF camp entry gates and especially the "HaKirya", the IDF nerve center in Tel Aviv. Three agents also covered the three entries to the check-in area of Ben Gurion Airport. None of these agents were Asian. Some were disguised as volunteers in communal towns spread throughout in Israel, some worked in other foreign embassies, and others came in as terrorists after a last-minute call. Everything was orchestrated from the Chinese Embassy in Tel Aviv.

M. warned his agents before departure to be aware that they might be followed from the second they left the building. Paranoia was the base instinct of an agent. M. changed the motto, "Trust and verify," to, "Don't trust and verify." Attacks always hit in unexpected locations when one was least prepared.

Chen's cell pinged an alert. A text message between the agents in the airport terminal read, "Panda Arrived"—"Panda" being the codename for Dan Eyal. The Chinese agents closed in to ensure that it was a positive identification. It was confirmed. It was 11:00 p.m., and only two flights were on the board. Both were direct flights to JFK—one departure via Delta Airlines at 00:30 a.m., and the other via EL AL Airlines at 11:50 p.m. They exchanged agents, and two left the airport, leaving one agent to find out which of the two flights Dan would board.

CHAPTER SEVENTEEN

D an acclimated to his new place quickly and enjoyed a little bit of the Florida sun. South Beach was his favorite place in the evenings, with all its restaurants, bars, and colorful people walking along Ocean Drive's sidewalks in search of excitement. Restaurant workers tracked down tourists and shoved menus at them, offering discounts and other freebies to get them into their establishments. *Competition is a bitch*, Dan observed.

He entered the Ocean Seafood and Grill and was directed to a table in front of the congested sidewalk. He sat down and inhaled the glorious early evening. He waved to the waiter and ordered a Mojito that arrived in a huge glass with a two-for-one deal. *This is a gallon of alcohol*, he laughed to himself. Most of the tables overlooking the sidewalk and beach were still empty.

A woman walked in and chatted briefly in Spanish with the hostess. She was seated at the table next to Dan.

"Impressive," he mumbled himself.

The woman had a striking resemblance to some Latin actress whose name escaped him. For a moment, Dan even thought it was her. Her dirty blonde hair was long and straight. Her almond eyes, pouty lips, and beautiful face complemented her body, which was covered only with a white cutout top, black leggings, and white sneakers. Dan noticed her designer bag when she opened it to check her makeup. Suddenly, as she read a text, she erupted with laughter and shook her hair, briefly exposing a small tattoo of a cobra on her neck.

Cute, Dan thought.

When the waiter returned, she pointed at Dan's drink and ordered one of her own in Spanish. She smiled brilliantly. Once her drink was placed before her, she remained happily busy on her phone, lost in her own world.

He was tempted to talk to her when her perfume struck his nostrils from four feet away. Dan returned her smile when their eyes met for a moment, and then she went back to texting.

Dan's chicken fajitas were served with a second Mojito, even though he had consumed only about half of the first one. *Whew*, he thought.

Surprisingly, the woman took a few more sips from her drink and then left after placing a hefty tip on the table.

The waiter approached Dan and asked if everything was satisfactory.

"Yes, thank you," Dan said. "Tell me, was that Sofia...?" He could only remember the actress's first name.

The waiter scoffed and replied, "Oh, no—she just looks like her." He shoved the tip deep into his front pocket.

Dan returned to reality. He was married and followed the strict Mossad rules, one of which was to be very careful about beautiful flirting women. He extinguished his desires quickly.

Dan chose to move onto his next step: a visit to Cape Canaveral as a visitor (before receiving his official security clearance). He was to meet with the chief of security to assess the procedures in the area prior to the rocket launch. It was on the schedule for the following month, weather permitting. The mission was critical due to its military nature, and tensions, as always, were high. The Mossad, CIA, and FBI were scrambling to ensure the safety of the launch and monitored every move for miles and miles around Cape Canaveral and Merritt Island.

For a month, Dan and his colleagues kept a low profile, as instructed, changing their appearances daily. They didn't stay in the same place twice and moved from apartment to apartment and motel to hotel. They were on the move constantly to avoid being tracked by the enemy.

They didn't keep a daily routine. "Be calmly paranoid," M. had regularly said in Mossad briefings.

Dan, Joan, and Ran's tourist visit would give them a mental layout of the establishment, and the excursion was for both fun and business. The security clearance would take a while, even if it went into an accelerated approval process due to his status. The FBI and CIA coordinated their efforts, but Dan didn't count on them.

They entered the visitor parking lot in two separate rental cars. The three easily blended with other visitors. Dan's colleagues followed in his shadow at a safe distance, posing as a married couple—despite their age difference. It was late morning and a passing rain moved east and allowed sunshine.

The tour at NASA started at the IMAX Theatre which screened a launch of the Space Shuttle Atlantis—and it was as close to reality as standing beside the craft itself.

At some point, Dan started heading to the washroom. A moment later, Joan followed him, making subtle eye contact. Dan turned right down the bathroom corridor with Joan still behind. As she passed the men's room, she heard struggling and the clanking of metal from behind the door. A Middle Eastern man appeared behind her, signaling for her to disappear before he walked into the men's room. She peeped through the crack in the door and saw Dan struggling against another unknown Middle Eastern man. At that point, both of the strange men tried restraining Dan—but Joan didn't think twice. After sending a quick text to Ran, she drew her pistol, burst through the door, and fired a shot into the man gripping Dan in a stranglehold. Dan writhed against the choking hands until the wounded man fell dead on the floor.

The other man then swiftly kicked Joan's pistol from her hand. The gun flew through the air and she groped after it, wincing from the kick, but the man was much quicker. He caught the pistol in midair. He struck Joan with the butt of the gun and she hit the floor. Dan pulled himself up by the sink, eyeing the enemy now pointing the gun directly at his chest. The door blew open again, and Ran stepped in and instantly shot the second man dead with a single bullet in his temple. The body collapsed on the floor. Joan's gun slid to the corner of the bathroom through a pool of blood that had spread over the tile.

With no time to thank his colleagues for saving his life, Dan started to frisk the bodies.

"Let's go now before anyone else comes," urged Ran through clenched teeth.

"Watch the door; I need to identify these men," Dan replied calmly.

Joan pulled herself to her feet, and she and Ran stepped out of the bathroom. Dan quickly emptied their pockets and snatched their wallets. He left the guns but swiftly snapped a few pictures of the bodies on his phone.

"*Quick*," Ran pressed from the other side of the door. Dan escaped the bathroom and moved to the building's exit. He glanced at his fellow agents and muttered, "They're gonna send a freaking army here now."

Dan was concerned that the photos on his phone might be proof of the altercation if he were caught, but identifying those men was worth the risk. He'd noticed a small tattoo, about half an inch in size, of a cobra snake on each of their necks—identical to the tattoo he'd seen on the blonde woman in the restaurant.

The three agents slipped right back into the IMAX Theatre, thinking that it was the right move.

"Did either of you see any cameras?" Ran asked quietly.

"I avoided them," replied Dan.

"Me, too," Joan echoed.

Ten minutes passed, and suddenly the lights went up. The screening froze just as the ship opened its cargo bay door to release the Hubble Telescope into orbit. Everyone looked around and murmured, wondering what had happened.

A few security officers walked in and blocked all the exits. Two other officers appeared and asked people to leave for the hallway through the last door on the right. The muttering crowd moved quickly; Dan, Ran, and Joan joined the stream of people.

As Dan passed one of the security officers, he asked coolly, "Is everything okay, officer?"

"Yes—please move on, sir," he answered politely, even though his gaze was cold.

From the hall, the crowd was escorted through an emergency exit to a parking lot behind the building. The forty-some tourists in the group, many assumedly from Europe and South America, stood there as commanded by the security officers.

Emergency vehicles made their way to the other side of the building and stopped by the main entry. Curious chattering sprung from the crowd, making the officers visibly nervous.

Joan remembered that she'd left her pistol on the bathroom floor in all the commotion. She whispered this to Ran.

"Better off in case they frisk us," Ran whispered to her calmly.

Dan made sure his shirt was appropriately tucked in and put his sunglasses on. He was unsure if the parking lot was monitored with cameras, so he focused on blending in. He didn't exchange any words or gestures with the others.

Another officer showed up and discussed something with the two lead officers who'd told everyone to exit the theatre. They then directed the visitors back inside and into a private room where they could wait comfortably.

Through the window, Dan watched two ambulances leave the parking lot without their sirens sounding; he assumed they carried the men's bodies.

Then the security chief hushed the group and made a quick statement. "Ladies and gentlemen, we've experienced a serious security breach. The rest of the tour is canceled. We are sorry for the inconvenience. We must ask you to show your identification and proof of where you're currently staying so that we may reimburse you for your tickets and potentially contact you for questions in the future."

They improvised a table and asked everyone to line up. Joan and Ran were among the first in line. Dan was much farther behind. Then he saw that unforgettable face—the blonde woman with the cobra tattoo. *Sofia.* He sucked in a breath and glued his eyes on her. He knew that it could not be a coincidence; he'd seen way too many cobra tattoos recently. Even more pressing was that these people could be affiliated with the assassin who wanted to send Dan home in a coffin.

Sofia didn't look at him at all and tried to sneak to the front of the line to get out of the room faster. Dan followed her, getting dirty looks from the officers and tourists alike. Sofia managed to get to the front, and Dan, frustrated, signaled Ran and Joan to watch the woman in the black jacket and pants.

It was too late. Sofia got her clearance from the officers and quickly took off. Dan could hear police officers and FBI agents flooding the hallway.

The three agents took their turns showing their passports with A-2 diplomatic visas; they told the officers they were working at the Israeli consulate in Miami and it was their first time visiting Cape Canaveral. The officers swiftly released them. They were instructed to leave the Cape immediately and exited the room without looking back.

In the parking lot, the three separated without further communication, each to their own rathole. The lovely afternoon had ended with two dead bodies, very close calls, and heavy frustrations.

"What a day to die," Dan mumbled to himself.

Dan surreptitiously searched for leads in the parking lot, but no car showed any obvious clues as to its owner. He assumed the Middle Eastern men had probably arrived in a cab—or someone dropped them off.

"Of course! *Sofia!*" Dan exclaimed.

CHAPTER EIGHTEEN

The Oval Office

The security meeting started at 7:00 a.m. with a briefing from General William Fox, the NIO director responsible for satellite- and cyber-intelligence gathering. He worked closely with the National Reconnaissance Office, which handled the deployment of military space equipment. The president invited the CEOs of large tech corporations to join and be part of the solution, as well. "They must have something to share; something outside the box," Cole had stated, probably trying to convince himself more than the others.

General Fox didn't look like a classic military man. On the contrary, he looked like an aging college professor—a soft-spoken, non-tempestuous man, barely carrying his short frame into the room. His belly hung lowly and threatened to pop his buttoned shirt, but his round face radiated with the opportunity to show how much he knew about cybertechnology.

Fox began with some background on why so many social media and streaming services crashed regularly. The primary culprits were computer entities that took over and attacked smartphones, smart TVs, and smart home systems. There were three or four assumed major players, but there was no clue whether individuals or countries ran them.

"We should assume the worst and take it from there," interjected President Cole. Despite his decisive statement, he usually did not encourage his top brass to convince him to wage war on adversaries without explicitly clear and present danger.

General Fox nodded his head and continued explaining the cyberwar arena as the group watched the corresponding video on their tablet screens. "All the smart home equipment can be connected to one worldwide network and synchronized to create a monstrous entity capable of attacking all our infrastructure. You can't pinpoint them because they have no server, just like the Stuxnet computer worm that destroyed the Iranian nuclear infrastructure software during Clayton's administration. It left not a single trace."

"Can you explain your meaning in simpler language, please?" requested Cole.

"They can watch and hear you from your webcam—even if your computer is turned off," Fox said conclusively. His smile didn't fit the mood of the room whatsoever. Cole wanted to smack him but realized that it was essential to know if this man could help. His temper needed to sit this one out.

"We call it the IoT—the Internet of Things," General Fox continued. "There was an enormous attack by someone called CMIYC, meaning Catch Me If You Can. They attacked smart home equipment and prevented it from receiving the services intended by their companies. Another entity is fighting them to re-hack the smart home devices and debug them from CMI-YC. As you can see, it's a computer war that's already started!" Fox's voice rose an octave. Apparently, the fight against hackers was the first phase before controlling home equipment for military purposes, such as intelligence gathering, communications, and service interruptions.

"The other entity named itself Lom—meaning crowbar in Russian. Don't forget—this is just a name, and there is no affiliation with the language or country of Russia," Fox added.

His eyes widened as if to ask the morons in the room,
understand?" Fox looked around and then asserted, "
or distributed denial of service, can affect both serv
the military. Therefore, hackers can easily win the next war
by utilizing cybertechnology alone."

The CEOs nodded their heads.

President Cole asked, "Does anyone have plans in place to
prevent this?" He looked around at the faces, hoping briefly
to get an answer from someone in the room, but it was in vain.
He was all alone.

Then a top cyber-intelligence officer spoke up: "Mr. President, we first need to stop the attackers. Second, we must
require manufacturers to always install antivirus chips to
prevent their products from being attacked."

The CEOs had seen that coming and, of course, resented
any idea that would hike up the cost of what they sold to the
public.

The president looked at them with a wrinkled face, and,
deciding to put the country first, he declared, "Unless you
have a better idea, I will ask my secretary of commerce to
start those new regulations immediately, without delay!"

General Fox nodded vigorously and said, "Anyone who
is connected to our defense systems or intelligence departments should be aware of the danger. Spying may be
happening through their smart home devices. I will draft a protocol within twenty-four hours and send it to you for approval."
Fox felt he had gotten the message across.

The door opened after a quick knock, and without waiting for permission, the chief of staff walked in with a grim
face and put a sealed note in front of President Cole. The
president opened it and read it to himself. *Two murdered,
unidentified men...suspected foreign agents...Cape Canaveral.
Under investigation.*

"Where there's smoke, there's fire," mumbled Cole, trying to connect the information to other current events.

He hadn't taken the time to learn all the government protocols and rules, which he would've ignored anyway, and he handed the note to Gene Bennett without mentioning anything out loud.

Secretary of Defense Wezniak carefully watched Bennett read the note.

Gene digested what he'd just read and decided to coordinate with his colleague in the FBI—but he didn't know that the FBI was already on top of the case.

The president ignored the inquisitive faces throughout the room and said, "You know what to do, Gene. Just don't start a war."

Gene nodded and handed the note back to the president. His face was fallen. He felt it was time to mention that the coordination among all military and security agencies required a Czar to oversee and brief everyone about incidents, discoveries, and plans; it was now a necessity.

"Mr. President, no agency takes orders from us," Gene said calmly. "There should be one office that links all our ranks and communications together." Gene's gaze stopped on Wezniak. The CEOs blinked in confusion.

"Done!" growled Cole, thrusting an angry finger at the secretary of defense's nose. "Wezniak will handle it."

CHAPTER NINETEEN

Colonel Warren Campbell spoke clearly but heavily: "Houston, we just observed an object passing by us here," declared the ISS Commander. "It was moving at enormous speed and dangerously close to the currently docking Soyuz capsule."

Campbell was surrounded by flight engineers working on the procedure to lock the Russian capsule into the ISS, as it had done many times.

"Stand by," Mission Control in Houston replied and copied the ATV Control Centre in Toulouse, France, which was the hub for the automated transfer vehicles that supplied the ISS.

The unexpected alert by Colonel Campbell was critical; the crew aboard the ISS could've been in danger. The ISS Mission Control crew, which was equipped with an advance warning debris detection system, was surprised that nothing had alerted or warned them.

"Houston, can you fix our debris alert remotely?" asked Campbell, floating through the space station.

"Checking that; stand by," was the reply.

"And are we following through with the docking?" Campbell asked, watching the Soyuz capsule through a window.

"Affirmative," was the laconic response.

The Russian Soyuz with seven tons of supplies and experimental equipment began its automated procedure, approaching the ISS docking hatch slowly, navigating itself to the entryway with precision accuracy.

"Docked!" announced Campbell with satisfaction, waiting for the alert control to indicate it was ready to open the hatch. First locking phase of the capsule to the station was secured and then its second phase performed an airtight maneuver because the vehicles were pressurized.

It had been about twenty-four hours since the Soyuz had fired its engines to change course and approach the ISS. The tension was nerve-racking at that point, and the ISS's team of six astronauts focused fervently on the mission. They closely watched the last phase on the monitoring screens and the round ISS hatches.

At the same time, technicians on Earth examined the external ISS camera systems carefully, trying to identify the unknown speeding object's origin. The object had been five hundred yards from the Soyuz, which was dangerously and catastrophically close by NASA standards.

"ISS, this is Houston," called the control room manager with concern. The manager remembered how calm Gene Krantz had been during the Apollo 13 incident and tried to follow suit, but it was hard.

"Go ahead, Houston," replied the ISS.

"Go, Colonel Campbell!" the manager ordered decisively.

"Roger that," replied Campbell, the forty-four-year-old commander of the International Space Station. Campbell, a tall, thin commander. He was extremely handsome with light green eyes, was a former fighter pilot who'd participated in the first Gulf War. A graduate from Harvard with a degree in biology, he truly was more suited for a career in business, yet he was a courageous fighter pilot who volunteered for the most daring missions the Air Force could offer. He'd dedicated his life to his high school sweetheart, who was handicapped by polio before they got married; her struggle had only brought them closer together.

"Campbell, we don't know where the object came from. It was orbiting retrograde, opposite to the ISS—which is orbiting with the Earth's rotation," said Jim Mason the operator of Mission Control over the communication system at Vandenberg Air Force Base. "We analyzed the photos, but they're not very clear. We compared the object with our database and think it changed orbits...therefore, it wasn't registered as a threat, but we will keep an eye on it."

"Roger, Jim," replied Campbell who always used Jim's first name, even in professional situations, as they knew each other from mutual visits and meetings on the ground or at NASA events. It was a deep friendship that had lasted decades.

Watching and monitoring radar for space debris was Jim Mason's duty as the Trajectory Operations Officer. Jim's team regularly altered the ISS's and other space vehicles' orbits to avoid destruction or loss of life during space missions.

Jim, also the director of Vandenberg's SCC (Space Control Center), monitored over eight thousand objects in space, updated every quarter to the hour. Most debris gathered below the five-hundred-mile zone from Earth, and little junk orbited above it. Also, most debris came from the Chinese satellite explosion and previous collision of the two satellites. Although Jim's team's debris maps were highly accurate, they could not spot anything smaller than a tennis ball and weren't very effective in detecting objects in extremely high orbits. This gray area was an issue that now caused headaches for the engineers in the control room.

The SCC also monitored objects around the ISS's orbital path, computing their speed, size, and probability of hitting the station. When the chance of a collision was high, the station was relocated to avoid an impact by using its control momentum gyro (CMG).

An officer who worked in tandem with Jim was part of a team called the Attitude Determination and Control, and he dictated the maneuvering of the ISS and whether it was kept in the same orbit. The station rotated and yawed with the thrusters on the service modules. They needed to calculate the mass of the station, including its docking Soyuz capsule, to finalize their next step. Jim and his team then decided to change the ISS's path.

"ISS, this is Houston," called the manager from NASA's control room.

"Go ahead, Houston," replied Colonel Campbell calmly.

"We are going for maneuvering procedure."

"Roger," Campbell confirmed.

Campbell trusted the folks at the Houston control center. They were a group of dedicated and motivated men who never left even the smallest detail uninvestigated. They knew of past errors that had caused devastating disasters due to faulty mathematical calculations or technical failure. They didn't stand for sloppy installation and refused to become a statistic.

A huge screen in the Houston control center marked the location of the ISS's orbital track and its position on Earth. In the top left corner of the screen, a box showed the ISS's positioning and attitude data and other related data about the space vehicle. All information was synchronized between the ISS and SCC, and they were ready for the burn procedure.

"Going for the burn in thirty seconds," said Jim.

"Roger, Houston," Campbell acknowledged. He knew that the entire maneuver would be commanded and controlled from Earth via computer. The ISS crew had braced for the burn due to the motion reaction they'd experience from the thrusters.

"Countdown...we're going for a thirty-seven-second burn, Campbell!"

Jim was on the controls in case of a failure to move the station to a higher altitude. He clicked a few functions on his keyboard in front of three large, colorful screens showing data, graphs, and tables as the engines went on. Then he started the reverse thrusters to maneuver the station until they reached the desired orbit.

The Soyuz added mass to the ISS, but the mass was not a significant issue for the maneuver, other than the recomputing of the orbit and position for the Soyuz's return.

The ISS crew was then free to transfer the Soyuz's supplies and equipment into the station.

According to laws of orbital mechanics, the height of the orbit determined the speed of the object in orbit. Based on the technicians' calculations, the ISS completed a circle every eighty-six minutes, and the dangerous object that had passed them was twice as fast. That meant that the next rendezvous with the object was predicted to occur in forty-three minutes.

The ISS began orbiting at its new altitude of two hundred and sixty-five miles from Earth, and at that point, it was not considered to be on a collision course with any other satellites or known debris. Usually, the ISS orbited between two hundred and two hundred and seventy miles from the Earth's surface, completing slightly over sixteen orbits per day.

"Got you out of danger, Campbell," Jim said cheerfully.

"Thanks for that, Jim!" laughed Campbell with relief.

Due to orbital decay caused by the atmosphere and dust particles close to Earth, the ISS, like any other artificial satellite, would lose speed and elevation and eventually fall back to Earth. Jim knew that a long time would pass before the next altitude adjustment. Without any sign of the mysterious object angering the Soyuz, the capsule automatically unlocked itself and slowly pulled back from the ISS after six hours.

About a kilometer from the station, the unbelievable happened, leaving the ISS crew frozen with gaping mouths and wide eyes. The mysterious flying object reappeared, having changed its orbit again, navigating itself close to the ISS. The object slammed into the Soyuz capsule, shredding it to pieces.

The heat of the impact caused an explosion, even though space was devoid of air. Materials melted and vaporized and created hot plasma, which expanded rapidly and spewed debris in all directions.

The blast impacted the ISS, and the crew stumbled, grabbing onto anything they could. Some grabbed the exposed hose, others a computer—some just bumped against the station walls.

The master alarm system sounded when the direct current switching unit was tripped by the blast. The short within the channel cut the power to all systems.

The backup system activated immediately to keep the command control and guidance navigation operating.

"Holy shit!" screamed Campbell while looking through the ISS hatch, witnessing the Russian spacecraft's execution. Campbell was convinced it was an act of terrorism—the first one seen in space.

"Did you see that, Jim? Jim? Should we prepare for Mode One emergency egress?" Campbell hollered through the intercom. "God, we didn't even have time to evacuate anyone onto the emergency Soyuz capsules..."

Jim and his control room team were speechless. Chills traveled down spines as some remembered the wrenching sight of the Columbia disintegrating into pieces.

"Stand by; we are checking the space station's status and assessing the systems," Jim finally replied, struggling to stay calm. He monitored the screen that showed the ISS spinning out of control, propelled deeper into space by the explosion.

"Jim—we lost power," Campbell breathed nervously.

"Your problems are greater than that," replied the Mission Control manager. "Stand by!"

CHAPTER TWENTY

The FBI investigators at Cape Canaveral concluded that the men found in the bathroom were killed by fatal gunshot wounds. One man was shot with a 9-mm bullet and the other by a Smith & Wesson Bodyguard .380 that was found on the floor. The investigators noted that type of gun was used regularly by women. They also immediately spotted the matching cobra tattoos on the victims' necks and assumed they were gang members. The crime-scene photographer snapped pictures to send through the lab and facial recognition programs. Since the men appeared to be Middle Eastern, the FBI also sought to inquire with intelligence agencies around the world about their identities and tattoos. The FBI then requested that ECHELON, a division of the NSA, assist with any communications and information connected to the two unidentified dead men.

"It could've been any one of the visitors," claimed the soft-spoken local police detective who'd been dispatched first to the scene. The investigative team hoped ECHELON could help, because no additional information could be drawn from the dead bodies—no one had claimed them or reported anyone missing.

Dan had done a thorough job, leaving no trace between the victims and his fellow agents, and the investigation came to a halt while awaiting any further evidence.

Hoping to revive the case, the lead FBI agent said to his assistant, "Jennifer, we need to check with local hotels to see if any guests abandoned their cars or left abruptly or without paying...maybe they even left unused travel tickets in their rooms. You know, the usual inquiry routine."

Jennifer wrote her instructions on a pad and nodded as her boss spoke.

Dan flew down I-95 in his rental car, desperate to get back to the embassy. His head spun around the day's events and the reappearance of Sofia. "It's like I'm obsessed," he murmured.

Dan hoped that she would revisit the restaurant on Ocean Drive where he'd seen her the first time. He considered interrogating the waiter who'd served them about whether he'd seen her there before, although Dan was pretty sure that she'd only been there to identify Dan and his general location. He pictured Sofia leaving the restaurant and getting back in the car with the two Middle Eastern men, preparing to follow him once he'd finished his dinner. "But how did she even know I was in Miami at all?" he asked himself.

Were the men Iranian? Turkish? Sofia spoke Spanish, but that's all Dan knew of her culturally. *Figuring this out is imperative before the next Canaveral satellite launch*, he thought.

Dan was sure that the FBI would use all the tools available to identify the dead men and find out who killed them. Perhaps he could convince his superiors to share information, but that would disclose that Israel might be behind the killings. Dan knew that the Mossad and CIA had a backdoor communication channel for emergency situations like this. The first close ties between the agencies had formed nearly a century before when the CIA gave the Mossad the most advanced spying equipment and technology. Dan was sure that

M. would get a call regarding the situation via the encrypted red telephone line.

Wound up in his thoughts, Dan failed to realize he was slowing down and eventually following a sluggish SUV. He blinked, looked at his speedometer, and immediately began passing the vehicle. Glancing briefly at the driver as he went by, his jaw dropped.

Sofia.

"Holy sh—" Dan stuttered and then hollered with a surge of adrenaline, "Going back to Miami, huh, baby?!"

She caught his eyes, and when she realized who he was, she stepped on the gas. The SUV surged ahead, still going the direction Dan was.

Dan slammed on the gas pedal and didn't let the distance between their cars increase; he tailed her, trying to figure out how to get her to pull over. Other drivers on the highway beeped and cursed at them, thinking two lunatics were racing and recklessly showing off.

Dan's car, a massive Dodge Charger, slammed into the SUV's bumper; to avoid an accident, she quickly swerved off on the exit toward Marco Polo Boulevard. Sofia had a handle on the car and did not slow down. Dan missed the exit by a few yards, screeching his tires and then reversing to maneuver up the exit. He lost sight of her, but the road only went to the west, so he stomped the gas down to the floor and kept it there. The engine roared and obeyed his request like a mechanical genie.

An intersection for Route 1 drew close, and he wasn't sure if she'd gone northwest or southeast. Traffic was light, but without any overhead intel, he couldn't figure out where she was. He slowed down as he approached Route 1—then, off to the side, he saw a dust cloud billow over a dirt road just before the intersection.

"Gotcha!" he yelled and veered onto the dirt road.

Without realizing that Dan was back on her trail, she turned left onto another dirt road into a thickly wooded area. Dan carefully followed at a safe distance and spotted the SUV parked behind some trees. She'd clearly hoped Dan would miss her, but the hiding spot was directly in his line of sight. He approached and stopped his car about fifty feet behind the SUV. He waited.

The road was so narrow and tightly packed with trees that the only way out was forward. Dan's GPS showed that there was another route about two miles south, but there was no connection between the dirt and asphalt roads. Sofia was trapped.

Dan pulled his gun from the glove compartment, got out of his car, and slowly approached the SUV from behind, trying to stay out of the view of Sofia's mirrors. Suddenly, the SUV took off again, speeding down the ever-narrowing dirt road.

Dan ran back to his car and pursued her, carefully navigating the thin gravel path. After a moment, he saw a canal off to one side with a small grassy area in front.

The SUV blew on ahead, bouncing out of potholes and ditches. Dan didn't slow down. The SUV excelled on dirt, but the gap between the two cars closed quickly. *This time she won't get away,* he thought.

Suddenly, the SUV hit a deep pothole. The vehicle took to the air while turning onto its side, hit the ground, rolled a couple of times, and ended up in the canal. The water quickly covered the upturned vehicle, threatening to drown the woman.

Dan pulled over a short distance away and watched. The driver's side was submerged in two feet of water, and the woman was still in her seat, upside down and motionless.

He ran to the SUV and realized she was dead or would die if he did nothing. Losing no time, he tried to open her door. It was stuck. He slammed the window with his gun and shattered it. Quickly, he pulled out her limp body through the rushing water, bringing her head to the surface as quickly as possible. Dan hauled her up onto the grass, lay her flat on her back, and when he noted she wasn't breathing or waking up, he started CPR immediately.

She didn't respond to the rescue breaths.

"Come on, Sofia!" he hollered. He tilted her head back farther, pinched her nose once more, and exhaled deeply into her mouth again.

Dan then rhythmically pressed his interlocked hands into the center of her chest. Suddenly, she lurched up, coughed, and spewed out spurts of water. She gasped for air, and Dan leaned back to let her breathe. Then she groaned in pain and rolled over onto her side. Dan realized that she'd probably sprained her neck or worse. He shifted and stabilized her head between his legs on the ground to keep her airway open. She opened her eyes and looked up at Dan hazily, confused. She didn't seem to recognize him.

"Where am I? Who are you?" she whispered and winced.

Dan felt pity for the woman, and his immediate human instinct was to call for emergency medical help, but the agent in him took over. He demanded, "Who are you, and why were you following me? Who were the two men who tried to kill me at Cape Canaveral?"

She groaned loudly and groped her broken leg. "Help me," her voice cracked, and tears burst from her eyes.

"I will save you if you answer my questions! Who sent you?"

"They will kill me," she whispered.

"You will be dead if you don't answer me," growled Dan. Then he tried a different approach: "I promise to help you if you help me."

"Albika," she murmured and gasped for air as the pain sent a shockwave up her spine.

"Albika? What's Albika?" asked Dan. He quickly surveyed the dirt road for any company. They were still alone.

"My boss. Albika."

"What does your cobra tattoo mean?"

"Gang membership," she said. She coughed and spat blood onto her chin. Dan worried that she wouldn't survive her injuries, as he couldn't be sure of their severity. He was unsure what to do next. There was no promise of getting any more info out of her. If he wanted to save her, he needed to get help right away. Then he noticed a pool of blood beside her leg.

He took off his shirt, tore it into pieces, and bandaged her leg. He left her lying on the ground, brought his car closer, and slowly carried her to his car. She groaned loudly, clawed at his chest, then lost consciousness again.

"Damn," grunted Dan.

Dan put Sofia in the backseat and searched his GPS for the nearest hospital. But when he turned around to check on her before turning his car back to the road, she was already dead.

CHAPTER TWENTY-ONE

M., also called "Memune" in Hebrew ("the appointed"), instructed his agency immediately to find out everything they possibly could regarding the name "Albika" and the cobra tattoos. M. also considered asking the NSA and ECHELON for help, but he reconsidered after his assistant reminded him that his Israeli agents were operating on American soil in secret without coordination.

Fearing that his agents would be discovered and exposed by the FBI, they were instructed to leave the United States as soon as physically possible. M. wanted to avoid an international incident—and the FBI running to the press with the story for credit.

Later that day, a pair of joggers discovered Sofia's body beside the canal and called the police. The FBI also arrived and swiftly connected the two dead men in Cape Canaveral to the woman by the water. Of course, Dan had taken her ID with him, even though he assumed it was fake, so the investigators couldn't identify her, either.

The SUV in the canal had been rented in Miami with a credit card issued by a Swiss bank under the name of Greg Bolton. It was quickly unearthed that this man didn't exist. The rental car company's security cameras had footage of the man who'd rented the SUV—but his identity was hidden beneath a cowboy hat, beard, and mustache.

The investigation hit a brick wall. The FBI assumed that the deceased belonged to an international gang operating secretly on American soil for an unknown purpose. They'd entered the United States under false names and used cash for all transactions except the rental car, which had required credit. The FBI would clearly inquire with the Mossad, who would play dumb about the case—but the FBI already knew about the Mossad agents who'd entered the country with diplomatic visas. But tying the agents to the deceased wasn't yet possible.

"It's odd," muttered the FBI investigator. "I know it's probably them. But I can't nail down motives—and why were they all there, of all places? I can't figure out the root of the conflict."

Dan contacted M. in Tel Aviv to check on the status of the case.

By that time, M. had unearthed more details. "The name Albika and the tattoos are linked to a gang in Chechnya."

"Wait—didn't we do business with those assholes before?" asked Dan. "Is Albika their chief these days?"

"The Albika profile is vague. It doesn't readily show any connection to the gang's leadership. I'm sure the entire organization is operating undercover by this point. Definitive info will be inaccessible." M. sighed, but added with confidence, "We will activate our cells fishing in Grozny, Chechnya, and Russia."

"Tell them no stone unturned. Seriously," Dan added.

"Yes, we need to find a probable connection between all these events before anyone else does. I'll use every resource we have—you needn't worry about that," M. asserted. "And now it's time for you and your colleagues to get your asses out of America."

"Yes, sir," Dan replied.

That same day, Dan arrived in Montréal and situated himself in a secluded, private apartment on Elm Avenue, close to the Consulat General d'Israël. Ran and Joan left the United States separately, one to London via a direct flight from Miami and the other to Paris, each reporting to their respective consulates for assistance. The upcoming rocket launch would have to be monitored by other agents already on the ground in Florida, which had been the secondary plan.

Dan's first time in this two-bedroom apartment felt good and comfortable—he felt okay with vanishing for a while. The unit was stocked with food, clothes, and fresh bedding. He also had a fax machine, computers, and a shredder. A Mossad agent from the DIAMOND (DIA Mission On Demand) checked the unit for bugs with his electronic devices and found it clear. The procedure did not ensure that the phone wasn't tapped remotely, but the room itself was secure.

Even though it was merely a block away from the city's business district and commotion, the tree-lined avenue was relatively quiet and peaceful. A row of low residential buildings on each side provided a great background, and Dan hoped that the Chinese had no leads on his safe location.

An expected consulate messenger—or, more likely, a Mossad intelligence officer's assistant—came to his apartment the next morning. The young man handed Dan a bunch of documents in a sealed envelope and briefly explained them to him. Dan had expected the man to be an old traditional clerk behind thick spectacles...but this man, in his early twenties, was well-built under his expensive Italian suit. He could've been a Calvin Klein model. He was an international Israeli student working as an assistant while studying computer science at a local college.

Dan already had two cups of coffee streaming through his veins, so he got straight to reviewing the papers.

There were photos of a woman who appeared to be in her forties, fashionably dressed and donning designer sunglasses. Some pictures showed her in a black Mercedes-Benz E300. More notable was that she was always accompanied by the same two or three security guards. *That's a tight circle,* Dan thought. The photos were taken mostly in Grozny, the capital city of Chechnya. *So, this is Albika.*

Albika operated an underground club and casino in a city where such things were not permitted. Western entertainment did not meet the city's religious standards.

Albika was a Russian woman with a tall, slim figure, long wavy blond hair, and big blue eyes. However, something did not add up. Dan thought that she didn't seem like a businesswoman who managed gangsters and operated illegal businesses—she was more like arm candy, and there was something else that he needed to find out. *Who is really running this operation?* And there it was, one of the photos of Albika showed her hair up in a French twist, exposing her neck and clinching her connection to the deceased in Florida.

We've found the assassins' origin, but what is their connection to Chang and the Chinese agency? Dan wondered. *Unless they were hired by Chang as proxies to do the dirty work. Retaliation for Dimitri's death?*

The second bunch of papers in the envelope included technical data, tables, prices, and photos of MRI equipment to help Dan pose as an MRI salesman visiting hospitals.

The Mossad had already confirmed two meetings at St. Petersburg hospitals and two in Grozny. The Mossad was entirely prepared if a deal was struck, since the sales department of the MRI equipment company was a Mossad collaborator in the United States—a win-win situation.

Despite all the new information he needed to grasp and squeeze into his brain in a short time, Dan was confident. He reviewed some more material on his flight to Amsterdam and on his connection to Moscow. The Aeroflot plane landed a day later on a cool, rainy, miserable morning.

He used a passport of his native country, Canada, under the alias Jack Cross; the Mossad believed no one would think he was Jewish with such a name. Under his new guise, he departed from Moscow to St. Petersburg for a series of business meetings before taking a train to Grozny later that evening.

Even with his many precautions, he knew that the FCS, the interior Russian intelligence agency responsible for monitoring all diplomats, journalists, and businesspeople for domestic espionage activities, would monitor his steps. Dan made sure he left traces of his activities up to a certain point or until he met his colleagues.

He was supposed to meet his assistant field operator and DIAMOND agent first, after confirming his meetings with the hospitals from his hotel room. Too many Russian agents roamed hotels and other popular tourist locations, so they chose to meet at a place on Prospekt Kadyrova. It was a simple spot that offered an easy escape route, which Dan quickly memorized. They ensured they weren't followed by using collaborators who sympathized with Israel or other Jewish people who owned businesses frequented by the Mossad agents. The assistant field operator and DIAMOND had gone to a store owned by one of the collaborators in their civilian clothing and walked out as local religious Imams. They were betting on reverse psychology—they dressed to draw attention, but the culture's religious respect let them go unbothered. In Chechnya, being a Muslim religious figure worked—ninety-five percent of the population was devout Muslim.

Dan was sure he'd be followed to the coffee shop and used all his tricks to lose any possible trackers, as working for the Mossad was enough to get them immediately executed.

They entered the shop one at a time, and each of them ordered and paid separately. The two dressed as Imams would attract less attention to Dan, even though he was dressed differently.

Away from other customers, they sat on wooden chairs around a table and whispered in Hebrew. They made sure to be heard speaking Russian occasionally.

Dan got straight down to business. "What do we know?" he calmly asked while eyeing the entrance.

The Imams pulled out a few pieces of paper just as two local uniformed police officers walked into the coffee shop. The officers looked around with their chins pointed arrogantly upward and cut through the short line to the ordering counter. The server gave them what they ordered, and Dan, who was seated directly facing the entrance and the counter, noticed that they didn't pay. No one complained—just shrugged.

The Imams concealed the papers and began chanting verses from their open Qur'an. The officers sat at an open table beside them, talking loudly and greeting the Imams.

Dan quietly left the table and walked out the door, paper coffee cup in hand.

CHAPTER TWENTY-TWO

John Fisher and his crew did refresher trainings daily on what they'd learned when they were younger astronauts. The trainings had been easier back in the day when they'd had more enthusiasm, but they still did well—better than expected—based on the medical and training reports. Their situation was not a drill. NASA told the trainees that the equipment they'd use to fly to space would not be tested; their first launch was the closest they'd get to a test flight.

"What a marvelous way to die," John joked with his crew and encouraged them to train harder and strive for the best possible results.

The crews visited and observed the spaceship rehab, asked lots of questions, and refreshed their knowledge of operations and safety fixtures. *They're smart guys; we can't fool them with simple explanations,* thought General Bloomfield as he accompanied them.

The Area 51 NASA technicians tirelessly prepared the equipment for the Moon mission and returned the ships to their original glory. They left no detail unresolved and were proud to take ownership of such an important project.

The chief engineer confidently addressed the astronauts: "Our technicians had to replace over two hundred thousand feet of electrical wiring and the fuselage insulation throughout the craft. They removed and replaced all the oil tanks and other hazardous chemicals to make space-worthy shuttles. Any questions?"

No one asked anything, so the chief engineer continued. "Some of the technology was replaced with more advanced and sophisticated systems that we annexed from our military vendors. The upgrades were installed on a speedy schedule and rigorously and repeatedly tested."

"And let me remind you," Bloomfield interjected, "not a single thing you see or hear in this establishment leaves. At all." The astronauts widened their eyes but nodded in understanding.

Along the tarmac of Area 51 the LLMs were tested, and the astronauts scheduled the upcoming flight. The Apollo Lunar Landing Module similar to that Neil Armstrong had tested, was refurbished quickly and the teams practiced with it to sharpen their skills.

The astronauts were training and experimenting with a confidential space weapon under an accelerated development schedule with tools never before used by them or anyone else—and the feeling was surreal. Some felt like they were watching a sci-fi movie in 3D Virtual Reality. These preparations dwarfed any concerns regarding the recent space incidents between global superpowers. At their ages, the former astronauts' senses of adventure were not as robust—risking their lives over ideology was not their priority.

Some of the retired astronauts and engineers considered that the mission may not even happen. They thought maybe the mission was the product of the new administration's paranoia or its urge to dwarf the accomplishments of the previous administration.

Many missions had been canceled in the past, even after billions of dollars had been thrown at them. "I'll be very happy to wake up laughing from this dream," John said in one of many conversations in the cafeteria during lunch.

Daily news of space incidents was broadcast in the NASA corridors, cementing their leaders' reasons for keeping the program alive.

General Bloomfield gathered the two shuttle crews and their substitutes for a meeting, disclosing a change of plans due to "new circumstances."

"As you know, we planned to launch two shuttles in tandem to the Moon, one after the other...this plan will now be altered a little," Bloomfield said. He adjusted his glasses and read from a written note: "The ISS is drifting into deep space. Colonel John Fisher and his Atlantis Shuttle crew may be needed to rendezvous and rescue the ISS crew. From there, they will fly to the Moon to join the Shuttle Discovery. Enterprise will be on standby."

Bloomfield waited for the chatter to recede and pointed to John, who had raised his hand.

"What about the two Soyuz capsules?" John inquired.

"They will use them only in an emergency. Those were never tested for viability," Bloomfield retorted.

"Shows how much you trust Russian equipment," chuckled John, and the entire forum laughed.

John then asked, "How many people are currently on the ISS?"

"Six," Bloomfield replied. "That means the ship will need to be altered to host six men in the redesigned cargo bay."

"Unless we can utilize the pressurized LLM to seat their crew," John countered.

"Theoretically. But we have our engineers working on that. They're considering adding a new capsule that will be mounted on the cargo bay, but we fear that will delay the Moon landing. And that's not what the President wants." General Bloomfield glanced around the room for reactions, and then he explained what had happened in the previous few hours with the ISS.

Bloomfield's job was to ensure that all his astronauts' doubts and uncertainties were assuaged. Concerns that the ISS was incapable of docking with the spaceship were dismissed. Even though John doubted that the whole thing would be successful, he led his crews to believe that it was all under control.

New concerns of a potential space war hit Cole's administration like a tornado.

"How unprepared are we?" Cole was asked in a Space Security Cabinet meeting.

"The many current disputes and territorial demands among the superpowers will never go away until one country controls the others—or controls the world, either by economic or militaristic means," Defense Secretary Wezniak responded.

Scientific magazine covers around the world illustrated the space activities with great accuracy. The globe was awed by how many countries were involved in space missions—some on their own, and some through joint ventures with other countries sharing mutual goals.

Generals informed the President of the progress that NASA and the military had made. They extrapolated on the current events and their possible connections to other countries. Cole kept spirits high and motivated his men to make sure there was progress. The astronauts' simulation training in Area 51 was being strictly monitored by the President's cabinet to ensure the refurbished equipment would ready to launch in six months. The schedule was tight; days and weeks were flying by, and the curriculum was massive. Three shifts worked around the clock to make the old equipment space worthy one more time.

Cole was informed that the old ships were refitted with new directional thruster engines, fuel tanks, emergency evacuation capsules, and modern computer and space avionics systems for the long trip to the Moon. The LLMs were refitted to connect to the cargo bay fuselages and could be released by the flight engineer using the Canadarm from the orbiter's control panel. The astronauts' entering the LLMs while in the cargo bay required new logistic planning from NASA engineers, as the original bay was not pressurized. In the mid-eighties, engineers had pondered the idea of having passengers in a pressurized bay, but it hadn't become reality until now.

The orbiter had side vents to depressurize during ascent and reentry. The cargo bay doors were not structurally designed to keep pressure in space; therefore, the additional pressurized capsule to house the rescued ISS crew had to be created from scratch. For that, the engineers needed to either redesign the cargo bay or invent a pressurized tunnel adapter that the astronauts would enter at the back of the cargo bay.

The astronauts trained underwater in pools to learn how to enter the LLMs and lock the doors from inside. A spaceship flight engineer would disconnect the module from the tunnel adapter and depressurize it before the arm could be used to release it into the Moon's orbit before landing.

The tension was palpable in the White House due to the recent space collision and explosion. The looming fear of space terrorism was at an all-time high. The Department of Defense used the term "DEFCON" (defense condition) for readiness levels, where DEFCON 1 was the direst situation or full nuclear war, and DEFCON 5 was a normal, everyday situation. It was suggested to raise to DEFCON 4, and the President scolded his top brass for escalating the pressure unnecessarily.

"One or two connected events might start to show a pattern, but it's not a reason to pull the trigger," Cole growled and then coughed lightly, caught in a moment of excitement.

"To be ready is not the same as waging war," replied Joe Wezniak, trying to stand up for his idea.

"If you declare DEFCON 4, wouldn't it be noticed by our adversaries?" Cole countered.

"I didn't say that," Wezniak said defensively.

"Whatever we do must be done confidentially, without talking too much—and no one squeezes any triggers without my command!"

Joe continued to explain his position; he mentioned to the forum that in space, the alert-level protocols were not determined yet. Therefore, verbal alert levels were raised from "severe" to the "conflict" level, which required the military and NASA to enter the conflict-preparation phase. A counterattack was imminent.

"No alert of any sort—just monitor the situation and report to me," instructed the President.

NASA was investigating the possibility that the ISS caution and warning system (C&WS) alarm for debris had been hacked and failed to signal the crew of the incoming object. There were a few different alarms: emergency, caution, warning, and advisory, all connected to the overall system, which was linked to Mission Control, enabling teams to view the signals on their screens. The hacking could've occurred through the COTS (Commercial Orbital Transportation Services), a proxy and partner to services and other licensing partners.

John Fisher assembled his Atlantis and Discovery crews in the cafeteria to calm concerns and offer casual conversation, coordination, and updates on training issues. It was essential to have cohesive teamwork while in space, since everyone on the teams depended on the others for survival and to complete the mission successfully.

Sometimes they needed to exchange feelings regarding the training difficulties and old equipment they needed to use. Trusting the system to perform impeccably seemed like a lot to ask.

"We will do what we were trained to do," John said in typical military style without challenging the authorities.

As part of the hybrid/nonlinear war strategy that Cole had chosen, the White House consultants decided it would be beneficial to spread disinformation. They had certain politicians take part in the sabotage, starting with POTUS himself. He would visit the Far East and meet with Chinese and Russian leaders to discuss new trade deals, then spread false news that they were handling everything necessary and would make any decisions when the time came.

CHAPTER TWENTY-THREE

May 23rd, Current Year

C hang's ILD agents, who specialized in tracking people, worked in conjunction with the CSIS, the notorious secret intelligence agency in charge of operations abroad. The agents had tracked down Dan and tightly followed him since his departure from Israel.

Chang's agents had not made any connections between Dan, Joan, or Ran, but they knew that Dan would likely not work alone.

Once they'd found that Dan had headed north from Miami to visit Cape Canaveral, they'd activated the assassination team, a ruthless proxy he used from time to time to ensure they didn't leave any tracks.

Chang had received a diplomatic bag holding the Mojito glass and flatware Dan had used in the restaurant in South Beach. Sofia's hefty tip for the waiter had been in exchange for those items, then she sent them to China to have DNA identification tests performed in a Beijing medical lab. They sought a match for the skin cell DNA collected from under Dimitri's nails. It took forty-eight hours for the confirmation, but it was a perfect match. They had the first potential clue regarding their rocket's destruction.

Chang prepared to execute his plan once he had confirmation that the assailant, Dan—the killer and Mossad agent—was present and witnessed the destruction of the launch pad in Kazakhstan.

Chang asked himself, *Why would the Mossad have been involved with the explosion? Was it just a random chain of events? After all, the Israelis had their own satellite in there; they were victims, as well, unless the Mossad discovered the plan to hijack Orbixeye.* Chang was confused, but he decided to eliminate Dan anyway as a form of revenge—not to mention he was a threat that could cause great damage to Chang's plans and organization.

The two Middle Eastern men, now deceased, had been sent to interrogate Dan first, then squeeze and drain his brain for information. They had to know why the hell he was so close to the launch pad so quickly after the Proton rocket's explosion. What he was looking for? Only after they secured that information were they ordered to kill him.

Chang knew that sooner or later someone would connect the dots, and hell would break loose. But, until then, he stuck to his agenda.

Chang's mission to protect the confidential Chinese space program went into an aggressively higher gear, aided by the Chinese space agency, STD.

A network of twelve attack satellites deployed in a short time—four in low orbit, four in high orbit, and four in geosynchronous orbit, all ready for the first combat command if their government authorized it. The satellites were equipped with laser beams and electromagnetic guns capable of destroying other satellites without using kinetic energy.

More satellites were scheduled for launch, but China's next step was to prevent other nations from conducting experiments or launching their own spy satellites. That was the more significant task, and it was equal to a declaration of war.

On the battleground, generals were always developing tactics to win wars; they experimented in the realms of psychology, disinformation, sabotage, technological and cyber-attacks, boots on the ground, and, most importantly, constant intel gathering. This was truly where nonlinear war came into play. Superpowers would attack small groups that seemingly could never win. Space, a dimension without boots on the ground, was called the "Space Army" by President Cole.

M. figured this a possibility and informed his Israeli government, which had already chosen to launch all their satellites from Palmachim Air Force Base just southwest of Tel Aviv. The base beefed up security with the "Iron-Dome" air defense system, and "Arrow" antimissile network, to intercept missiles in a variety of trajectories. On the other hand, China started launching their rockets from the new Cosmodrome, even though it was not completed—but included all the vital components for safe and confidential activities at that point.

Russia checked how the global situation could benefit them, and, as always, they danced with two partners at the same time. Running hot and cold relationships with other nations was the Russians' best strategy. On the ground, Russia was up to their necks in the Syrian conflict mess, preventing the oil and gas pipelines from flowing to Europe and making other countries buy gas only from them, all while keeping one eye on space while the other on helping dictators stay in power.

The first threat was when Russia warned through TASS, their news agency, that the Chinese were provoking war if they continued their aggressive experiments in space and damaging Russian equipment in orbit. Was this disinformation? Or was it a real threat?

Tim Woodward, as the American National Security Agency director, was responsible to figure this out.

The Spax rocket was ready for launch with three satellites on board. The first satellite was an experimental military attack satellite equipped with laser guns and electromagnetic-pulse launchers, developed in the previous decade but completed in the last year with extra funding from the White House. The other two were the Israeli satellites Ophir 1 and Ophir 2; their names had been changed from Amos to cover intentions—one of them carried the new Orbixeye system. America and Israel had reached an agreement to share technology with a license to use freely, but the tech would be maintained by Israel. In the future, it would become a business model for fee.

This agreement was settled between the two countries' leaders to expedite the control of space.

The security at Cape Canaveral tightened; no visitors were allowed. NASA security, police cars, and helicopters patrolled the area. In addition, two F-16D fighter planes from the Eglin Air Force Base took off with two drop tanks full of fuel to patrol the waters off the coast, ironing the skies around the launch pad.

CHAPTER TWENTY-FOUR

I t was early May, but the weather on the eastern coast of the Mediterranean was hot and humid. The weather didn't spoil the party on Gordon Beach in Tel Aviv, where a mixed crowd of Asian and Israeli people prepared lunch, drank, and killed time with loud Middle Eastern music.

Hanyu Chin-Li had changed her name to Naomi. She was a mid-thirties Asian woman who mingled among the celebrants, looking much younger than her age in a tiny tight bikini that would put a supermodel to shame. She had long black hair, lush lips, and black, almond-shaped eyes.

No wonder her husband didn't let her get away and captured her in his passionate web. She was the perfect bride, and on top of that, she had chosen to convert to Judaism and join her husband's faith.

Hanyu was an infant when her parents escaped from China to Japan in the 1980s after the state labeled her father an enemy of the people. Her entire family fled and boarded a smuggler boat, ripped away from the little they owned. The vessel sailed on open seas for days, as no port accepted the human cargo—and the conditions onboard deteriorated and neared catastrophe. Going back to China only meant death and was not an option. A miracle occurred when they were intercepted by an Israeli Navy missile boat, putting an end to the suffering of the immigrants. They were scooped up and headed to the southern Israeli port of Eilat.

The boat's refugees were taken in with open arms, unlike the Jewish holocaust survivors on a refugee boat in WWII that no one had accepted; those people had been sent back to Nazi Europe and murdered in a concentration camp.

Naomi's husband was an officer in the IDF's Department of Intelligence; he was on duty and not at the beach party. Therefore, there was no one to help Naomi expel the flock of admirers congregating around her beach umbrella.

Avi, twice Naomi's age, sat under his own large umbrella, reclining in his seat. He read the local newspaper but watched the young woman that the Mossad had targeted as a possible recruit—without her husband's consent.

Avi was an agent of the UMINT division of the Mossad recruiting department. He sought an opportunity to start a conversation with Naomi, but he needed to shoo away the men that started playing virtuosic racquetball just in front of them. He was patient; as he always said, "They all need to eat and shit." He'd find the right time to speak with her.

And Avi was right. Eventually, Naomi broke away from the clan and headed in the direction of the nearby restaurant bar, still chatting with people as she went.

Avi followed her casually, keeping an eye on her location while using a unisex shower to rinse off the sand. He then took a seat in the restaurant overlooking the beach, watching her meander over to the bar with her towel wrapped around her torso. He was seated near her return path, and when she passed by on her way back to the water's edge, he said, "You look familiar!"

Naomi stopped and eyed him. She figured that this senior citizen was attempting a cheap flirtation trick, and she even smiled at the idea. He was probably harmless, and it was flattering, regardless, since Avi was a handsome older man.

She gave him another penetrating glance, nodded her head respectfully, and then tried to continue her walk back to her umbrella.

Avi didn't give up. "Do you have a moment?" he asked, and something in his voice intrigued her.

Naomi let her curiosity take over, and she sat at the table with him. "If you think you know me, how am I familiar to you?" she asked and smiled.

"You're Naomi, right?" Avi inquired.

"Yes. Have we met before?" She raised her perfect eyebrows.

Avi decided to get right to the point of his mission—a direct approach that usually worked for him. "Naomi, you and your parents were embraced by this country, if I'm not mistaken. Have you ever thought of helping in return?"

"Helping what? Giving back or something?"

"Somewhat."

"How? Who are you?" she questioned, her face growing grimmer. She hesitated, shaking her head slightly. Avi then spoke about her life, including all her school achievements, medical records, interests, and her loud social media opinions regarding defending Israel.

She was stunned. The more Avi detailed, the more overwhelmed she grew. "How do you know all this?" she asked.

"Look, if you're interested to know more, here is my card," Avi said calmly. "Keep it confidential, including this conversation."

She took his card and slid it into her bikini top. Her heart twinged; she thought she might know who this man was. His card had no other information beside a phone number.

"Not even your husband," Avi added firmly.

Naomi was shaken but remained composed.

Avi noticed the demonstration of her ability to veil her emotions. As he left the beach restaurant, he smiled to himself. "She will work just fine," he murmured, satisfied.

Naomi had always blended well in Israeli society, and she'd even served in the military. Her husband had informed her that if she were married, she didn't need to serve. He would've preferred her by his side, but she went ahead with it anyway. The country had saved her family, offering them the human dignity they deserved. Deep down, she never thought she gave enough.

"How did he know all that about me?" she whispered to herself as she walked across the sand. She shivered. "I don't even know his fucking name...he totally controlled me; he fucking hypnotized me."

I can't even tell my husband, she thought once she was seated back under her umbrella. She peeped at his card again with just a phone number printed on it. *I'm sure he's watching me from a distance,* she realized. *Who can I ask an opinion? Well, apparently no one.* Thoughts dashed across her mind quickly. The encounter had sapped the fun out of the beach party. Somewhat reluctantly, she considered contacting him. But just to ask more questions.

Two weeks later, Naomi called the number on the card. After telling her his name, Avi immediately put her through psychological and IQ tests that further enhanced her curiosity. Psychiatrists analyzed her character, strengths, and weaknesses, and worked with her to sharpen a new personality. She learned how to use a gun, lie, cheat, and flirt with men as she'd never done before. Her instructors at the Mossad taught her catlike skills— how to follow people, lose trackers who followed her, how to hide and mingle in the crowd, and how to steal food from market counters.

Her husband thought she was working in the family restaurant, and her family thought she was hanging out with her husband; no one knew anything about what truly kept her busy.

She trained hard, and the more she trained, the more she got into it; she quickly rose to the top of her class.

One evening, Naomi met her husband in their apartment in Herzliya, north of Tel Aviv.

"Rafi," she said, making sure she had his full attention. "I have to tell you something." She hesitated briefly, but he nodded for her to continue. "I was selected to be a part of a diplomatic team. I will travel and be an assistant for the foreign affairs department."

"What? How?" Rafi demanded, staring at his wife with wide eyes. "Who in foreign affairs contacted you? I know them all."

Naomi grasped her mistake and sighed. Rafi held his sharp gaze while taking off his uniform and slipping into a comfortable training suit. He had dark skin, black eyes, and a tall stature with medium build.

Naomi remained silent.

"Naomi, you know that I'm a high-ranking intelligence officer," Rafi said through an exhale. "If this is something you can't tell me, I probably already know what it is, so don't breach your confidentiality." He pursed his lips.

She nodded slightly, and her eyes begged without a sound, saying, "Let me do this."

He understood her expression, but he was not sure about his wife's qualifications. "Going to China, I presume?" he stated.

She nodded and let her husband guess the rest. As an intelligence officer, he was too smart to not figure it out. *How has the Mossad trapped my wife?* he wondered. *Why is she a good candidate? Is it the language? Her looks? Intelligence?* And he'd thought that she was working hard in the family restaurant for the last six months. He scoffed to himself. *Were there qualities he didn't know about his wife?*

"Ezra Maman?" he inquired about the captured Israeli scientist who'd disappeared after the explosion in Kazakhstan.

She shook her head and still said nothing.

Rafi sighed and understood not to ask any more questions. He hugged his wife tight and said, "Good luck, and come back home safely."

Naomi would enter China as Naomi Davidi with her Israeli passport. She'd left behind her given, registered name, Hanyu Chin-Li. Her new code name, "Shkedia," the term for an almond tree, had been shortened to the nickname "Shaked" during her training.

The fact that she possessed strong Chinese features wasn't expected to raise any concerns. She had a cover story—Naomi's biological mother had abandoned her for being born female, and Naomi had been taken in and adopted by Vietnamese parents.

CHAPTER TWENTY-FIVE

an walked away from the coffee shop in Grozny, leaving his two fellow agents to secretly watch him from inside. He looked around for any trackers or suspicious cars but saw none; he also determined that the two policemen he'd evaded were unaware of who he was or who the Imams actually were. "Better safe than sorry," he murmured to himself.

The humid, muggy day added some discomfort, and Dan started to sweat under his well-tailored suit. The mid-August sun baked the ground, pounding it with heat. The streets emptied as civilians looked for shelter.

The two Imams left the coffee shop and got into a car parked nearby, ignoring Dan. He got a signal to follow them in his own car, which was parked a block away. Dan's vehicle had been rented by a Kurd recruited by the Mossad to perform lending services without the standard paperwork. After a short while, the Imams spotted Dan following their car, and they continued to an undisclosed location. The two vehicles drove along the Sunzha River. A few minutes outside the city, the geography changed; a green forest blanketed the landscape. Being the only two cars on that route, they kept a considerable distance between each other. The two agents ahead of Dan made a turn to the right. Dan slowed down, and when he approached the turn, he saw the new road was a dirt path. After about one hundred yards, the dirt path ended at a small, treeless clearing. *A perfect place,* Dan thought.

They all stepped out of their vehicles, and the Imams spread out their papers on one of the car hoods.

"Not a very good shot of him," said the taller Imam as he showed Dan a portrait of a man in a karate outfit. The taller Imam's code name was Asman. "This guy is Bico, the head of the Cobra gang."

As Dan reviewed the Mossad profile of Bico, his eyes grew large. The man had quite a list of crimes beside his name—money laundering, drugs...anything that made quick money.

Dan kept reading as he asked, "So, who is Albika?"

"She is Bico's girlfriend, companion, high-priced Russian arm candy with ambitions," replied the tall Imam.

"I bugged their office and villa in the mountains," added the other agent from the DIAMOND squad.

"This is his villa," he said and showed Dan a photo of a beautiful mansion with a pool and modern architecture. Dan examined the picture and asked about the villa's security and systems, specifically focusing on entry options and escape routes.

"In this file, you will find information about the gang," Asman directed Dan, his fake beard swaying in the wind. "They operate internationally for the highest bidder. The Russian authorities know about them, since they've used the gang on numerous occasions to murder and smuggle people. Most popular with Russian officials was to have the gang members get rid of journalists or political opponents. Very dangerous. Be careful."

"Where can I find Bico?" asked Dan after swallowing the information now stuck in his throat like a chicken bone.

Asman replied, "Go to his club first; he's the only one who can operate a casino locally. It's a popular place for Western tourists and high-ranking politicians who want to have some fun."

"Since his office and villa are bugged, we will not see each other again—unless it's an emergency," Dan said to the agents.

"Wait," interjected the DIAMOND agent. "This is the key to the safe hideout apartment on Gutserlyeva Street. The apartment is part of a private house, so if you need to disappear, then we will meet there. I checked the house; it's clear. No bugs."

The agents then showed Dan, Bico's psychological review, as prepared by a Mossad psychologist. The report revealed Bico's lifestyle, including his sexual preferences, eating and drinking habits, friends, and close family members. While memorizing the information, Dan felt he knew Bico better than he knew his own brother. *Although not exactly a flattering comparison,* Dan thought.

"What about going to the club as a guest? Do I need to buy a ticket? Will they frisk me?" Dan asked his agents.

"You can get into the club as a paid guest. However, they have metal detector gates, so you can't go in with a weapon," Asman said, hoping the information would help Dan. It was clear to Dan that his Imams didn't know what exactly the Mossad was looking for within or regarding the Cobra gang. Not sharing those details was a precaution in case any of them were caught—they wouldn't know anything, so they couldn't confess to anything.

But Dan knew why he was there—Sofia was directly linked to Bico and Albika. The Cobra gang knew more than just whom they were ordered to assassinate. Dan and the Mossad had to infiltrate that club to get their hands on Bico and more underlying information.

Dan and the two agents returned to their cars and drove back onto the dirt path, and as the other two turned left on the road, Dan took a right, swiftly getting as far away as possible.

An hour later, Dan went back to his hotel room and then took a taxi to the Black Belt Dragon Club. The name was appropriate, since Bico was known as a martial arts expert. Bico specialized in Aikido and Jujutsu, Japanese styles of barehanded, close combat for defeating an armed and armored opponent. Dan was grateful he knew this information before provoking the martial artist with a big ego.

The evening was cool due to the breeze from the mountains, and Dan wore loose clothing and a light black jacket. He stepped out of the taxi and stood at the address that his agents had given him, but something was wrong. He didn't see any club entryway, box office, or typical signage. The street was dim and narrow and made Dan uneasy. The taxi driver mentioned the fee from his lowered car window, and Dan handed him the rubles.

"*Podozhdite!*" Dan asked the driver to wait, using some of the Russian he'd learned while working with Russian immigrants in Israel.

"*Chto?*" asked the driver, glowering at Dan.

"Black Belt Dragon Club?" Dan asked, hoping the man would know what the English meant.

"Building entry, right there," the taxi driver pieced together in broken English. "Press first button on bottom." The driver gestured toward the building and then sped off.

Dan was still uncertain. Russians' impatience with foreigners was well known, and he hoped the driver hadn't dumped him in the middle of a sketchy street for some Dobermans to tear his guts out.

On the side of the building was an intercom panel with two buttons and a camera. Dan was not sure which one to press, so he pressed both. A man's voice lazily asked, "Yeah, who's there?" in Russian. Dan, without delay, said the name of the club in English. The camera moved from left to right, examining him.

Dan pressed the button again after a moment of silence, and the door opened after the camera studied him once more. The bouncer inside resembled the feared André the Giant wrestler and gave Dan a nasty look. Then the bouncer nodded his head and directed Dan through the first set of fancy glass doors and into the vestibule.

"*Spasibo*," Dan thanked him. The man didn't respond and returned to his high-top chair. *I guess that's his entire job*, Dan mused and then moved through the second set of fancy doors into a small lobby with two elevators.

Beside the elevators, an usher in a black tux with a gold-toothed grin said, "Take the left elevator and press at the bottom."

Dan nodded and said, "Thank you." Dan noticed the bump on the usher's upper left chest—he was armed.

The elevator slid down a couple floors and opened to an upscale reception hall filled with hundreds of small LED lights. The hall led to a large, Las Vegas-style casino.

Two women dressed like Playboy Bunnies smiled at him as he approached the casino's entryway. Inside, a bar with dozens of seated people was situated on the left, enclosing the two female bartenders who shook and stirred alcoholic beverages for visitors from around the world.

A man in an off-white suit directed Dan to go through the metal detector before entering the bar area.

Once Dan passed through the gate, he scanned the crowd and then said, "Stolichnaya on the rocks."

"Right away," replied one of the women wearing oversized bunny ears.

"Size matters," mumbled Dan.

The woman who'd taken his drink order looked to be in her late twenties. She wore a small bra that barely covered her nipples and tiny denim shorts that showed her glinting belly button piercing. Dan imagined the women had to meet certain criteria to get those jobs. *A perfect ass is obviously a requirement,* he chuckled to himself.

Dan gazed about the casino. *Perfect tourist trap.* The establishment appeared to only employ beautiful women to attract customers, although some patrons clearly preferred to bring their own arm candy to show off. The security jobs apparently went to men resembling gorillas.

Dan's drink was served with its bill in rubles, equaling about sixteen American dollars. *Reasonable, I guess,* Dan thought as he found an empty spot to lean against the bar. One of the sexy bartenders noticed him and politely asked, "Where you from?" in broken English. She flashed him a perfect smile that could have donned the cover of a fashion magazine.

"Canada," he lied.

"Is it beautiful there?"

Dan didn't have a chance to answer her, as a drink request came from two heavy men who looked American. She pardoned herself and jumped to the new customers after collecting Dan's money. She served the men their drinks and returned to chat with Dan.

"Yes, Canada is beautiful...but nowhere near as beautiful as you," Dan complimented the bartender, and she blushed— even though she'd heard it countless times. She giggled and bent forward, resting her breasts on the counter, pressing them against the wood in front of Dan. She gave another dazzling smile and said, "My name is Natasha."

"I could have guessed," whispered Dan, and she laughed again when he extended her another five dollars as an additional tip.

Dan sipped his drink for a while, watching the crowd. When Natasha came back and winked at him, he smiled at her, gauging the situation. Then he asked her point-blank, "Where can I find Bico?"

She froze at once, her face falling. Hesitating, she lolled her head slightly to the left so no one could hear her. "Do you know Bico?" she asked in a much darker tone.

Dan nodded; at that point, he had nothing to lose.

"Wait here," she whispered.

A few minutes later, Natasha returned to the bar accompanied by a man resembling a hunter who was about to get his shot at the elk.

"And you are?" he asked Dan arrogantly.

Well, back to the gutters of being an agent, Dan sighed internally.

"You can call me Jack," answered Dan confidently.

"What brings you here, Jack?" the man thundered.

"Well, I heard about this beautiful place, and I wanted to tell the owner or Albika how much I appreciated their present when I was in Florida."

Dan watched the goon's face for a reaction, but the man didn't stray from basic disdain. *Perhaps he didn't get the message*, Dan considered.

"I hate Americans," the man said, leaning in closer, and Dan could smell the Beluga Vodka on his breath.

"I'm Canadian," Dan replied curtly.

"All the same to me. But you are a client. So, I like you," the man said and erupted in a short and emotionless laugh. "Wait here," he said and disappeared behind the blackjack tables.

Natasha leaned over the bar toward Dan and asked loudly, "Do you want another?" Then she quickly whispered to him, "I don't like that guy. Be careful."

Dan waited at the bar for a bit longer but then decided to try his luck and sat at the nearest blackjack table. The female dealer looked like she'd just finished a beauty pageant before clocking in at the casino. *Where the hell did this guy get these women?* Dan thought, his eyebrows raised.

He was alone at the table. He cashed five hundred rubles and bet twenty-five. She dealt the cards. He got an ace and a two, and the dealer got five. He doubled, and she gave him one card. It was a six. She showed her other card; she had fifteen. Then she pulled another card—a five. She'd won. Suddenly, someone grabbed Dan's shoulder as the dealer cleared the bet.

"Come with us," said the man who'd escorted Dan through the metal detector. He had another gorilla beside him who also wore an off-white suit. *If I ever open a casino, I gotta re-member—bouncers in suits and girls in strings*, Dan mused to himself.

The gorillas led Dan through the half-full casino; smoke climbed to the ceiling, and half-empty vodka bottles were scattered across the tabletops. Bunnies offered drinks and flirting smiles, squeezing the customers' wallets as much as they could.

Toward the back of the casino was a stage where a woman sang the blues, moving her body like performers one might have seen at B.B. King's club on 42nd Street in Manhattan. A few men, ignoring the music, lounged with girls on their arms—drinking, making out, shoving hands down the girls' denim shorts. It was obvious where they would end up soon.

The guards directed Dan through a huge steel door with sculpted metal figures in martial arts poses. When they opened it, there was another set of doors that led into a big, apartment-style office.

The entire length of one of the walls was a one-way, bulletproof mirror, showing the whole casino floor to a man who sat on a couch. A woman mixed drinks at a bar beside a kitchenette on the other side of the large space. The apartment was dressed with the best modern interior décor and devices, showcasing the expensive taste of its occupants.

Dan's escorts stopped him a few feet away from the man on the couch. The man leaned in assured relaxation, almost bored. The guards pulled Dan's jacket down to pin his arms, and he did not resist. But with one tiny lift of the man's brow, Dan was released from the guards' hands. He yanked up his jacket, giving the gorillas a dirty look.

"Sit, please," the man said politely while signaling for the woman to bring Dan a drink.

Dan sat down in the chair that the man nodded toward. Dan crossed his feet to look relaxed, assuming that this man was Bico, based on the photos his agents had shown him.

Dan recognized the woman, too. Albika. Only she was more beautiful in person than in the pictures. A high-class model. With another signal from Bico, the guards reluctantly left the room like trained dogs.

"My name is Bico; this is Albika." His voice was rough as a hacksaw, but his English was perfect.

"I know who you are," replied Dan nonchalantly.

"Did you come to sell me MRI equipment? If so, I am not interested," Bico chuckled and sipped from his drink. Albika also laughed as she moved about the room with her cocktail. She took a seat away from but directly facing the men.

Dan smiled; they'd called his bluff. Dan knew Bico had the right connections and probably already knew him and his purpose. Bico most likely knew too much and was the one who sent the assassins. No reason to pretend. Time would tell. "No," Dan answered jovially and continued joking as friends might, "your casino doesn't appear to need MRI equipment." The couple laughed again, glancing at each other.

Bico was stocky, in his mid-forties, dressed casually in Nike sneakers, and unusually short. Noticing his overdeveloped muscles through his clothes was easy. He was solid rock. Many photos of his martial arts competitions hung on the walls. An eighty-inch television screen sitting on a low stand flickered a live soccer game on mute, and every once in a short while, Bico checked the score and cursed in Russian.

"So, what is a Mossad agent doing in my club?" Bico asked with a chuckle.

"Well, you're trying to kill me," Dan stated calmly. He looked at Bico with a penetrating gaze, waiting for an answer.

Bico's eyes remained glued to the screen for a second, as if Dan's statement had not been directed at him. He did not seem surprised—still almost bored. *He did already call my bluff,* Dan thought.

Albika was silent. Bico put his glass on the coffee table and leaned back. He put his hands behind his head and stretched his torso, seeming thoughtful—or perhaps he'd already made his decision to shred Dan to pieces.

Bico then stared at Dan, leveling their gazes. "It's business. As I understand, you killed my soldiers in Florida," Bico said and finished his drink in one swallow. Slowly and deliberately, he lit a Marlboro cigarette and offered one to Dan, who politely declined.

"So, you wonder why I don't kill you now, right?" asked Bico as he inhaled the smoke. He exhaled the plume toward the ceiling.

"Yes, I do," Dan responded. "You probably also know the reputation of the agency behind me, correct? If you kill me, you're a walking dead man. You and your entire family."

Bico burst into laughter, and Albika joined him, albeit nervously.

"I know the Mossad, Dan," Bico remarked. "Perhaps you don't know that in my early career, I was a KGB agent. I know your agency; I know your methods. The Mossad made deals with people like me in the past. I am quite aware of their reputation. We are all alike—one working for his government, the other working for himself, only on opposite sides of the fence for the moment. I give you credit for killing my men in Florida."

"You don't care?" Dan challenged.

"They are collateral damage, Dan. Professional paid soldiers. They knew the risks of working for me."

"And Lyudmila," added Albika from a distance. Dan assumed she was talking about the woman that he'd called Sofia. Dan wondered how Sofia had spoken such good Spanish with the waiter, as her real name sounded Ukrainian.

"We are businesspeople and want to make money—a lot of it. We do not kill for fun," Bico said casually. "The contract on your head was easy. But tell me: how did you find me?" Bico raised his eyebrows, extinguishing his cigarettes in the huge ashtray.

Dan tapped his neck with his finger. Bico did the same, touching his small cobra tattoo that he and his gang all shared.

"Oh, I see. The reputable Mossad knows everything," Bico laughed.

"As a matter of fact, it was the ECHELON agency from the United States that helped," Dan countered. "Your gang was under surveillance for having guns for hire, so you understand that I didn't come here to die. If necessary, I will kill you."

Bico laughed again, harder this time, and slammed the table with his palm, rattling the flatware. Albika anxiously joined him again, curling her lips.

"We are not a gang, Dan. We are an organization working for other intelligence agencies around the world—and there's a big difference," Bico said, suddenly serious, his face tensing.

"We can work together. If you listen to me," Dan said and surprised himself. He tried to stay cool to see if Bico would once more call his bluff. Dan knew that he had no chance of survival if Bico did decide to kill him; after all, Dan was in the cobra's den.

Dan trusted his intel's assertion that money was Bico's only concern. It was a gamble to have come with nothing to offer, betting his life on Bico's roulette wheel; it could work, or Dan could die. The agent inside Dan continued to press the issue.

If Bico were a real businessman who cared only for money, he would negotiate his way out and try to make a profit along the way. That was what Dan hoped. The first step was to try recruiting Bico to work for the Mossad and then figure out what he knew.

"Really, Dan? You came all the way here to tell me you could kill me, then offer me employment?" Bico asked, cracked a smile, and pointed with his muscled hand to all the martial arts photos around the room. Albika giggled, believing it was a good joke.

"I am aware of your reputation, actually," Dan stated, sarcasm filling his tone. "A former KGB agent whose claim to fame was killing other agents across the globe. Did you have fun?"

Bico chuckled. "You did your homework, Jack, the MRI salesman—I mean, Dan. Wouldn't you do the same for your country?" Bico lit another cigarette with a confident smile.

"We don't kill journalists for disagreeing with the government. We also know what happened in London with the former Russian agent who defected. Was it you?"

"What do you have to offer?" Bico snapped, changing the subject. He signaled for Albika to make him another drink.

Dan felt he'd made progress. This was exactly where he'd wanted the conversation to go, even though he'd been forced to wade through Bico's macho contest.

"May I offer you another drink?" Bico then asked, his manners returning.

"Sure," Dan said, okay with calming the tension.

Bico made the same hand sign, and Albika gave Dan Absolut with lime juice without asking what he preferred. Then she brought a bottle of mineral water and a few small plates of appetizers from the refrigerator.

"Caviar?" Bico offered with a chuckle. "The best. And it's kosher."

Dan laughed out loud, thinking it was Bico's first genuinely good joke. Dan scooped some caviar with a sesame cracker and took a gulp of his drink that sent a cool wave down his spine.

Bico continued speaking casually. "By the way: I've always wanted to ask the Mossad if they knew anything about a shipment transported by truck a couple years ago in Afghanistan. Was it intercepted by the Mossad?"

Dan coyly played dumb, even though he knew the answer. "What was in the cargo bed? Nuclear waste?"

"Ten pounds of nuclear fissile material," Bico replied. "And the truck disappeared."

"I heard the story but know nothing about it."

"I lost fifteen million dollars on that deal. Commission fee," Bico said, his lips pursing slightly.

"You had no concern about how it would be used?"

"Pakistan is under the International Atomic Energy Agency's surveillance. I am merely a businessman, and it was legal," Bico said, sticking to his motto.

Dan remarked, "I'm not sure if they signed the nonproliferation agreement to not spread nuclear materials. Where did it come from?"

Bico realized he'd hit on a sensitive issue for the Israelis. Any nuclear material that could find its way to a terrorist group or adversary would be intercepted, destroyed, or disappear mysteriously. *When something like that happens, the*

Mossad is involved in one way or another, Bico mused to himself. Bico decided to speak no further on the subject.

Bico and his organization dealt in a range of different activities: murder, smuggling people or nuclear material, weapons deals. If money could be made, Bico would be there. That's why he put Albika's name in front of his organization. The members worked for Albika; she recruited and employed them. That was why Sofia/Lyudmila had mentioned Albika and not Bico. Lyudmila and the others had never met Bico.

Bico recruited informers and collaborators from the Russian spy agencies—including police officers. All were paid off handsomely for their information and covering for Bico.

"The caviar's great. Best I've ever had," Dan said coolly. "By the way, who paid you to kill me?"

Bico jutted out his chin, signaling for Albika to leave the room and close the door behind her. Apparently, she was kept ignorant of certain operations involving governments and other corrupt regimes. Bico had his own reasons, Dan was sure.

"The body that agreed to pay me two million dollars to eliminate you canceled the deal," Bico said nonchalantly. "You owe me that money unless I kill you. But I feel you are worth more than that if you're alive. My client knows you are not dead; they were there, observing. They have informants everywhere."

Both men paused and watched the soccer game for a moment. Dan's mind shifted into high gear. He knew that Bico was shrewd and probably wouldn't pass up the opportunity to do a business deal with the Mossad. Or perhaps Bico was playing with his mind. Again, time would tell.

"My agency will reward you if you share information that is valuable to us," Dan said assuredly. "We both have too much to lose by not working together."

"Goal!" Bico screamed and threw his hands up in the air, slamming his Nikes on the floor. "Now we are qualified to play in the European championship." The soccer game was clearly more important than other things.

Dan silently challenged Bico to calm down and return to reality by watching him carefully, intensely.

Bico took a deep breath. He exhaled and then said in a whisper, "Maman."

Dan was stunned. Bico's intel and potential cooperation rang loudly in the silent room.

CHAPTER TWENTY-SIX

The security at Cape Canaveral remained tight due to constant whisperings from Israel and the Russian Foreign Intelligence Service. It was rumored that an attack on the rocket was imminent. No other concrete information was found. Rumored threats were monitored closely in case further security measures were necessary.

On a perfect afternoon, the Spax rocket was ready for launch, its valuable cargo heading to space in a prograde orbit. The Mission Control techs were anxious to find out the results of Orbixeye operating in space.

The two F-16D fighter jets continued surveilling the skies from north to south over the tranquil Florida coast, ready to intercept any given challenge. Drones and Apache helicopters equipped with missiles hovered over the Cape for hours before the launch, monitoring every move. It was total lockdown.

Since the loss of the satellite in Kazakhstan, the Israeli industry had created two separate Orbixeye systems to be launched one minute before midnight. Backup launch was scheduled for the next day if the necessary circumstances arose.

The weather forecast was clear skies and light wind, with the possibility of a passing thunderstorm about eighty miles south of the launch pad. Something to watch in the control center.

The rocket was locked into position and being fueled.

The FBI and other federal agencies were on location and communicating with the monitoring network to ensure a safe launch. The F-16D pilots spoke with the helicopters on a different frequency to coordinate the coverage tightly. The fighter jets were at a higher altitude than the helicopters, but all actively used their radar. No aircraft, boats, ships, or jet skis were allowed within a one-hundred-mile radius of the Cape. The orders were to shoot down any suspicious craft not authorized to be in the area.

Around the control center and Cape, others monitored with dogs and binoculars to spot any suspicious activity. It was T-minus one hour and three minutes to launch.

"All is well," declared the top security officer to himself, satisfied and proud of the arrangements.

Immediately after the rocket's fueling was the most dangerous time; it was nerve-wracking for the technicians while the Israeli agents stood watch.

The launch director began the readiness poll, and after a green light, the technician started loading the kerosene to the rocket tanks, which took twenty-five minutes. At T-minus thirty-five minutes, liquid oxygen was loaded for another twenty-eight minutes. Then the required engine chilling lasted for six minutes—until T-minus one.

The flight computer demanded the final prelaunch checks; the propellant tank was pressurized for flight at T-minus forty-five seconds. The director verified launch readiness for the last time at T-minus three seconds, and then the engine controller started the engine-ignition sequence.

"Alpha Whisky, my radar is showing a low-flying object heading from inland toward the rocket," reported one of the pilots. "Sixteen miles away, speed of sixty knots, altitude of one hundred feet. Heading toward the launch pad."

The report struck like lightning. Even with all the precautions and equipment, an object had managed to cut through the tight security.

"I've spotted it—foreign object is a drone!" declared an Apache pilot. At night, the helicopter pilots could not see objects without technological help. The crew relied on a new night-vision system called the M-DSA, which gave the pilots crystal-clear vision, even in total darkness.

The high-performance turboshaft engines were pushed to the limit as the pilot headed toward the object that was now dangerously close to the launch pad. The launch director listened to the chatter on the emergency frequency, frozen in place. The clock moved to T-time with no emergency stop.

"I'm locked on and ready to fire," called the F-16D pilot. Without delay, a loud whoosh was heard as a pair of AIM-7M missiles launched, but they missed the target. The Apache then closed in on the foreign drone as the window of opportunity quickly dissipated.

"Target now sighted at point-nine miles," the Apache pilot yelled and turned on his laser cannon. "I'll splash this son of a bitch."

The Apache's laser radar locked on the drone, sending out a long green ray in a fraction of a second. A short signal told the pilot that the system was ready to fire. Without hesitation, the pilot pressed the red button on the controls. With a *poof* and tiny explosion, the mysterious drone splashed into the Banana River, two thousand feet from the Spax rocket lifting off with its precious cargo.

The Apache helicopter had successfully hit an unmanned target with a laser gun; the pilot thanked the weapon's manufacturer in his mind while watching the Spax rockets roar to heaven.

The FBI and Cape Canaveral security immediately began investigating to find the drone's origin. They also desperately needed to know how it got past their multiple levels of surveillance and security.

The moonless night favored the attackers who'd fled the scene. The police and FBI sealed the finger of Florida from Charlottesville in the north to Key West in the south. The attackers had almost succeeded once, and it was feared that they would be encouraged to try again.

The FBI and CIA checked their intel to see if any other smuggled attack drones had been found in the country. They considered moving future launches to the Vandenberg Air Force Base in California for further security.

It was directly and calmly announced in a news conference that the event was a terror attack, and the President promised to find the responsible entity and retaliate. All finer details were kept entirely confidential at that point.

CHAPTER TWENTY-SEVEN

It had been quite sometime since the explosion in Kazakhstan when a light, early snow covered the ground with powdery flakes.

Dan sat frozen in his chair, speechless. Bico's murmur of "Maman" ran through his head on a loop.

Bico stared at him, victorious. His dark eyes could send an electric shock up anyone's spine.

An arrogant smile crossed the face of this mysterious man who seemed capable of anything. His soldiers, as he called them, were paid well for their unfaltering loyalty. They were well trained in underground tricks they learned from their boss and his knowledge from being a former agent.

"What do you know about Maman?" Dan finally asked, breaking the thick silence. Was it Bico who'd helped smuggle him out of the Cosmodrome?

They both stared at each other for a while, their thoughts distracting them.

"That information will cost you twenty-five million dollars—plus expenses," Bico answered flatly.

This son of a bitch knows where Maman is, Dan thought with a scoff. That was the first time he'd ever heard such a high price for cooperation with the Mossad—or was it extortion? Or worse—both?

Big appetite, Dan thought, but he knew that it was essential to find out what happened to Maman and what the

Chinese were doing. Dan immediately thought about inform-
ing his superiors of this development; and if Bico was lying,
he'd join his ancestors.

"What can you tell me about Maman that's worth twenty-
five million? Sell me the package," provoked Dan.

Bico knit his brow, relaxed back on his couch, stretched
his arms, and said, "I could've killed you with a second cell of
soldiers in Florida, but after the first attempt, things changed."

This is getting more interesting by the minute, Dan thought.
He wondered how much Bico paid the assassins he deployed
around the world. If the FBI investigating in Florida had found
a second group of assassins, that would've been significant
information to share. Perhaps the drone operators at Cape Canaveral had seen something.

Bico looked at Dan as if he were reading his mind and
growled, "They've already left the United States. The FBI and
CIA failed to catch them."

"I need time to communicate with my office," Dan said.

Bico grabbed a phone sitting on the credenza and handed
it to Dan.

"I have to go to my hotel room and call from there," Dan
explained.

Bico shook his head. "Until we've shaken hands on a deal,
you're my prisoner. Either we make a deal, or I kill you to get
my well-earned money from Fei."

The name Fei, a Chinese name, sounded familiar to Dan. *Is
that who hired Bico to eliminate me?*

It seemed that Bico preferred to have the Mossad and Chinese secret agency fighting each other for his services. He'd
use them against each other to get the highest bid.

"Refresh my memory: who is Fei?" Dan inquired calmly.

"Don't be naïve, Dan; you know who Fei is. You do know
who you killed in Kazakhstan, don't you? To refresh your

memory, as you requested—does the name Dimitri ring a bell?"

Dan wasn't sure what Bico knew. But this was more proof that Bico knew more than he was openly sharing. Dan assumed that the Chinese Secret Intelligence Services had hired Bico's organization to perform an assassination on American soil and stop the Orbixeye without incriminating the Chinese. The Chinese didn't want to confront the Americans or Israelis while they were all trading with each other.

Dan was skeptical and curious as to how the Chinese had linked him to Dimitri's death, even though it was true.

There's probably only one reason why Chang wants to interrogate or silence me, Dan thought. Something Dan might've found out that the Chinese agency wanted to keep quiet. The reason for the explosion in Kazakhstan was perhaps information that should not be shared with anyone, punishable by death if it was released.

Dan wasn't sure what the Chinese thought he knew. It was ridiculous, but they clearly weren't taking any chances. Bico had been offered a decent chunk of money to leave none of the Mossad's stones unturned. This was what Dan had to disclose to his boss on the phone.

Dan knew the Mossad had a long history of collaboration with the Chinese Secret Intelligence Services. He knew how the CSIS operated. However, the situation had changed; what was once a mutual goal was now a difference in government priorities. Fifty years earlier, it had been the African Theatre, and now it was the Asian Theatre.

Dan was sure that Bico knew well how to choose a work partner. As a former agent, Bico knew how the KGB had lost time after time to the Mossad and CSIS duo.

"May I use my phone instead?" asked Dan, pulling his own cell from his jacket pocket. "Yours is probably bugged."

Bico nodded, so Dan dialed an encrypted secure number.

It was late evening in Tel Aviv, but Dan caught M. still in his office. The only other person with M. was his second in command.

Dan spoke in Hebrew, using slang only the Mossad knew. Understanding that his call could be recorded—or even filmed—Dan used code and covered his mouth while discussing his status. M. agreed with Dan about the risks of being live bait and was a little concerned about Dan's safety. "But Bico knows better than to touch a single hair on your head," M. assured.

After about five minutes, Dan hung up and turned to Bico. "He needs an hour," Dan said simply and nonchalantly.

Bico agreed and continued watching the end of the soccer game, consuming expensive caviar by the pound between sips of his cocktail.

"So, they won?" Dan asked lightly.

"Yes. Otherwise, I would fire the coach," Bico chuckled, then changed the subject. "There is a martial arts competition tonight, and my team is participating. Join me as my guest."

"If we have a deal, will you tell me why you're willing to switch sides?" Dan remarked.

"I can do better business with the Jewish people. Fei refuses to pay me for delivering Maman. They want the design and purpose of the secret satellite your country developed." Bico's tone implied that his and Dan's deal was already in his pocket.

"Hmm," Dan responded laconically. He wasn't going to say anything more than was absolutely necessary.

CHAPTER TWENTY-EIGHT

The Cape Canaveral drone incident embarrassed the intelligence agencies, despite their success in intercepting the foreign weapon before catastrophe. The attack took more skill than that of just some Al-Qaeda or ISIS organization. It clearly had been costly and required months of planning, and only a nation with hefty resources behind it could've pulled it off. The Cape's launch schedule was entirely confidential, as well as the details of the rocket's cargo; they feared that only a mole could've revealed this information.

Then, a group claimed responsibility for the attack. They called themselves "Bismillah al-Rahman al-Rahim" (which roughly translated to, "In The Name of Allah, Most Gracious, Most Merciful"). The investigators were skeptical but didn't altogether reject the idea. The group had no websites, social media accounts, or any traces of previous terror activity. Investigators couldn't entirely tell if the group recruited new soldiers or collected donations, and that signaled it might be a new organization previously unknown to the CIA, NSA, or any other foreign agencies.

Exchanging information with Israel revealed only the same conclusions. The assumption was that either this new group was a proxy for another foe seeking to destroy the rocket in retaliation for the ruin of the Proton in Kazakhstan, or the new group only existed as a distracting ruse. In Israel, it was easier to round up informers and collect intelligence on the streets, and the Mossad and Shin Bet set to that immediately.

Nevertheless, the foreign drone operators and their assumed "team" had attacked with stunning near success, especially as they did so on American soil. The drone wreckage was dredged from the Banana River to identify its origin and which weapons it possessed. Experts could not find any signs, letters, or decals revealing its source. No weapon was attached to its ten-foot wings. Traces of RDX, an organic-compound explosive, revealed that the drone was intended as a flying bomb—just one more headache for the NSA. How were the parts smuggled into the United States? How was the entire drone assembled, and where? Carried by diplomatic bag was the most plausible idea, as the bag's contents would've only been seen by its owner—outside airport x-rays. Neither the Israelis, the United Kingdom's security agency (MI5), nor any other friendly spy agency had a clue of its coming. It displayed a total failure of the security intelligence world.

Vandenberg Mission Control and the Operations Center in Santa Barbara, California (responsible for monitoring the Orbixeye alongside the Israeli developers), investigated the deployment of the two Orbixeye satellites. The drone incident was quickly ignored because the Spax rocket was on its way, leaving the security commotion on the ground far behind. The rocket accelerated and escaped the Earth's gravity as planned. Israeli satellites were placed in geostationary orbit with zero eccentricity and inclination to match Earth's rotation speed. This specific orbital placement was designed to offer NASA security the quickest warnings of danger. The two satellites hovered over stationary points on the equator, but each on the opposite side of Earth. The satellites were equipped with fuel tanks and thrusters to ensure their fixed positions and prevent drifting due to the Moon and sun's gravity.

The process took about two hours after the Spax's launch. Both the Mission Control room in Vandenberg and Palmachim Air Force Base just south of Tel Aviv displayed the data on large screens.

Scientists planned to eventually put a third Orbixeye into orbit for complete coverage of the atmosphere around Earth.

Once the final satellite positions were secured, the Israeli Mission Control's job was to unlock the password code—which was changed daily, due to Ezra Maman assumedly defecting. They activated the Orbixeye system, which was displayed on both control room screens and in POTUS's Situation Room simultaneously.

The Space Security Cabinet monitored the deployments, as ordered by the President. NIO director General William Fox, his chest covered in medals, also aided orchestration with Israel for the Orbixeye.

President Cole was briefed on all the events. He was concerned about the ISS situation and the other countries involved, but he kept that confidential.

In the meantime, Cole was satisfied with the satellite-launch results and eager to watch how the Israeli system worked. Fox walked into the room in a suit that looked like he slept in it, but he was totally refreshed and eager to show what he'd accomplished.

"Everything is ready," Fox stated, but no one was listening to him. The Situation Room, located on the ground floor, was officially named the JFK Conference Room and used for intelligence management. It had a long wooden conference table and TV screens on the walls. In one corner was a flag bearing the Seal of the President; the other corner's flagpole donned the American flag.

"It's on the screen," announced Fox, and the room went silent as all eyes locked on the television.

The screen displayed a three-dimensional map with dots all over it. Everyone had the same puzzled look, silently asking Fox for an explanation.

"It's downloading," Fox explained.

"Was this worth the free F-35 squadron we gave them?" President Cole demanded.

"We'll see," replied Joe Wezniak seriously. "I hope so."

The group returned to chatting amongst themselves. Cole, CIA Director Bennett, and Defense Secretary Wezniak made polite conversation with the Vice President, who was mostly out of the loop.

Secretary of State Cyrus Bradford was present and exchanged notes with Tim Woodward, the director of the NSA. The President had also invited Joint Chief of Staff General Mark Heller, who was briefed on the development of the United States Army's Space and Missile Defense Command (SMDC) under the direction of Lieutenant General Art Pratt.

Both men, the only uninformed people in the room, were to come up with a plan to ensure that the United States Army around the world was ready for escalation due to what would be the United States' preemptive first strike. They were surprised by the developments outlined in the briefs.

"Here it comes," declared Fox as data started appearing next to the map's dots. He looked outside the White House window as autumn's rusty mood changed the leaves to yellow and orange. Cool breezes engulfed the capital.

"Each dot represents a satellite's position relative to Earth," Fox began. "The data represents each satellite's speed relative to Earth, as well as its altitude, weight, and the frequencies upon which it communicates with its controller."

"Many satellites are missing data," Bennett observed.

"Those are debris; they have no frequency," Fox clarified.

"Unbelievable!" said the President. "It's remarkable."

"Which are ours? Does this map identify other countries' satellites, too?" asked Wezniak.

It was Fox's big day in the Situation Room, and he stood proudly before the country's top people. Finally, he could be valuable and add his thoughts to the security efforts after so many gray years of routine activities.

As Fox had detailed, the satellites in space used frequencies to communicate with their control centers on Earth. Orbixeye was equipped with a frequency and nuclear-material scanners. It would take time to scan and download all the data from the computer to the screen.

"The X band frequency, eight to twelve gigahertz, is usually used for military satellites to work with sensitive radar applications, pulses, and single polarization," William explained. "So, it works by elimination; we know which ones are ours, so every satellite using the X band frequency that is not ours is considered a foe."

"How many satellites do we have?" questioned the President.

"We have five hundred and ninety-three, and the Russians have over one thousand," interjected Bennett before Fox or Arthur Pratt could answer.

"There are many reports—and they are not all accurate," chimed in Lieutenant General Pratt.

"China?" asked the President.

"According to reports, China has about one hundred and ninety-two; most of them are disguised as military equipment with attack capabilities, but, honestly, we lost track of the Chinese satellites in space, so this might not be accurate," Fox said apologetically.

"Probably many more," remarked Lieutenant General Pratt. "They recently launched a bunch more than they had in the previous thirty years."

President Cole was overwhelmed by the enormous burden of a potential future war and what it could do to his legacy. The popular assumption that he was a warmonger only further pushed him to avoid a conflict. In the past, the United States had been brutally attacked twice, awakening the merciless, retaliatory sleeping giant. One was at Pearl Harbor, and the second was the terrorist attack on September 11th, 2001. Both times, America had been caught unprepared, surprised, confused, hurt, and unorganized. Cole could not let that happen on his watch, but he needed more confirmation before escalating the tension and declaring a higher DEFCON status.

If I leave this to the generals, we will immediately be in a terrible war, Cole thought. Therefore, the Moon excursion, even with its immense price tag, was the preferable way to deal with the situation. Cole worried that his generals were pulling his leg with the Moon camp photos, so he invited a scientist from MIT to the White House to offer another opinion. POTUS was cautious and calculated with every decision, as was his duty to the country.

Commander in Chief Cole wanted to wait and see what the Moon excursion unveiled. *Generals would always be quick to squeeze the trigger,* he reminded himself.

The old rules regarding declarations of war per the Geneva Convention were obsolete—dead. A surprise attack on a military foe was no longer an uncommon act of war; in fact, those types of attacks had only become more sophisticated. Nations regularly deceived others to gain the upper hand.

The Orbixeye completed downloading. The military then needed to ensure that its attack satellites were prepared for further orders from the President.

"Based on the data, we see some satellites traveling prograde and some traveling retrograde," Fox continued. "We must keep our eyes on those traveling retrograde, as they could be used as kinetic-attack satellites by increasing their energy during impact."

Fox and the agencies were unsure the types of weaponry the potential attack satellites possessed or how to identify them. Were they equipped with lasers or electromagnetic weapons? Could they attack targets on Earth? The CIA felt pressured to come up with the answers.

All eyes were back on NASA and the CIA as the ship's launch drew nearer.

CHAPTER TWENTY-NINE

After speaking with Dan tersely on the phone, M. swiftly called the Israeli Prime Minister's personal phone, even though it was late in the evening. The Prime Minister was at the wedding of a cabinet member's son.

M. heard the wedding band's music and cheering in the background. It was probably a bad time to call, but time was of the essence.

"We have our first chance to find Maman's whereabouts," M. stated quickly, and then his voice dropped. "But the information will cost us twenty-five million dollars."

M. then disclosed the necessary cooperation required of their agency. The Prime Minister, a previously high-ranking IDF officer, was concerned about the legitimacy of the source—especially since Bico was a former KGB agent.

"They are all liars who play both sides," the Prime Minister stated. But M. was convinced that Bico was telling the truth and took full responsibility for possible failure.

"I propose that we offer five million now and five million after he discloses the information and legitimately proves it," M. continued. "If he brings Maman back, he will receive the rest. Bico either accepts those terms or there's no deal. And—maybe—if the operation to smuggle Maman back to Israel is a success, we could offer Bico a bonus." M. knew that this mission would boost the reputation of the Mossad and raise his own ranking to the level of the legendary Mossad chiefs. The mission to return Maman would rival the Mossad's capture of Nazi Adolf Eichmann, who was tried and hanged in Israel. Regardless, M. was not looking for glory; but perhaps the Prime Minister was, considering the next election was about a year away.

M. emphasized the value of the information Maman could offer the Mossad, assuming that Maman wasn't already dead. "Not only that, it'll greatly help the FBI, MI5, and CIA," M. added. "It'll be worth the investment; and think of what Israel could then ask of the United States in return."

Dan and Bico rode in Bico's limousine to the wrestling arena, accompanied by Bico's entourage of bodyguards. Albika was also with them, her silence somehow sensual.

An SUV trailed closely behind them, full of Bico's protective soldiers who were equipped like a battalion on a military mission.

They reached the arena and entered through the VIP door, heading toward the front-row seating.

Dan was tense, as he was still waiting for a response from M. in order to move their plan forward. Somehow, Dan trusted that whenever a deal was sealed, Bico would honor it. *Definitely better to have Bico on our side—at least for now,* Dan thought.

The Chinese had gambled with a bad deck of cards, and it wasn't the first time they'd lost a game against the Mossad. China had seemingly let their ace, Bico, slip between their fingers.

The first match started when Bico displayed his wrestler in the ring. As Dan expected, Bico's fighter won. Another pair of fighters began the second round in front of the wildly cheering crowd—onlookers who'd probably paid handsomely to watch the match live.

Dan anxiously glanced at his phone from time to time to check for messages, worried about missing M.'s communications. No calls, no texts. Bico showed no sign of concern; he was obviously confident and assured that the Mossad would not pass up the opportunity once he'd laid out the bait. After all, Bico held the merchandise—their chief Orbixeye scientist Maman *and* Dan.

Suddenly, Dan's phone rang. M. asked to speak with Bico directly.

"For you," Dan said to Bico politely.

Bico raised his eyebrows and sucked at his teeth before asking, "Who is it?"

Dan didn't answer and merely pushed the cell toward Bico. Bico grabbed it. "Bico speaking."

M.'s metallic voice on the other end of the line was sharp and clear, despite the noise of the arena. M. did not introduce himself; instead, he immediately outlined the deal he'd agreed upon with the Israeli Prime Minister. Bico listened silently. Then Bico made a face like he'd been hit below the belt—his head jerked back as if he'd been struck by lightning.

But then, as if changing masks, Bico quietly rattled off a Swiss bank account number. Dan knew that the deal was nearly cemented.

Bico then casually and expressionlessly handed the phone back to Dan. After five minutes, Bico nonchalantly checked his bank account on his phone. Five million dollars had been deposited, as agreed. Bico tilted his phone's screen and showed Dan.

Dan nodded but was still confused by Bico's odd jerking reaction and facial expression from before. "What was that about? Looked like you got electrocuted."

Bico waved the waiter over and asked for a bottle of vodka, cups with ice, and lime. Upon the liquor's arrival, Bico poured it and toasted to Dan. "To our collaboration! *Salud.*"

"*Za zdarovje!*" cheered the others.

Bico had blatantly ignored Dan's question, but Dan didn't inquire further, as M. would probably offer details about the call later.

Then, Bico stood up and signaled for his crew to leave. Clearly, the main event for Bico had just ended. Dan followed the order, and they left in the middle of the fifth round.

CHAPTER THIRTY

M. didn't coordinate the mission he'd planned for Agent Shaked with his counterparts, the CIA, or MI5. Those agencies were busy trying to collect intelligence and plan whatever they could with that minimal intelligence, hoping some event would connect the dots for them.

The CIA, NSA, and NASA couldn't yet display for the White House any justification for the billions of dollars spent on training crews and flying refurbished equipment to the Moon. President Cole had already bought the plan, but they were still under pressure to provide more information about what was up there and what to expect—and what the Chinese space program's aspirations were.

The intelligence lacked clarity, but CIA Director Gene Bennett knew in his gut that the mission would be fruitful and unveil the information they hoped for. And he definitely knew it would be well worth it to demonstrate that the United States was still a major player in space.

Too many hints and puzzle-piece fragments of information came to Bennett's office from his field agents, scooped from the gutters of cities around the world. The field agents stealthily paid off hotel bellboys, restaurant hosts, credit card companies, and car rental agencies for following Chinese scientists when they traveled to participate in science events around the globe.

One such event was produced by the CIA in Geneva, wherein they hoped to catch the big fish. China was careful and followed Chang's advice for scientists to stay home, unless Chang gave them the green light to do otherwise. Chang advised them to leave their computers, laptops, and personal cell phones at home. He also required them to get new SIM cards from his agency, which had Trojan horses inside. That way, if a Chinese phone was stolen, the Trojan horse would send information back to China about what the thief was looking for. Also, Chang added a feature to the cell phones supplied to diplomats and other government agencies; the app would secretly track the phone's location so that China would know where the thief took the device.

The Chinese space facilities were under CIA surveillance. Bennett employed Chinese Americans with political backgrounds to spy on China. Bennett's big picture was not yet complete, but he could see it on the horizon of his vision. But explaining this to others was another story—especially the President.

The mole responsible for exposing the American network was assumed to have fled the country. The Chinese Embassy had probably equipped him with cash and a fake passport and helped him cross the Mexican border.

The Mossad had an ample presence on the ground, and it comprised more than Dan in Grozny and Shaked on her way to Beijing.

M. understood later that it was a logistical mistake to not plant a closer eye on the Chinese space program. He'd only said no to selling Israeli technology to China, including the sale of the Israeli satellite company to the Chinese. M. was sure that his refusal to support the sale made him a target and prime suspect for the Chinese regarding the destruction of the Protons— regardless of the event's collateral damage for Israel.

CHAPTER THIRTY-ONE

The beautiful Asian woman was examined thoroughly by the border police. She remained poised and unnerved.

One of the officers examined her diplomatic visa and passport extensively. She seemed relaxed and confident to him; he just wasn't sure how an Asian woman was serving the Israeli Embassy as a citizen.

Naomi wore simple jeans and a light cotton blouse, casually hiding her curves.

Finally, the officer asked her in Chinese, "Business?"

"Yeah; my entry visa says it all," she replied in his same language and dialect.

The officer raised his eyebrows and scoffed, "Are you Chinese or Israeli?"

"Both," she stated bluntly, narrowing her eyes.

Without moving his head, he darted his eyes upward, studying her from his chair behind the booth's glass. His palpable disdain, arrogance, and unnecessarily slow movements drove Naomi crazy. Eventually, he stamped her passport and signaled her to move on. *It's too early for hide-and-seek,* she thought.

An hour later, she met with the security officer for logistical assistance at the Israeli Embassy in Beijing.

The Chinese authorities had probably torn through her bags and followed her to her destination. She didn't try to cover her tracks.

Naomi opened Maman's classified personal folder and found out that he was a brilliant—but lonely—man. His wife had divorced him long ago and won custody of their two children. She'd turned them against their father, so they'd refused to see him when he'd tried to visit. He'd probably felt his entire world collapsed and that it wasn't worth the work. His life then changed and took a drastic change for the worse. Though treated by a psychologist for diagnosed separation anxiety, he could not recover, especially when the court hammered him with heavy alimony and maintenance payments that drained his bank account. He perpetually hoped for the social worker's mercy after losing the warmth of everything he considered home. He continued working for the technology industry, intermittently taking breaks to go somewhere else without leaving a trace; he was a perfect, vulnerable target in the midst of his meltdown. Then the CSIS appeared and convinced him to change sides and take revenge on his family.

The Chinese didn't skimp on him, quietly hoping he would unwittingly return the investment. They showed him the life he'd missed while in the traditional Israeli marriage institution.

Although under curfew and always escorted by a secret police agent to his hotel, Maman could go out for errands nearby without supervision—but only when equipped with a smartwatch and synchronized phone that tracked his location.

The planning division of the Mossad searched for ways to penetrate the facilities where Maman would supposedly be working. The assumption was that he'd be utilized as a researcher and developer for space, robotics, and artificial intelligence projects. His expertise would aid in developing a new Chinese version of the Orbixeye; the Chinese called it *Jiàndié Guǐdào Qì* (which roughly translated to "Spy Orbiter").

M. and his officers at headquarters discovered the footprint of the Israeli "atom spy" who'd been hijacked from Rome and hurriedly returned to Tel Aviv to stand trial. M. drew a parallel profile between Maman and the "atom spy". M. found a similar pattern: both people had similar backgrounds and defected with vital Israeli secrets to potentially share with adversaries.

"So, where is Maman?" asked Dan as he and Bico began planning.

"That was never mentioned to me," Bico replied. "I'll try to find out."

M. suggested that Bico call his contact within the Chinese agency to request his pending repayment—and, in the interim, ask questions that might shed light on Maman's location.

Bico thought it was a good idea. He called his contact and asked for Fei Liwei, the Chinese agent who'd hired him. Fei, a thin man, looked like a merchant in a farmer's market. He was smart, sharp as a razor, and used his unappealing appearance to his advantage as an agent.

"This is Fei," he answered in a friendly cadence. He already knew who was on the line.

"It's me," Bico said. "And you know why I am calling, right?"

A long silence followed as both men considered their next words.

"Yes, yes, yes. I know. I need more...time," Fei said apologetically.

Bico easily imagined the narrow man on the other end of the line, writhing in the discomfort of being the subordinate of another intelligence agency.

"You got the merchandise. I want my payment, or I want the merchandise back," Bico remarked firmly.

Dan could hear Fei's laugh through Bico's phone.

M. was remotely sending notes to Bico regarding what to ask Fei about. Greco, seated beside M. in Israel, tapped the phoneline to get the location to monitor future calls from Fei.

"Oh, no, that will not happen," chuckled the Chinese agent. "I will have to get back to you soon."

Dan wrote a quick note on paper and slid it over to Bico. It read, "Ask him if he knows where Maman is."

"Wait, Fei—you've already promised me a few times, and I cannot wait. What did they do with the merchandise?"

Deliberate silence from Fei followed. Bico cleared his throat to remind Fei that he was waiting for an answer.

"I promise to get back to you in an hour," Fei said, and the line was abruptly disconnected.

"Well, if the mountain will not come to Moses, Moses must go to the mountain," sighed M. through Dan's phone, referring to an old Arabic phrase. They had to change their strategy.

The phone rang one hour later—on the dot—and Albika answered it. "It's for you," she said, pushing the phone toward Bico.

Bico looked at his phone's screen and shot a thumbs-up to Dan. It was Fei.

"I'll have the money in twenty-four hours," Fei said. "Can you meet at my place?"

"Can you wire the money?" Bico countered.

"No; it's all cash."

"Okay. Let me check my schedule, and I'll get back to you."

M. and Dan immediately thought it was a trap, but it was also an opportunity to get themselves inside the Chinese intelligence security hub. Dan would enter China with his fake passport, posing as part of Bico's entourage. The Israeli Embassy would supply the logistical support to get them what they needed to perform their mission. The embassy kept a few rental apartments around Beijing and would utilize one for this plan.

Agent Shaked was informed that ever since Maman had crossed lines (and the explosion occurred in Kazakhstan), there was surveillance on the embassy and its diplomats. She needed to hone all she'd learned to avoid being stalked by other agents. She was to always use the front door when she left the embassy—never the back door.

For her to exit the embassy for a secret mission, collaborators would come disguised as civilian visitors. Agent Shaked would also put on civilian clothes and appropriate makeup to walk out as a different person.

Often, they couldn't keep accurate count of how many people had entered or left the embassy, so they kept records and photos to identify possible Mossad agents.

Shaked's job was to prepare the apartment and stock it with food and necessities without drawing attention from the locals. The apartment was registered in a local person's name so that they always could claim that strangers had broken in if questioned.

The chosen apartment was in a quiet residential building in the suburbs of Beijing. It was not far from the embassy and relatively close to the airport. Shaked's mission was to find Maman's location, kidnap him (with the help of the team), and take him back to Israel.

The Mossad operations department sent new passports to Shaked and her team in a diplomatic bag. All the passports were fake and used names "borrowed" from real people— some of whom actually resided in Israel.

Shaked regularly used her talents of observation to blow off her trackers, mingle, and blend with her surroundings to quietly uncover clues and move her mission forward.

Maman lingered in her mind day and night. She already knew his profile by heart—his desires, habits, and tendencies, all gathered from interviews with his acquaintances and family. As someone who'd suffered a harsh marriage to a cruel, controlling woman, he'd developed a taste for courting and sleeping with easy, beautiful women. It was not for companionship—he desired control.

One of Shaked's advantages was her ethnicity, which allowed her to easily move about the crowded Beijing streets unnoticed. She took full advantage of it but was never cocky.

Even though the Mossad had its own internal cybersecurity department, their agents needed more than decorated military histories. Their positions required upstanding personalities and the ability to plant bugs or infect computers with Trojan horses—and other hacking skills were a bonus.

Shaked had checked the apartment for bugs or other spying instruments and was satisfied that it was clean. She'd disguised herself and surveyed the city for possible escape routes or hiding places in case of a snag.

She was ready.

Bico and Fei compromised to meet in Kazakhstan, as it was between China and Chechnya.

Bico, Dan, and the Mossad still assumed that the deal with Fei was a trap to eliminate Bico. Bico was a nuisance and liability for the Chinese, so their intentions were easy to guess.

"With lemons, you make lemonade," recited Dan, repeating one of his Prime Minister's favorite quotes. The setup wasn't ideal, but it was their only option to locate Maman so that Agent Shaked could get to him.

Fei's superior knew of the arranged meeting in Kazakhstan. They planned for Fei to execute a fake transaction with Bico in a neutral land—then they'd blame a separatist group or robbers for Bico's murder to avoid too many questions. *No one would miss a meeting anywhere on Earth for millions of dollars in cash*, Fei chuckled to himself.

Although Fei had asked Bico to come alone to avoid unnecessary attention, Bico intended to bring his group of assassins and then escape back to China without being detected.

Zharkent in the Almaty Region of Kazakhstan was chosen for the rendezvous. Bico agreed to meet at a designated address near the Chinese border.

"So far, so good; things are moving according to plan," Fei reported to Chang, rubbing his hands together in satisfaction.

A small city twenty-five miles from the Chinese border and the Chinese city of Khorgas on the border were part of the plan to get in and out without any trace.

Dan and Bico were sure that Fei didn't intend to use the border crossing between the two cities on the Chinese Route G312 or highway A353 in Kazakhstan. From the Chinese border, the relatively short distance to the meeting point meant that Fei and his team would likely cross on foot. That night, Fei and his team planned to steal two cars on the other side, drive to the meeting point, shoot Bico (and his assumed entourage), and cross back into China with one car heading east on highway A352.

M. ordered his network to check the area around the meeting point and report to Dan and Bico. Dan and Bico would have minimal logistics; they'd primarily need to handle everything on their own.

The meeting was scheduled for three days later at midnight; they'd meet southwest of Zharkent on regional road R-21. The exact spot was right beside a toll stop about five hundred feet from a roundabout—which was the escape route Fei planned. M. and his team checked the address repeatedly, attempting to discern why an open area had been chosen for the event.

M. thought it best if Dan and Bico entered Kazakhstan illegally and then met up with Agent Shaked. After they returned to Grozny, they would then fly to Beijing, with Dan donning his MRI salesman identity again. At least he'd learned more about selling medical equipment since his stay in Russia.

Dan and Bico's getting to the meeting point had its challenges. The spot was sixteen hundred miles away. Dan hoped Bico's organization could help them. They considered taking a seaplane from the Caspian Sea to a lake near the rendezvous— or even parachuting. In the end, Dan and Bico chose to fly on a commercial plane and rent a car. Bico's soldiers would travel only by car from Grozny to Kazakhstan, and they left for their nonstop journey immediately in two separate vehicles.

The game had begun.

CHAPTER THIRTY-TWO

Aboard the crippled ISS, drifting somewhere in orbit

The backup power system was the only thing keeping the crew alive.

Once that power source died, the other ISS systems would shut down—and the vital life support and environmental controls would expire. It was likely the solar panels (the International Space Station's source of energy) were damaged.

The engineers at Mission Control were certain that an extravehicular activity (EVA)—a spacewalk—was imperative to avoid a total electrical failure. The control room would advise the crew if a spacewalk were required and alert them to the potential risk of electrical shocks.

After an intensive evaluation of telemetry data, Mission Control concluded that the sequential shunt unit was responsible for the power loss due to a faulty voltage regulation from the solar panels. NASA tied the loads from one solar wing panel channel to the second solar panel's channel in the Main Bus Switching Unit, which restored power to half capacity. The crew spent the next twenty-four hours rebooting power to the systems and reversing the emergency mode as the station spun along its own axis. A replacement sequential shunt unit was needed, but such a spare part was not on the station.

A chain of events then spread like a plague: first, the station's cabin lost 0.2 PSI of pressure every twenty-four hours;

next, the Elektron oxygen generator failed. The generator was vital; it used electrolysis to separate oxygen and hydrogen from water to replenish the station's atmosphere.

An air leak was detected through the pressure gauge and visual examination. The crew discovered that one of the air hoses was loosened and damaged after an astronaut held onto it during the explosion.

Mission Control had to either evacuate the crew (by moving three astronauts onto each emergency Soyuz capsule) or repair abundant damage without any spare parts.

The emotionless voice over the communication network left no doubt: "Mode One emergency egress."

The astronauts hoped it was just a bad dream. They'd never imagined having to abort. The station had served for more than a decade. Still, having no other choice, they made the final preparations to evacuate into the emergency Russian capsules, which were pressurized and could maintain life support for a limited time.

The three American astronauts stuck together and entered one of the capsules. The two Russian cosmonauts and the Japanese astronaut got into the second capsule after turning off all the station systems and bringing the Soyuz craft to life. An event that would've typically taken hours happened in a fraction of that time.

The Russian cosmonaut commanding one Soyuz capsule, Vladimir Bulanov, crammed into the spacecraft with his two colleagues and signaled to Mission Control that they were prepped for undocking procedures.

Since the ISS was spinning, the attitude control thrusters required activation to reduce the station's motion and bring it to equilibrium. A series of burns maneuvered one capsule downward and away from the station. The second attached

Soyuz capsule was docked on the opposite side of the station, awaiting the signal to complete the same procedure.

While drifting about sixty feet from the station, the automated controls fired the engines to push the first Soyuz into the precise orbit and angle to enter the Earth's atmosphere.

A little over three hours later, Bulanov and his crew landed on Kazakhstan's grassy ground, relieved that their ordeal was over.

Luckily, whatever object had hit the ISS spared Bulanov's Soyuz on its way back to Earth; now, all eyes were on Colonel Campbell and his team.

Minutes after the American astronauts took their seats and strapped in, they started the emergency routine to check the capsule systems, turning on switches and going through the undocking checklist.

Campbell gazed at the ISS for the last time before declaring to Mission Control that they were ready to undock. That procedure would separate the two spaceships by opening the latches holding the Soyuz to the docking port of the ISS.

Mission Control's response took longer than expected, and Campbell waited patiently; although nervous, he didn't show it. He remained composed when the communication hissed.

Then he finally heard Jim: "Stand by, Campbell; we're experiencing an undocking malfunction."

"Roger."

A few strained minutes passed, and the urgency to get them on their way filled the capsule. Debris started flying into their orbit, which confirmed the collisional cascading theory developed by NASA scientist Donald Kessler in 1978. Time was of the essence, and the Space Shuttle Atlantis was three days away.

The astronauts made the appropriate adjustments to monitor and verify the manual mode in case the automated system failed.

"Switch to command set point for a manual undock—and then standby," Mission Control remarked when the automatic controls failed.

Campbell handled the undocking activities while one of his colleagues maintained contact with Mission Control for search and rescue.

"Campbell, EVA requires you to unlock the capsule," Mission Control stated.

Mission Control switched to emergency mode.

At Cape Canaveral, NASA was ready to launch the two spaceships with their crews for the risky journey to the Moon—and to assist the ISS astronauts.

CHAPTER THIRTY-THREE

After the first five million dollars hit his bank account, Bico felt like the chief club member for the best team on the planet. Information about Bico's partnership with Chang and Chinese spy agencies piled up, and the Mossad were amazed that the intel hadn't surfaced earlier.

In Beijing, Chang prepared profiles on everyone in the Israeli delegation who'd participated in the rocket launch. But the Chinese government was still buying Israeli technology left and right, as doing business was something neither country wanted to quit.

Behind politicians' smiles were agents rushing to get intelligence from each other in the alleys of Tel Aviv and Beijing. As agents were trained to be secret soldiers, they specialized in absorbing and delivering data. They roamed every capital, contacting their informants and meeting their collaborators in search of more intelligence with unparalleled ambition. There was no limit to what they could do or use to achieve their objectives.

Chang's watchdogs had lost track of Dan and his team in Florida. Greco couldn't answer any questions; he was frustrated and looking for any clues. He was ready to make a call to Bico himself and find out what had happened to the hired assassins in Florida, but such a conversation would not have gone well. His gut told him that the Mossad had crossed the finish line before him again. He needed to know if they were involved—or not, which was his greatest fear.

Chang had told Bico that the payment for smuggling Maman from the Kazakhstan Cosmodrome to China also included the identification, interrogation, and elimination of Agent Dan Eyal. Therefore, the payment had been canceled due to a failed delivery. The Chinese had changed the rules, claimed Bico; those were two separate deals, but they'd combined them and then refused to pay.

But now Bico was in bed with the Mossad—and M. requested that he play the game and keep communications open. Bico had asked Chang to forward him at least one million as a deposit for his incurred expenses, but Chang had refused. "You know how our agency works; you know it's useless to ask for anything," Chang had retorted.

Although the game remained civil and Bico assumed the Chinese knew nothing of his deal with the Mossad, the Chinese were not dumb—they'd already planted an agent to track Bico's activity.

The Mossad in Tel Aviv again warned Dan that the meeting with Fei was likely a trap, but Dan and Bico had already carefully planned their steps. They were to be the executioners—not the executed.

In the limousine on the way to Bico's mansion, with the driver removed from their conversation by glass, Dan felt relaxed enough to open serious conversation: "So, the money transferred. What information do you have on Maman?"

"Oh, yeah, that," Bico replied casually. "Your scientist was not hijacked. It was all a front. He defected."

"What? Are you sure?" Dan pressed, anger rising inside him. "What are you telling me? Who—how?"

This new information reshuffled the cards. Now, someone would have to pay the price, as was expected when the shit hit the fan. Spy agencies had no mercy for people who switched sides...or attempted to play both.

"I can tell you this," Bico said, "it was my mistake to deal with Chang; and my other likely mistake was dealing with the Mossad. You're both brutal agencies. I would've been better off sticking to my own business." Bico's voice trailed off, and he stared at his reflection in the tinted glass window.

"Well, what's done is done," replied Dan coldly. "You must deliver Maman back to us."

In the past, many agents and collaborators had given their lives for their countries. The Mossad, like many notorious and remorseless agencies, was not opposed to punishing those who betrayed them. No agency executed and terrorized their enemies (and their enemies' homes) quite like the Mossad. After the Munich Olympic games terrorist attack in 1972 and further terror attacks in the streets of Tel Aviv, the Mossad had buried each and every culprit, one by one. None remained to tell their story. And now Maman was on the top of their list.

Dan ran previous events through his head like a movie montage. He assumed that the Chinese were now salivating to get their hands on him. *This opportunity could have been their best*, he thought, and a chilling spasm sidled down his spine.

Why did Maman desert? Dan deliberated, furrowing his brow. That was of highest concern—that, and whatever damage the Israeli space agency would incur if Maman shared his expertise with the Chinese.

Two things had to happen simultaneously: finding Maman's whereabouts and starting damage control for potentially leaked intel...assuming the information Bico had provided was accurate. Cyberattacking the Chinese space agency would then be Greco's task.

"Bico, if you're even telling me the truth, how do I know that Maman is still alive?" Dan asked. "What else can you tell me?"

Bico took a few moments to digest Dan's questions and gave his driver instructions in Russian as they approached the gated mansion.

"I think I know where Maman is," Bico remarked, suddenly examining Dan's face. "I am not sure what he was up to, but this plot was hatched less than a year ago. Maman was approached by the Chinese on his last trip to China. He was a delegate of the Israeli science team at that time, apparently. The Chinese dug up his profile and took the opportunity to sway him. They presented themselves as saviors—Maman took the bait."

The limo drove into the compound, and they were greeted by servants as they entered the massive circular foyer.

"You will stay tonight as my guest, right?" Bico asked with a smile, pretending like Dan had a choice.

"Of course; we're partners now," Dan shot back with mild sarcasm.

Bico giggled.

Albika immediately took charge as the lady of the house and threw orders at the housekeepers. "We will have dinner in forty-five minutes in the main dining room," she announced to Bico and Dan. "Meanwhile, you may help yourselves to drinks at the bar."

It was close to midnight. *The Russians like to eat late...very late*, Dan thought as his stomach growled, reminding him that he hadn't eaten anything for a good while.

Bico's villa rested on the edge of Grozny; its view of the mountains was spectacular.

Dan was escorted to a private room that he assumed was bugged and equipped with cameras. He turned on the shower to drown out the sound of his voice and made a call to M.

M. looked at his watch and cursed when his phone rang. His wife grumbled about who was calling in the middle of the night—as if it were the first time.

M. grabbed his phone and went to his kitchen. He rubbed his eyes and answered shortly, "Yes." He already knew who was calling.

Dan talked, and M. listened. After three minutes, M. responded with frustration, "Just this information about Maman alone is worth five million dollars! We completely failed to see he was emotionally vulnerable to manipulation."

"What would've been his motivation to join the Chinese?" Dan asked.

"We'll doublecheck his profile and question the psychiatrist who saw him," M. said sleepily. "Maybe we should re-interview some of his family or friends. I doubt his motivation was money. Did you find out if Bico knows his location?"

"It's on the agenda," Dan sighed. "Bico said he knows, but I'm starting to doubt it."

"Okay. Be careful out there," M. mumbled and hung up.

After more thought, Bico and Dan decided against flying to the meeting with Fei. Instead, they and a few other gang members left in two cars for the three-day trip to the Kazakhstani town. Their black Land Rovers had double roofs to store their weapons.

Equipped with passports and visas to enter the country, they crossed the Caspian Sea via ferry to reach Kazakhstan.

Any discovered drug or weapon smuggling would lead to a trial and harsh penalties—perhaps even life in prison—and the failure of their mission.

During the sea journey, Bico ascended the ferry bridge and spoke with the captain. As Bico walked away, a set of eyes locked on his back, and a shadowy figure then approached the captain, too. Despite his time in KGB, Bico seemed to have lost his sixth sense that had made him legendary.

CHAPTER THIRTY-FOUR

A gent Shaked, situated in her apartment, dug into her investigation to find Maman. She developed a plan to penetrate the space and research facilities; she called to ask for a tour, presenting herself as a reporter from Xinhau News Agency. She stole a badge in the agency cafeteria and copied its design to create a new badge donning her fake reporter name.

It was painstaking work to get permission to enter the facilities. Finally, she scored an interview with the China National Space Agency (CNSA), who'd split from the Ministry of Aerospace Industry to create a second agency, the China Aerospace Science and Technology Corporation (CASC). Shaked felt that was a decent start.

Each of the agencies had a few departments; one of them was the SASTIND—the State Administration for Science, Technology and Industry for National Defense. A couple of secret departments were not on the long list of subordinate agencies.

Equipped with a camera made in China, microphone, recorder, and badge to add to her new image, she dressed like the reporters she'd seen on television.

She made sure to flash her Huawei cell phone when she entered the lobby and asked to meet with the press secretary.

A short, thin man in his late thirties came out in a tailored suit. He greeted her with a bow and handshake.

He introduced himself as Jing Yapin, the head of the press office. "I checked with your agency," Jing said to Shaked in a hushed tone. "Your name was not on their lists."

He studied her badge closely, but Shaked didn't lose her cool. She stated confidently, "I'm Liu Zhongyi. I just joined the agency a couple weeks ago; perhaps they haven't updated their lists yet. I'll clear that up with my office when I return."

Jing nodded his head and asked her politely to follow him to his office. "Please refrain from taking any pictures on our way," Jing added.

She followed silently. She gazed around, but all she saw were long corridors with many sealed doors with small placards.

One placard drew her attention, and she memorized it— "The Department of Artificial Intelligence." Shaked was curious about the department, but it likely wasn't connected to the missing scientist. Still, the fact that China was stretching their long octopus arms everywhere intrigued her and would be interesting intel to pass along to her superiors.

They reached Jing's minimally furnished office. The press department was a one-man show: no secretary, assistant, or even office activity.

She started with routine, casual questions that she'd prepared, and Jing answered them with no issues. They both felt mostly comfortable, but Jing attributed the slight nervousness in her voice to excitement about her first interview for a new agency. She asked permission to shoot photos. Then she nonchalantly added, "Rumors in my agency require me to ask you, Mr. Yapin: is an Israeli scientist working in your agency?"

Jing shifted nervously in his chair and scowled. He paused and glared at her with his charcoal eyes. "I can't comment on that question, as I am not aware of any Israeli scientist working here." Jing attempted hiding his surprise and potential lie, but Shaked's knowledge of body language paid off when he refused to meet her gaze.

"Fair enough," she replied calmly and smiled at him. She continued with her prepped questions.

Jing decided not to ask her about her unexpected inquiry. He would do his own investigating later. He then refused to discuss the scientists' daily routines and future missions with her—and swiftly asked to end the interview.

Shaked's gut feeling was that Jing knew about Maman. Perhaps he was working just behind the door down the hall—who knew? Jing's pupils had dilated when she'd asked the question. His polite and easygoing tone had turned nervous, impatient, and snappy. Shaked would relay these details to M. later on.

She left as quickly as she could. She knew Jing would call the news agency again—or maybe even the Chinese intelligence service so they could track her. She felt cold but sweat ran down her neck. She tried not to look back. She took random turns to lose anyone potentially following her. Every now and then, she'd open her makeup mirror or stop beside a store window to see behind her.

Then she rushed onto a crowded bus and looked around her for stalkers. She felt safe but didn't directly return to her apartment. She changed her clothes twice in department stores, picking cheap clothes and paying only in cash to easily mingle with the crowds.

.

CHAPTER THIRTY-FIVE

"Where were you?" Dan asked Bico, who'd come back with sandwiches and a smile.

"You want one?" Bico asked, offering a sandwich to Dan. "I just went to meet with..." Bico's voice then trailed off as he searched for something in his pockets with his free hand. "Oh, I left my phone on the Captain's bridge." Bico bolted back in the direction he'd come from.

When Bico returned to the stairs to the bridge, he saw a suspicious man out of the corner of his eye. Bico sucked in a breath as the figure moved closer.

Upon realizing who the shadowing stranger was, Bico released a groan. "Damnit," he said through clenched teeth.

It was Anatoly, Bico's driver. Bico shook his head, realizing that someone had apparently hired Anatoly to spy on him.

Bico let Anatoly pass by without calling out to him. Bico then rushed back to Dan and their accompanying gang members.

Bico immediately explained the situation to Dan and they decided to eliminate Anatoly as soon as possible. They couldn't take any chances. They wondered what Anatoly had already seen and disclosed to Fei and Chang.

"Watch him," Bico whispered. "I'll be right back."

Dan nodded.

The captain recognized Bico from their earlier conversation and smiled nervously. Deep in the captain's pocket was the money Bico had offered in exchange for his gang's skirting the Kazakhstani border police. The captain handed Bico his phone.

Bico then asked directly, "What did the man with the blue shirt want?"

The captain had no intention of returning Bico's money, so he answered immediately: "He asked me about you."

After Bico ran back and grabbed Dan, the two slid into the Land Rover Anatoly drove and asked the rest of the gang members to move to the other car. Bico locked the doors, and Anatoly became visibly nervous.

Bico narrowed his eyes and grilled the driver: "Why did you follow me to the bridge?"

Anatoly, who had worked for Bico's organization for a couple years, mumbled inaudibly. Bico encouraged Anatoly to speak as Dan gripped him from behind the seat.

"Money? Is that why you backstabbed me?" yelled Bico.

Anatoly squeezed his eyes shut and nodded.

"Damn you, Anatoly! I could kill you right now," Bico spat. "Did you think they would actually pay you for spying on us? What did they want to know, huh?" Bico's lips nearly grazed Anatoly's ear.

Dan cut in and asked, "Who else is on the ship with you? Who hired you?"

Anatoly stiffened. His situation was dire.

Bico, despite his friendly appearance, was a ruthless killer. Nothing could stop him from hitting his target.

"I...I just had to...report all your moves..." Anatoly whispered slowly, his voice shaking. "Weapons, if any. Suspicious thoughts or strategies."

"Who wants to know?" Bico hollered, hitting the driver on the back of the head.

Anatoly winced, hesitated, and finally murmured, "I don't know his name. He is upstairs in the passengers' lounge."

"So, you have company on the boat, do you? Any other friends you want to tell me about?" Bico snapped. "Speak!"

Anatoly remained silent.

"Okay," Bico growled. "We're going for a walk."

Dan released the driver and Bico stepped out of the car to explain the situation to his gang. "Anatoly leaked that we are on the ferry, so there are agents onboard to eliminate us," Bico reported. His men clenched their fists and scowled.

"Anatoly mentioned one man in the lounge, but there are likely others he doesn't know about," Dan warned. "We have to find them before we reach the dock."

They split into two groups, and each one went to the passengers' deck, leaving their cars in the lot below. From a distance, both groups made eye contact and shared signals. From a safe distance, Anatoly reluctantly identified the man who'd hired him. Dan lingered safely behind them, already considering this man's presence an act of the Chinese agents.

Suddenly, the man spotted Anatoly with Bico.

The man was cornered, and he quickly walked toward the exit leading to the exterior corridor—but Bico's other group of men had sealed the doors.

Bico and Dan rushed after him, leaving Anatoly behind. The man was unsure how to escape, debating whether he should run to his cabin or the upper deck.

The man then rushed up to the heliport deck but found himself pressed against a barricade with nowhere else to turn. Bico easily wrestled him down to the cold steel deck.

The ferry crew on the bridge in front of the heliport were completely unaware of the drama unfolding behind them. Bico pulled the man up by the neck, glared into his eyes, and bent him backward over the railing, threatening him with a freefall into the chilly waters below.

Dan surveyed the deck to ensure no one would intrude on their business.

The man gasped for air. Bico promised him a bath if he didn't answer questions.

"Who do you work for?" Bico yelled. *I've been asking this question a lot lately,* he thought to himself with disdain. When Bico received only silence in response, he bent the man farther over the railing, cracking his spine.

"Wait," the man cried out. "Fei activated me to monitor you and...and I hired Anatoly to get more information."

"Where is Fei now?" Bico snarled.

"I don't know!" gasped the man. Bico studied him for a moment before deciding to believe him. Despite getting what he wanted, Bico continued to push the man backward, heaving him by his leg. Flailing, the man pulled out a small handgun from his pocket as a last resort.

"Damn," Bico grunted. "Fuck, I thought everyone was frisked for weapons before boarding."

Bico sighed and released his grip on the man, preparing to let him plunge into the Caspian Sea. Before the man slid entirely over the railing and to the water below, he fired one bullet directly at Bico's shoulder. The sound of the gunshot blew away in the sea wind, unnoticed by any crew.

Quickly, Dan helped Bico back to the car below so they could assess the wound. Dan sighed with relief when he found the bullet had only deeply grazed Bico's flesh.

Anatoly rushed up to the car and was immediately more concerned for his life when he saw that Bico had been wounded.

"I don't think Fei actually intended to meet us at that roundabout in Kazakhstan," Dan said flatly as he bandaged Bico's shoulder. Bico winced and nodded.

"He planned to follow us and attack at a point when we were vulnerable and unprepared," Dan continued. "Anatoly and that man were scouts."

Their hope of interrogating Fei to squeeze out information about Maman had gone down the drain. The mountain would not come to them, so they had to go to the mountain.

They arranged to take the same ferry back to Grozny.

Shaked prepared to set a scouting point and watch who entered and exited the main doors of the space agency facility.

Beijing's street corners were full of homeless people. Some had small children with them as they begged for charity, and others were disabled people to whom destiny had been unmerciful. The next day, Shaked collected some old worn clothing and blankets smelling of urine. Cloaked as a beggar, she situated herself some distance away from the agency. She wanted the police and regular pedestrians to get used to her presence there. Each day, she moved a few yards closer to the facility's luxury entrance, equipped with a hidden camera and communication system.

M. informed Dan that Shaked had a lead on Maman, so Dan needed to get to Beijing immediately and meet her at the apartment.

Bico was not happy to see his profit dissipating when his plan to deliver Maman had failed. He needed to find a way to get back into the picture, and the only way was to convince the Mossad that he could help smuggle Maman back to Israel. M. considered the idea, as it never hurt to have another set of hands. Seeing as though Bico also had experience as an agent, M. cautiously agreed to keep him on the mission.

Shaked moved closer to the facility with each passing day, and at last, she could clearly see every person filtering in and out.

She saw the usual and expected people—like Jing—but there was no sight of Maman.

Once they arrived in Beijing, Dan and Bico waited in the apartment. Shaked reached them through their communication systems. After that, the men disguised themselves as tourists exploring around the facility, throwing coins into Shaked's straw hat on the concrete.

A local security agent from the embassy drove past Shaked every day to keep an eye on her and ask if she needed any help. They were all connected to the same communication system in case of an emergency.

On the fourth day of Shaked's beggar ruse, she spotted a man resembling Maman—at least based on the photographs she'd memorized. She used her hidden GoPro camera to take pictures for identification. She immediately sent the photos to the headquarters in Tel Aviv, which immediately analyzed and matched them with their records. Dan and Bico received the pictures next.

"He gained weight, the son of a bitch!" M. shouted angrily.

Maman's height matched. His body was a bit fuller, perhaps due to high-calorie Chinese desserts—but Maman still kept his hair short and without sideburns. A small beard covered his face, but Dan recognized his walk; his shoulders were permanently slumped forward.

"That's him," said Bico excitedly, and he recognized Fei walking beside Maman as a bodyguard. "Time for payback."

Dan met Bico's eyes and they nodded at each other in agreement.

Shaked gathered her junk from the street corner and slowly followed Maman and Fei. The two men got into a car. Shaked signaled the embassy security agent parked nearby, silently telling him that the subject was en route to an unknown location. Shaked remained slouching on the sidewalk with her torn blankets, gathering looks of both empathy and scorn.

Her colleague in the vehicle passed by her and followed the black car carrying Maman. A second embassy security car joined the first one, and they traded off trailing Maman to avoid either being noticed. However, the trip was shorter than they expected. After ten minutes of driving around the crowded streets of Beijing, past vendors' wagons, bikes, and motorcycles, the black car stopped at a hotel. Fei and Maman got out and walked into the lobby.

Shaked needed to disappear from the scene, and she carefully made sure she wasn't followed back to the apartment.

The trio's next step was to lure Maman to their apartment. This task was for Shaked and her unquestionable sex appeal.

Within an hour, the haggard, dirty beggar woman transformed into a fresh beauty that could dizzy any man. Naomi was a makeup master, regardless of whether its application was for a nightclub or gutter. She examined her reflection in the mirror and received excited nods of approval from Dan and Bico.

The field agents were informed once Shaked headed toward Maman's hotel. Dan and Bico followed but stayed safely behind to wait.

At the same time, the aiding security agent parked his car a couple blocks away, entered the hotel, and situated himself at the lobby bar. Luckily, it was an American chain hotel packed with Western businessmen, so he easily blended in.

Shaked walked in thirty minutes later.

"Fei dropped him and left; Maman might be alone in his room," the security agent whispered in Shaked's direction from behind his hand.

They both combed the fancy lobby and spotted a few people that might've worked for Fei.

The security agent checked the dining room, bathrooms, and stores on the lobby level. "He must be in his room," he reported once he rejoined Shaked, and she nodded her head.

Shaked took a seat at the bar, facing the lobby entrance in order to visually cover the entire area. She ordered a glass of red wine, and then she waited. Despite the crowds of businessmen, she was not the only woman at the bar. Two young ladies in chic modern clothing chatted in Mandarin three stools away from her. They examined Naomi up and down, eyeing the newcomer—the competition—and opened a polite conversation with her. Naomi quickly ended their interaction, telling them she was just there for the day with no intentions of roping any men; it was her day off.

Perhaps Maman ordered room service, Naomi thought after more time passed.

An hour later, Naomi had just ordered a second glass of wine when Maman came in wearing causal clothing. He headed straight to the restaurant's dining room. He was alone, and it seemed like this was his evening routine since he'd had a few months to acclimate. He walked confidently. Naomi looked over at her security agent sitting in an armchair with a glass of vodka in front of him. He assured her with his eyes that no one was watching her.

Naomi passed by Maman, letting him get a whiff of her perfume. She smiled and politely asked his pardon when she brushed against his arm. Maman smiled back and nodded in return. *That got his attention,* she thought.

An agent standing watch in the lobby was replaced by another one and delivered the update: "They made contact. Standby."

A waiter offered to seat Naomi in the dining room, but she pointed to Maman and said in fluent Mandarin, "He was here before me; I don't want to be rude." She made her voice flow like honey. Maman was escorted to a table, but he glanced back at her one more time. She flashed him another smile.

Maman had been advised by Fei to be on the alert for traps of any kind. *No, she couldn't be with the Mossad,* Maman thought. He was accustomed to high-end escorts flooding American hotel lobbies, aiming to snatch Western businessmen and empty their pockets. However, this woman was different—beautiful like the others, but with flowing grace and seamless class. Maman hadn't seen a woman quite like her at his hotel before. And she didn't hang out in the bar with the other escorts; she ate with the guests in the dining room.

A waitress sat Naomi at a table for two; Maman was directly behind her. She sat so that she faced his back, and then her phone rang. She answered, making sure to speak in English just loudly enough for only Maman to hear.

"Hi, Arthur, baby," Naomi cooed. "Long time no talk." She paused, pretending to listen to a voice on the other end of the line.

"Yes, yes. I'm free," Naomi said enthusiastically. "In my apartment tomorrow evening at seven, then. Confirmed." After another smooth pause, Naomi giggled, "Yes, yes—you know you're my favorite regular. Bring plenty of money this time; I'm feeling creative."

Naomi ordered a simple rice noodle soup with tofu. After the waitress delivered her dinner, Maman set down his menu and turned around to face Naomi.

"What's that you've got there?" Maman asked her with a simper.

"Pho," Naomi replied kindly. "Vietnamese soup; it's very good for you."

"Good idea. I'll get the same," he said but seemed more eager to continue their conversation than order his food. "Are you alone?"

"At the moment," she chuckled.

Once Maman ordered, his soup also arrived quickly. But instead of enjoying his meal, Maman kept his eyes on Naomi.

She looked up at him and scrunched her nose charmingly. "Sir, you need to eat; it's getting cold."

"What are you doing later?" Maman inquired with excitement, completely ignoring her previous statement.

"What's on your mind?" she countered.

"May I ask you to join me later?" he asked, his voice and gaze eager.

She laughed to herself. "Men are all alike."

"I'll pay for your time," he assured quietly.

She raised her eyebrows and studied him. Maman was nervous for a moment, fearing he'd misinterpreted her profession.

"I heard your phone conversation," he explained.

"It will cost you," she whispered curtly.

"I know," he replied with a hungry nod.

"We can't discuss this here," Naomi murmured and set her chopsticks in their holding dish. "Meet me at the entrance."

She left the table, leaving him to pay the bill.

"Sure thing," Maman said softly as she passed by him.

Maman wasted no time; he fervently tossed money onto the table without touching his dinner or asking for change.

Maman rushed into the lobby just as one of the Israeli agents walked out to hail a cab—but Maman was unaware of the agent's identity. Another agent entered the lobby to replace the previous one and briefly made eye contact with Naomi as he walked by her.

Maman approached her, wringing his hands together.

"Five hundred dollars cash," she stated before he could speak.

"Let's go to my room upstairs," Maman replied.

"No, the hotel doesn't allow call girls in the rooms," Naomi said. "If they catch me naked in your room, I'll be banned from the hotel. Besides, my apartment is only ten minutes away."

He agreed, and as they walked out, the agent in the lobby whispered over the communication system to the agent in the car outside, "They're exiting the lobby together."

"Confirmed. I see them," the other agent replied.

A cab pulled up beside Naomi and Maman, and the scientist opened the door for her. Maman had a moment of hesitation before getting into the cab as Naomi gave instructions to the driver in Mandarin.

"Are you coming?" she asked with a coy smile. She licked her top lip playfully.

Maman looked around as to see if he was being watched. "Damn," he murmured to himself in Hebrew, knowing his hormones wouldn't relent. He hopped into the cab, wrapping an arm around her hips.

The Israeli agent in the lobby watched them from a distance, speaking quietly into his comm that they were on the way to the apartment. The agent in the car followed the cab to its destination, where Bico and Dan waited.

In the espionage world, one's first mistake was usually their last.

CHAPTER THIRTY-SIX

Presidents of the United States tended to see the world in black and white: there were those who were with their country—and those who were not. There were only foes or friends.

Generals and cabinet secretaries had shared that philosophy until President Cole's administration, which had changed decades of foreign strategy. He was a master of the disinformation game, especially regarding his planned trips to Beijing and Moscow.

The Mossad decided it was a good time to also push their agenda further. With the media's cameras aimed at the President, they could perform acts in the dark alleys.

This particular morning was not one of President Cole's better ones. Mounting piles of issues delivered by his generals in the daily briefing weighed heavily on him. He was not a military man and could not weed out the rubbish. He skipped a couple of briefings, not only to handle problems in space but to also monitor the tensions with North Korea and Iran, which directly threatened the planet's stability.

"Can I get the real picture here?" Cole barked in the security cabinet meeting.

The south windows let the rising sun into the room, which lightened the heavy mood—despite the snarl in the President's voice.

Secretary of Defense Wezniak was quick to answer: "Mr. President, North Korea is a proxy of China, and Iran is a proxy of Russia. We think there might be an underlying plan. The more the proxies howl like mad dogs, the less we pay attention to the real issues. And the more we stretch our neck into space, the more intercontinental ballistic missile and nuclear tests are conducted by NoKo and Iran."

Secretary of State Cyrus Bradford, who would accompany POTUS on his upcoming trip, noted that he'd devised a plan for asking each country to control its proxy to avoid war. But there would be no mention of America's space developments.

CIA Director Bennett joined in the conversation: "I had a meeting with the Chairman of the Federal Reserve, Mr. Schwartz. He's an unparalleled expert on precious metals and their importance in a volatile global economy. I brought to his attention that China is aggressively buying gold in hopes that he may help me connect some dots. Apparently, China's gold reserves have increased to 3,389 tons in the past three years. They're just ahead of Germany now. They're drinking the stuff like water."

President Cole listened politely for a bit, which differed from his usual nature, but then he snapped, "Is this a security meeting or an economy lecture, Bennett?"

Wezniak came to Bennett's assistance, trying to suppress a chuckle, "Sir, if China is buying gold above market rate and at an alarming pace, it should be investigated. Wars are not fought only with missiles and bombs. Money is a powerful weapon."

"Okay, I get it, Joe. So, what you gonna do? Buy gold?" POTUS asked incredulously.

"It may not be a bad idea; it's at least worth exploring," Wezniak replied. "If we start buying gold at a higher rate, we'll get to see how China and the market react—and maybe discover something we don't already know."

"I need more resources," interjected Bennett, who wanted to take the opportunity to increase his budget. It had been depleted due to activities in the Far East.

"Fine, Bennett," Cole groaned. "Keep watching the Chinese, and I'll get you more money."

"Yes, we're watching—and making sure the enemy is looking in the wrong direction," Bennett replied with a smile. That was his expertise.

It was reiterated to the President that if a war did break out—and America didn't control the most important economic commodity—they could potentially face something akin to the Great Depression. They couldn't let that chaos ensue.

Someone reminded the room that many countries wanted to dethrone the American dollar as the prime global currency, but the United States had no intention of losing that status.

"I know China," the President added after some thought. "I know their manipulative currency behaviors. I used to sell them scrap metal, and now I regret doing business with them."

"Imagine your scrap metal helping them build a weapon to use against us," remarked Bennett cautiously, fearing he'd anger Cole—even though it was true.

"Everyone just keep praying," the President said under his breath.

With that, the sun disappeared behind a blanket of black clouds. Thunderstorms rolled in and swirled above the capital, sparking bolts of lightning and pouring rain until night fell.

CHAPTER THIRTY-SEVEN

March 6th, one year after the initiation of NASA's new program

The countdown had begun forty-three hours earlier when the test director ordered the other stations to perform their systems verifications.

The ships were in excellent shape and ready to go. They were flown on refurbished Boeing 747s to Cape Canaveral and prepared in the vehicle assembly building (VAB).

The spaceships were then moved on the crawlway to the pads for launch preparation. The Shuttles were close to each other, with Atlantis on Launchpad 39A and Discovery on Launchpad 39B, mere feet away from the Atlantic Ocean. The Enterprise was on standby.

The massive Shuttles were hooked into the launch towers and could be seen from miles away. In the past, their solid rocket boosters had come from a manufacturing facility in Utah and their external tanks from Louisiana. This time, the Shuttles and their parts came entirely from Area 51. All their remaining segments had arrived in Cape Canaveral by train for the final assembly. During that time, the space vehicles had waited in the Orbiter Processing Facility. After the tank assemblies were completed, the orbiters were attached to their solid rocket boosters and external tanks.

John Fisher chose his breakfast carefully that morning. He then let the engineers dress him in his spacesuit and check all its connections. The two separate crews boarded the Shuttles at T-minus three hours after traversing the White Room and elevator, sticking closely to their schedule.

John noticed that the LLM crew assigned to land on the moon carried a white bag resembling a briefcase. He hadn't seen that before, since some of the LLM training had been kept confidential. The LLM crew had signed nondisclosure agreements. When John asked them about it, he was politely rejected with a joke—"Yeah, we packed some boardgames to keep us entertained on the moon," one of them laughed.

John felt uneasy and hoped that NASA knew what they were doing.

Between T-minus three hours and T-minus twenty minutes, the crews were strapped in on their backs and performed communications tests, checking all switch system configurations and completing all closeout preparations. Between T-minus forty-three minutes and T-minus three minutes, the Shuttles were fueled and ran testing procedures while the control room monitored the weather.

John saw the main engine light turn on, and the engines rumbled. Seven seconds later, the rocket engines ignited, lifting the hybrid Atlantis vertically up to the sky.

The vehicle vibrated violently, and the ride was rough on the crew. It had been quite some time, outside of their recent training, since they'd experienced such intense g-forces. For the first two minutes, they were smashed back against their seats, feeling crushed by twice their body weight.

A big flash of light signaled the separating fuel tanks, and they fell back to earth.

The ride got smoother in the thinning atmosphere, but the vehicle increased acceleration, bearing down on the crew and pressing the air out of their lungs. They endured the eight minutes after liftoff the best they could, and then the main engines stopped.

They were in space.

John checked the systems once more. His long year of hard training came down to this single mission—these calculated, careful moments.

The Discovery lifted off a minute later, and then both Shuttles began their uncertain voyage to the dark side of the Moon.

The crew felt the expected headaches and dizziness while in zero gravity due to fluids shifting to the upper parts of their bodies.

The Atlantis crew's first task was to intercept the ISS and its stranded American astronauts.

After a quick burn of their engines, both ships escaped Earth's gravity. The Discovery angled straight for the moon, but orbital calculations directed the Atlantis toward the ISS on a slightly divergent route.

Colonel Warren Campbell received the good news that Atlantis was on its way to rescue them. They were holding up but praying that no debris would hit them. There was no way they could maneuver to escape a collision. Atlantis was a day away from manually docking with them.

Once Atlantis reached the stranded astronauts, the first challenge was to stabilize the ISS's rotation using the Shuttle's thrusters. The maneuver was dangerous, as the Shuttle first needed to synchronize its spinning with the ISS for successful docking. Its difficulty called for a skillset like Fisher's.

"Houston, I have visual," called John through the communication system.

"Roger, John. Go for manual docking maneuvers," Houston directed.

Atlantis approached the dead space station slowly and carefully. There were three available docking ports of the ISS's original four, and John needed to select the one that would be appropriate given the grave situation.

"I'm happy to see you guys," Campbell rejoiced from his Soyuz command chair, wedged between his two colleagues.

"I've docked the ISS a few times, but I've never seen anything like this," John said through the comm. "I'm happy to see you, too, buddy." A moment passed, and then John asked, "Are the capsule engines operable?"

"I hope so; we haven't tried them," Campbell replied.

"Atlantis, the Soyuz capsule engines will assist in stabilizing the station and will go for a short test," Houston said.

"Roger," confirmed Campbell. "Waiting for a countdown."

Campbell needed to select the correct thrusters to turn the station against its axis. The engineers calculated the mass, speed, and other data for the proper burn; once those were determined, they were all ready for the test.

Atlantis hovered a safe distance from the nearest solar panel wing.

"Going for a ten-second burn," Campbell declared and counted down loudly.

From a distance, John watched the ISS's spin, controlled by the smaller spaceship. It slowed down until it floated weightlessly in the high orbit (nicknamed "junk orbit"). Junk orbit referred to where all the dead geostationary-orbit satellites were abandoned at the end of their useful life.

"Houston, it worked," Campbell said excitedly.

"Atlantis, continue docking maneuvers," Houston ordered.

"Roger," John responded.

John's piloting skills were put to the last test of his career in this unusual circumstance. He firmly controlled the Shuttle's systems to gently dock the ISS port.

"Docking maneuvers completed," John confirmed calmly.

Campbell and his crew left the pressurized capsule through the station, which was dead silent after so many years of activity. The astronauts boarded Atlantis. They were ready and informed Mission Control of their intention to abandon the ship. In junk orbit, there was no chance the ISS would reenter the Earth's atmosphere; it would float forever in the space graveyard.

"ISS crew secured," announced John.

"Atlantis, let's join Discovery and get to the Moon," the Houston control manager replied, relieved.

CHAPTER THIRTY-EIGHT

At Vandenberg Air Force Base, the Orbixeye system amazed its operators. The entire planetary satellite system was displayed on the large screen, strangely resembling a giant computer game.

The American attack satellite logged and synchronized with the Orbixeye system, locking on all their adversaries' satellites. They were ready in case POTUS ordered an attack.

On the other side of the globe, Maman followed Naomi to her apartment on the ground floor through a back entrance. As M. always said, "When you enter through one door, always escape through another." Two means of egress was the Mossad protocol.

The apartment was dark, and Naomi let Maman enter the foyer first while she followed closely behind.

Like a lightning strike, Bico and Dan covered Maman's mouth and sealed his lips with duct tape. They immediately bound his hands behind his back with the tape and threw him on the floor.

Maman was unable to react and totally paralyzed. He tried to look up at Naomi, his eyes wide in terrified questioning.

"What's your name?" Dan demanded in Hebrew removing the duct tape from his lips. He sunk his elbow into Maman's lower belly to encourage an answer.

"Maman," the scientist growled. "Ezra Maman!"

Dan nodded his head and said, "We have positive identification."

Agent Shaked turned on the lights and observed Bico and Dan pressing down on Maman's torso. Maman gasped for air, and she told her colleagues to ease their grip.

"Welcome home, Ezra," she said equally sarcastically and sensually. Ezra scowled.

Dan sent out an encrypted message: "Subject is home."

M. knew that the CSIS would not rest until they could stop Maman from being smuggled out of the country. The Mossad agents and Bico had no time to spare. The mission's second phase commenced.

Their nonstop flight from Beijing to Tel Aviv was already boarding and scheduled to depart in a mere forty minutes. After a few phone calls, M. got the flight delayed due to "technical difficulties."

With skilled hands, Naomi prepared an injection to knock out Maman. His eyes popped out of his skull with fear. He knew—deep down—that no one would probably know he'd been captured until the next morning, unless someone had trailed him. Naomi stuck the needle into the scientist, and he swiftly fell into a deep sleep.

They put Maman's body in a large suitcase that was specially designed for the occasion. The embassy's diplomatic mail truck stopped in the dark alley behind the apartment building and loaded up the suitcase.

Dan and Shaked had previously received airline tickets using their diplomatic passports. They joined the mail truck and then looked back at Bico, who would remain behind.

"I have unfinished work to do," Bico said with his usual smirk.

"Fei?" asked Dan.

Bico nodded.

"Take care, Bico," Dan said. "You were a great help." The two men—maybe now friends—shook hands. Dan promised to arrange the final payment of Bico's entire promised reward, even though things hadn't gone as planned. *At least he's staying behind to clean any other evidence,* thought Dan.

"Don't worry about my money," Bico said calmly. "I'm sure that we will work together again. You can pay me then."

Dan grabbed his handgun from the diplomatic bag and handed it to Bico.

"Watch yourself," Naomi said, sad to see a colleague go.

The vehicle and its live cargo left for the airport.

Half an hour later, Shaked and Dan entered the airport through the diplomatic entrance and passed through security with no issues. The large bag holding Maman's sleeping body was delivered to the airplane's underbelly in a security car. Dan and Naomi boarded the Dreamline aircraft that waited on the tarmac just for them. The technical issues were miraculously resolved at the same time. Dan almost joked with the captain about keeping the cargo bay pressurized and flying as fast as possible.

Maman was in Israel before the Chinese even knew he'd been taken.

CHAPTER THIRTY-NINE

The Discovery entered lunar orbit as planned and then waited for Atlantis to join them a few hours later.

They planned to orbit the Moon for twenty-four hours and check the LLM systems before separating the orbiter from the LLM. The Shuttle would remain in orbit and serve as a communication platform between the LLM and Mission Control.

The chosen landing site was near the Moon surface's equator.

The ISS crew was solaced to have been saved and didn't mind the extra voyage to the moon.

"What's going on?" Campbell asked John.

"Well, I guess you could call it 'war games,'" John replied seriously and pointed to the crew of the LLM still carrying the big white suitcase.

After a moment of looking at the LLM crew, John asked, "Shiké, can you finally tell us about your confidential training?"

Shiké, or Colonel Isaac Holmes, the commander of the three astronauts who would land on the Moon with him, didn't see the point in keeping the secret any longer—as far he was concerned, confidentiality only applied on Earth.

Shiké kept his voice low and calm, making sure the external intercom was off. "There is a secret facility in Area 51," he began. "That's where NASA and the military are developing new millennium weapons. Bullets, guns, and missiles will not be able to win future wars."

"What's in the suitcase?" Campbell pressed.

"Electromagnetic gun poles and a laser gun—in case we're met with hostility on the Moon," Shiké replied.

"Really?" John said in disbelief, almost joking. "Well, apparently NASA was able to develop a powerful new electromagnetic gun that only five years ago was the size of a house."

"The new laser gun works based on heat up to a thousand degrees, melting anything in its path," Shiké clarified seriously. "The state military attack satellites were equipped with the same powerful laser technology...both in this case."

"Is that true?" Campbell asked in John's direction. Campbell wasn't sure what to believe, as he'd been out of touch and on the ISS for over a year.

"We don't know, but better safe than sorry," said John.

After a few more hours, the Atlantis entered the same orbit as its sister, Discovery.

In twelve hours, the two LLMs would separate from the Shuttles. This allowed the Atlantis LLM crew to go through the same procedure of checking the control panel, switches, and communications system. If there were a malfunction, they would be stranded on the surface on the Moon. The crews knew the risks involved with their mission and were ready to start.

"The Kessler Crater near the equator on the dark side was chosen as our landing site; it's about two miles from the suspected camp," Shiké explained to those who were not part of his excursion.

They all knew that humans had never landed or walked on the dark side of the Moon before. If anyone wanted to cover his activities from the prying eyes of Earth, the dark side would be a suitable choice. Tension filled the cabin.

The systems seemed to be operational, so the two LLM crews carefully entered the vehicles with the mission specialists' assistance.

The mission specialists in charge of the arm were ready and signaled for the captains to open the cargo bays and expose the LLMs.

Faint light penetrated the LLMs as the cargo bay doors opened, and Shiké understood that they would be in orbit soon. Communications were linked with the Shuttles' crews and Houston to orchestrate that release into orbit. Both Shuttles carefully followed Houston's instructions.

Time passed, and the LLM crews were left with only the sound of their breathing.

CHAPTER FORTY

Maman was checked by a physician who reported that he was in good health after his long period of sedation.

They took the defector to the basement of the Mossad building, and a special investigator began questioning Maman while Dan, M., and a few operations officers watched through a one-way mirror.

Maman was broken, tired, and confused—definitely not the wizard he'd once been considered. He was a scientist with the spine of a shellfish—a wayward man who'd prioritized improving his personal circumstances over any allegiances. But he hadn't done so due to political or cultural alliances. Maman's motive puzzled the investigator.

"What did you work on?" the investigator pried.

Maman felt (and looked) like the traitor he was. He knew a great deal about the Chinese space program and their plans, but he refused to speak.

M. didn't wait for Maman to soften. He'd already convinced Maman's ex-wife and children to come to headquarters for a couple of hours. They were in the waiting room, and the investigator took Maman to them in handcuffs.

Ezra hadn't expected to ever see his ex-wife or children again—and especially not like that. The scientist burst into tears and cried out, desperate to leave the waiting room. And that was all it took.

The family went home, and Maman cracked open; he answered every question the Israeli scientists who joined the interrogation, could ask.

M. was interested in the Chinese space agency's agenda and future projects, but those details Maman didn't know. M. then assumed that the Chinese had not trusted Maman enough with their "big picture" or secret plans and only kept him on because he could help with the Orbixeye and other engineering responsibilities.

"What did you work on?" the investigator again demanded.

"I helped develop artificial intelligence for their robots that work on the Moon," Maman murmured, staring down at his feet.

"Robots...on the Moon?" the investigator stumbled.

The Israeli scientists were floored. They could not comprehend what China's technology had apparently achieved in the previous ten to twenty years—all without anyone noticing.

The scientists squabbled amongst themselves while throwing questions at Ezra simultaneously: "Why do they have robots on the Moon?" and, "What do these robots do? What type of AI did you develop?"

Maman sighed, his eyes glued to the floor, and went on to explain what he knew. The robots were workers who sent small spaceships, each the size of a refrigerator, to an asteroid named 16 Psyche. These tiny spaceships utilized modern energy theories that China had combined and functionally implemented. And the asteroid was made entirely of heavy metals—including 90% gold.

"Is this a pitch for your new sci-fi script?" an Israeli scientist yelled.

"I'm telling the truth. The Chinese want the gold," Maman exclaimed. "Would you unhandcuff me, please?"

M. narrowed his eyes on Ezra but then nodded. An officer removed the bindings.

Maman rubbed his freed wrists and then asked, "May I see my family again?"

"Yes," replied M. "They left for home."

M. rubbed his temple and paced for a while. "Damn, China probably invested trillions of dollars," he mumbled to himself, "which would put pressure on the Chinese economy. But it was money they earned as a byproduct from the fueled American economy. It's national security for Western civilization."

"True," Dan commented, bewildered. "From time to time, they manipulated the currency to cope with the financial burden and gain more profits from their unfair trade deals, primarily with the United States. That probably helped bring their adversaries to their knees in total economic breakdown."

"That's a national security threat," M. uttered.

"How did they do this?" the investigator asked Maman.

Ezra looked worn, and his eyes had glazed over. Eventually, he spoke again: "The small spaceships travel from the Moon to the asteroid on minimal fuel—they primarily use sails powered by the solar winds, sun's rays. The asteroid is around one hundred and forty miles in diameter. Its heavy metals have been valued around seven hundred quintillion dollars."

Dan whistled. Everyone else gaped.

"Earth's gold has been valued at over seven and a half trillion American dollars," Maman continued somberly. "Putting the same amount of gold into the market would drive the price of the commodity down; gold's value in the market would crash."

Dan commented, "The inflation would be unlike anything ever seen. I have no idea how the global economy could recover from something like that."

"For any of this to be feasible, it must be economical to harvest an asteroid in space," M. said. "Mining pure gold—if that's what's even on this asteroid—is probably more profitable than mining on Earth, as processing gold here is expensive. If a country harvested gold in space, it could bring it down slowly, one load at a time; the price of gold would stay relatively the same or drop a little, but it would not cause a panic."

Maman nodded his head but kept his eyes on the floor.

"What's China's goal with all this? What is their target?" the investigator asked.

Maman merely shrugged. "Not sure," he sighed. "Perhaps to collapse all markets and then come in as a savior." China had done the same to Ezra, so to him, it seemed plausible they'd attempt it on a larger scale.

"How did they get the fuel to the Moon?" asked another Israeli scientist.

"They discovered water just below the surface many years ago after sending a probe to the Moon," Maman said. "They just separate the hydrogen and the oxygen for fuel and breathing."

"They have humans on the moon?" the scientist exclaimed. The rest of the room gasped.

"Yes. Two astronauts keep everything in working order," Maman said, finally looking up from the floor. "They are exchanged in six-month intervals."

"Are they armed?" asked the Mossad investigator.

"Yes, they are trained to defend themselves and attack if necessary," Maman replied.

"How long has this being going on?"

"Probably a few years...maybe ten...or even twenty," Maman guessed.

"What would happen if other astronauts landed on the Moon right now?" Dan asked.

"They would be destroyed," Ezra croaked.

CHAPTER FORTY-ONE

The commotion of POTUS's traveling was a mess: three presidential helicopters, four C-17 Globemasters, and a load of fully armed Marines...not to mention sixty journalists crammed into Air Force One.

There was a flurry of red carpets, anthems, flowers, and endless speeches with empty words. But POTUS and the Chinese president were only focused on penetrating each other's minds. *This is not a genuine olive branch event,* POTUS reminded himself and looked at the moon hanging in the sky.

While the media in China was distracted with POTUS's visit and meetings with the Chinese president, Bico had the perfect opportunity to take care of his business with Fei.

Bico shot Fei in the head and left him bleeding in his car in a Beijing parking lot after Fei had been investigating Maman's disappearance. Bico then smuggled himself safely back to Grozny, much to Dan's delight.

CHAPTER FORTY-TWO

"**A**tlantis, this is Houston," Mission Control said tersely over the intercom.

"This is Atlantis," John answered, wondering what was taking them so long to give LLM separation instructions.

"We've just alerted the LLM crew members that they will likely confront hostilities on the Moon's surface—Shiké must take major precautions," Mission Control explained. They quickly told John the information the Mossad had uncovered in Maman's interrogation.

"The robots have a small bump on their heads that is sensitive to heat. This bump is an antenna and an artificial intelligence nerve system," Mission Control continued hastily. "The crew must aim the laser at it, and this will shut down and deactivate the robots. They might be equipped to defend themselves, though, so extreme caution is imperative." Mission Control also alerted John to the armed astronauts managing the robots on the Moon's surface.

The element of surprise was on the Americans' side. John wished the LLM crews good luck and announced their new separation time—two hours from then—as directed by NASA.

In the meantime, the Shuttles orbited the Moon, and the crews watched the incredible sight of the Earth rising against the blackness of the endless universe.

During those remaining two hours, the LLM crews continued checking their systems thoroughly.

The Canadarm put the LLMs in orbit from the cargo bay in order for them to land safely outside the Kessler Crater. The LLMs then descended upon the Moon's surface, crossing many craters, rock formations, and deep valleys—an amazing journey that only twelve American astronauts had ever experienced. The dark side was completely surreal.

Shiké didn't have time to be impressed with the view and followed the automatic landing procedures intensely. The two LLMs communicated to ensure they wouldn't be seen by the prying eyes of the Chinese base. There was a lot riding on this mission—and the LLM crews were the first combat astronauts of President Cole's new space army.

Once the LLMs lost the last bits of sunlight, they couldn't reach Mission Control.

"The Osprey has landed," Shiké reported to himself, as no one could hear him. He imitated the famous quote from the first man who stepped on the Moon. "Only this time, it's my final leap," he said softly to himself.

After a few tense minutes, the crews powered down their engines. They pulled all the switches to the off positions as they saw Moon dust rising over their windows.

The astronauts checked all systems and prepared the astronauts for departure. Then the crew members exited the Lunar Landing Modules. They stepped outside and crossed the Moon's surface with long kangaroo jumps, carefully heading toward the suspicious camp.

The Moon's far side was dark but somehow a strange glow radiated from space, reminiscent of the lighting in horror films.

Shiké prayed that they wouldn't lose their element of surprise. A little less than three miles was a long trip for moonwalking, but it was the only safe way to travel, considering the fighting ability of the robots.

Back on Earth, Dan sat alone, his thoughts heavy. Then a shock went down his spine. The strange object he'd found in Kazakhstan while fighting Dimitri was a Chinese robot's headpiece. The two blood types found on the helmet had been only Dan's and Dimitri's.

"Robots on the Moon..." John mused to himself, his crew, and the rescued ISS team. "Never too late to discover something new, I guess."

The LLM crews walked in a straight line, then switched to side by side, taking cover of the landscape elements. The laser gun and electromagnetic launcher were cocked and ready to fire in case of a clear and present danger situation. The camp finally revealed itself in the distance. They carefully approached the station and decided to split into two groups— each LLM crew was to flank the target on one side.

The Chinese camp sat at the foot of a rocky cliff created by a small crater. At the base of the cliff, they saw a few cylindrical pods connected in a cross-like shape–long arms on each side with large solar panels on both sides of the moon getting direct sunlight. A few pods with igloo-shaped tops were separated from the main station with no visibly connected energy supply—and they looked just like the structures from the MoonKAM photographs. They had no windows. The crew assumed the pods were either storage or the foundation of an unfinished construction site.

Shiké informed his colleagues that their priority was to eliminate the potentially armed Chinese astronauts first. They used sensored infrared binoculars to scan for thermal human imaging and catch any movement around the station.

After a while, the LLM crew found it odd that they hadn't seen any stirring yet. They carefully and methodically moved closer under the cover of the rocky landscape and heavily shadowed areas.

They crept closer to the first airlock door. Every single eye locked on that door. It was deathly quiet, and all they could hear was their own rhythmic, tense breathing.

"Bingo," Shiké said and pointed to the exterior cameras on the side of the structure. That was their first major mistake—not checking for cameras from a distance. They all froze in place, and Shiké ordered everyone else to take cover.

"I will proceed by myself—watch my back!" Shiké demanded.

If someone had been watching the camera feeds, the LLM crew would've already been shot down—but there was still no movement or response from the station. Shiké was skeptical and stepped closer to the airlock, watching for any surprises. Two cameras looked right at him, and he froze again. The rest of his crew watched from a safe distance, ready to fire their weapons if necessary.

Suddenly, the airlock opened wide, and a bright beam poured over the lunar surface. Shiké stood in the center of the pool of light. A man in a spacesuit stood on the threshold, casting a long shadow on the ground. Only six footsteps separated the two spacemen.

Shiké hesitated, unsure of the other man's intentions. They were both surprised by the other. Astonished, Shiké watched the spaceman raise his hand, hailing and greeting him with an open palm.

He thinks I'm here in peace—or does he think I'm his replacement? Shiké wondered as he angled his gun forward and toward the man's chest.

Suddenly, the man realized that Shiké was not friendly nor his replacement. He tried to get back inside the station and lock the door, but Shiké triggered the laser on him. The shot blasted the man's helmet, depressurized his spacesuit, and destroyed his life-support system. He collapsed on the metal landing and rolled down the steps to the ground, raising a small cloud of dust.

After seeing the attack on the cameras, the other Chinese crew member somewhere inside the station immediately manually locked the door and bunkered himself inside.

Out from the igloos swarmed an army of android robots, storming the area for a counterattack. *They're controlled by the astronaut in the station,* Shiké realized. Shiké's colleagues leapt out from their cover to join the fight right as even more robots appeared.

Amazingly, the androids were equipped with weapons nearly identical to those of the Americans. *Perhaps another successful Chinese hacking of stolen technology from the United States,* the thought passed quickly in Shike's mind.

The LLM crew acted immediately. Shiké yelled, "Aim for the bumps on their heads!"

Almost forty robots covered the area, running and shooting laser beams wildly. It felt like a 3D video game in virtual reality.

The robots' bumps were difficult to hit due to their erratic movements and speed. One astronaut shot a few robots in the legs so that they fell to the ground, making their bumps easier to blast.

The robots' thin green laser beams zoomed in every direction as they searched for targets, but their accuracy was poor. But more robots kept coming—no one had any clue as to how many there were. And the astronauts knew their suits had limited oxygen supplies.

Knowing that it was now or never, Shiké cried out, "Steam them up, boys!"

After a powerful, blinding laser assault from every astronaut in tandem, things went still. A few robotic limbs twitched, but their glowing lasers dimmed and died.

The sudden quiet was jarring and strange.

The astronauts checked on each other, raising their hands to confirm they were unharmed. The conflict had been quick, but the elderly astronauts were exhausted.

Shiké briefly investigated the igloos from which the robots had appeared and ordered everyone to leave the other Chinese astronaut in the bunker alone, as he was terribly outnumbered and no longer posed an immediate threat.

After things remained quiet for a time, Shiké removed the dead astronaut's helmet to gather evidence—but he was thrown deeply into shock. The dead astronaut was an Asian female—the same age as Shiké's youngest daughter. His heart ached. "What a waste of life," he murmured to himself, wincing.

A minute later, one of the American astronauts guarded the airlock door so that Shiké could investigate around the station.

The Americans still had no communication with Mission Control, and only when the orbiter was hovering directly above them could they communicate with John.

When Atlantis floated closer, Shiké made contact. "Robots," he reported to John. "At least forty of them, all currently deactivated. And we have one dead female astronaut. We don't know how many living astronoauts are inside the main station, we can't communicate with them to encourage them to surrender."

"Destroy the station and let him fend for himself," John replied.

"No, we achieved our objective," replied Shiké.

The update was relayed to President Cole, who had been in constant contact with NASA even while on the red carpet.

On the other side of the station, Shiké found a shadowed, unpressurized entryway. He decided to take a quick peek inside to gather more evidence for NASA. He stepped in slowly, not sure what he would see.

Once surrounded by total darkness, Shiké turned on his helmet's flashlight. He was surrounded by countless drawers. He opened one and cautiously peered inside.

"Gold!" he exclaimed in surprise. "I'll be damned!" He reached out to touch the glittering metal, even though he couldn't feel it through his insulated gloves.

He made sure his helmet camera was still filming. It seemed that the robots would gather gold for six months and then ship it to Earth when the Chinese astronauts changed shifts.

Shiké estimated that there was about one ton of gold— around fifty million dollars. Shiké looked around at the workstation; vessels the size of refrigerators stood here and there, their hatches open and exposing more gold.

What were the Chinese thinking pouring trillions of dollars into this operation? Shiké asked himself.

John asked Shiké to finalize the mission and get back to the LLMs as quickly as possible. Time is of the essence.

As a parting gift, the American astronauts quickly pitched every hunk of gold across the Moon's surface and damaged any visible computers, cameras, and monitors...then to their surprise, they saw a space vehicle resembling NASA's Eagle Lunar Module.

Shiké snapped one picture of the vehicle. "Who knew old technology could be so advanced. One vehicle... they can't have too many living astronauts in here," he muttered to himself.

The crew made their way back to the LLMs, carrying bags of gold for evidence. Once aboard the LLM, Shiké placed the gold in protective lead boxes in case of radiation exposure. He had no idea how much the stash was worth—or how much gold the Chinese had already harvested and shipped back to Earth.

Perhaps the Chinese space agency on Earth had seen the entire event through their Moon base's camera feeds—but perhaps not. The LLM crews didn't have the energy to care.

It was time to go home.

CHAPTER FORTY-THREE

News of the Moon base attack was whispered into the Chinese president's ear as President Cole stood nearby. The two leaders continued waving from the red carpet on the way to the podium.

Chinese intel had confirmed the attackers were American astronauts. The Chinese president kept a frozen face and took a quick glance at President Cole next to him.

From his post Chang could not stop the ball from rolling. His secret plan to alter the Chinese space program would now likely be revealed, as well as his collaboration with the head of the Chinese space agency. Gold had not been the Chinese president's objective. The moon base—yes. But the gold—no.

The Chinese President issued a verbal arrest warrant of Chang, his State Council and the head of his space program, once the anthems ceremony was over. Cole exchanged a few words with the Chinese counterpart and disclosed information about the gold on the Moon base as they walked away from the podium. Cole's actions against the moon base station infuriated the Chinese president who claimed he knew nothing of the gold operation.

The Chinese president then offered a list of excuses regarding the Moon base and its gold, and even though Cole didn't believe any of it, starting another conflict wasn't worth it. It was only a matter of minutes before Chang and his collaborators would become scapegoats. If it was true or not, it didn't matter.

Shortly after, upon seeing a battalion of the Chinese People's Liberation Army storming his compound, Chang knew the game was over. As a last-ditch retaliation, Chang quickly ordered an attack on American satellites, the American spaceships bringing home the astronauts, and the ISS.

At Vandenberg, the Orbixeye system detected the Chinese attack satellites' signals as they shifted orbit to strike.

Secretary of State Bradford approached POTUS from behind as they faced the American and Chinese flags, leaned over and whispered to him, "Our adversary's satellites are attacking."

The President, with one hand on his chest as the American national anthem played loudly, waited for the music to end before turning to Bradford. "Let them take the first shot," Cole said calmly through an unfaltering smile.

Orbixeye proved to be the ultimate detection system. Its connection to the American satellites instantly prepped for a potential counterattack.

At the political gathering, the Chinese anthem was now playing, but the Chinese president was visibly uncomfortable. He pressed on his earpiece to hear better and looked at President Cole, whose face gave nothing away.

Jim Mason, watching the system with his teams and the Israeli investors, noticed that one Chinese attack satellite was climbing to a higher orbit.

"Have they gone mad? What's it going after?" Jim yelled.

"ISS," replied a technician.

"It's abandoned," Jim snapped.

"Yeah, but they don't know that," John Fisher said to Jim through the communication network. "They might be looking for us, too."

"Look!" exclaimed the technician. They watched a group of Chinese attack satellites simultaneously zero in closer on their American targets. Jim felt sweat on his neck. They hadn't heard an order from President Cole.

Cyrus Bradford leaned toward Cole one more time and whispered again. Cole nodded his head slightly, but it wasn't clear if he'd given the order to counterattack.

"I guess our President really trusts your Orbixeye," joked Jim, glancing around the room. By the looks on the other faces, no one else was in the mood for comedy.

The Chinese anthem finished, and both presidents exchanged a stone-faced handshake. Then Cole turned around and caught Secretary of State Bradford's eye. Cole flashed Bradford an ambiguous thumbs-up.

Ten seconds later, Jim hit the attack button in the control room.

The Orbixeye locked on the locations of the Chinese attack satellites. Upon the electronic command, they released their powerful laser beams. One after the other, the Chinese satellites went offline, dead silent.

A nervous silence filled the communication network, as no one knew if it was over or not. Necks craned and brows furrowed in waiting.

Suddenly, Jim shouted into his microphone, "It's over! It's over, boys!"

The control room erupted like a football stadium after the home team scored the winning touchdown. The air filled with whistles, cheers, and ecstatic clapping.

Now that the Orbixeye's work was done, the dead Chinese satellites would drift until roped into Earth's gravitational pull. Then they would plunge into the planet's atmosphere and be incinerated.

"Atlantis and Discovery," Mission Control called. "You are both cleared to come home." John and his crew could hear the United States national anthem blaring through the communication network.

Later, when Vandenberg's long runway finally appeared through the clouds, John said from the cabin of the Atlantis, "Mission Control, our runway is in sight."

"Yea!" cried all of Mission Control.

Jim squeezed his eyes closed in relief and exhaled. Then he grabbed a bottle of Champagne, tore out the cork, and filled cups with the foaming gold.

CHAPTER FORTY-FOUR

The United States never admitted to the attack on the Moon base or destroying the Chinese satellites—but most knew that no other country could have done it.

America claimed that the Atlantis and Discovery had launched only to rescue the stranded ISS crew. Thanks was given to the Russians for their cooperation and letting the stranded Americans use the Soyuz capsule for survival.

President Cole, rather satisfied with his own handling of the situation, chuckled to himself and said, "All I wanted to do was cut new deals with China, but perhaps it was a bad time."

Cole instructed his administration to declare a partnership with their Russian and Chinese counterparts; he then wanted all countries to join and create an international satellite-monitoring organization. This United Nation organization was to end the use of strategic weapons of mass destruction in space. Only helpful satellites—those for communication, weather, and scouting Earth's natural resources—would be allowed.

This international collaboration was unlike anything seen before in Earth's politics; and it would also build and monitor a new station on the Moon for the betterment of all mankind. It was built by humanity for humanity, and it served as a springboard for missions to Mars and beyond. Astronauts from all corners of the planet trained and experienced living on the Moon.

The gold and 16 Psyche were left untouched. Asteroid mining was outlawed for the safety of the world's economy.

On the last day of Cole's visit in China, the Chinese president leaned over to him. "Good job, America," he whispered. "I was just informed that my head of intelligence and head of the space agency conspired together with our State Council on the mining plot."

"No need to congratulate me," President Cole replied kindly, his usual gruffness set aside. "Would you like to resolve this peacefully?"

"Absolutely."

"I came here to prevent a war—not start one," replied Cole.

The Chinese president said with a calm smile. "I want only to propose peace to you and your fellow countrymen."

The two leaders shared a knowing nod.

"Since we've got the entire world watching, let's give them a strong handshake," President Cole rallied.

And they did.

Sophie Fisher sprinted to her husband as he stepped off the NASA helicopter, still in his spacesuit. It was the same helicopter that had taken him from their home and to his last space mission a year before. Sophie was much happier to see that helicopter this time around.

"Well, did you save the world?" Sophie asked as she gazed at her husband, her arms wrapped tightly around him.

"Yes, I did," John sighed. He looked up at the sky and smiled. "I saw our herd multiplying from space."

They both laughed.

–The End–

ABOUT THE AUTHOR

W illie Hirsh has published three novels: *Regicide, The Shadow King* (2018), *Amongst and Above All* (2020), and *Constellation: The Second Race for Space Has Begun* (first edition, 2018) which was an American Book Fest Finalist in 2018.

Willie currently spends his spare time traveling, photographing nature, and painting landscapes in oil. He loves writing spy and political suspense books after a career in engineering.

willie@williehirsh.com
twitter-@WillieHirsh
Instagram
Facebook-The Odyssey of Art by Willie Hirsh

Made in the USA
Monee, IL
12 July 2020